THE SECRETS

OF

TAYLOR CREEK

AGENT JAXSON LOCKE FBI MYSTERY THRILLER SERIES BOOK 2

MICHAEL MERSON

Edited by: Angie Wade Novel Nurse Editing

Cover Design by: G•S Cover Design Studio
https://www.gsstockphotography.com/

Prologue

Sunday, April 18, 1965

It was a cool April evening in 1965. The loud music and laughter from the invited guests, the who's who and well-to-do of North Carolina, could be heard in the distance. Delia Snipes looked back once at the old plantation home that bordered Taylor Creek. She was tired, intoxicated, and ready for bed. Her red high-heeled shoes made her feet ache, and the flower print, form-fitting dress she wore was way too tight. Delia felt more comfortable in a pair of jeans and a loose shirt, but the man who had requested her presence this evening required her to dress how he wanted.

Ben Arrington made all the girls who were of mixed race dress how he desired. The lights from the house were but a small glimmer from the long, dark driveway that led to the main road. The shadowed figures of the drunk politicians, businessmen, and party "treats"—like Delia Snipes—danced past the windows to the beat of the Rolling Stones.

The house belonged to the Arrington family of Beaufort, North Carolina. To visitors of the area, the home was described as an antebellum plantation home. It was white with tall pillars that supported the roof, which extended over a large ground-level balcony. To folks living in the area, especially black folks, it was known as the Old Klan House on Taylor Creek.

Delia had made an early exit from the Gentlemen's Social through the servant entrance in the back. She was satisfied with the hundred dollars she had earned servicing the wealthy white men attending the social. Delia never gave much thought to the things she did for the men nor to their special requests at parties. Besides, she was not paid to ask questions. She believed it was a necessary means to an end. After tonight, she had enough money to move herself, her sister, and her mother to Virginia Beach, where she hoped they could all find work and a different life. Maybe they would head farther away, to Pennsylvania, where her aunt could help her get a job in a factory. Either way, she and her family would be leaving Beaufort just as quickly as she had left the social tonight.

Delia allowed her intoxicated mind to drift toward thoughts of Virginia and Pennsylvania as she staggered down the driveway in the direction of the main road. The driveway was long and dark. It was best described as more of a tunnel of Spanish moss that hung overhead from the rows of trees lining both sides of the gravel driveway. The farther Delia walked from the house, the darker it was. She always felt uneasy about the area and was more comfortable on the main road. From there, she hoped to catch a ride with the workers heading to the docks.

The feeling of someone watching her caused her to stop. She stood motionless and listened for a moment. She squinted her eyes as she peered between the trees into the dark brush on both sides of the drive.

There ain't nothin' or nobody out here but you and God! Stop imagining things. You just drunk! Delia told herself. Slowly, she walked forward once more while singing Shirley Ellis's new hit song, "The Name Game." When Delia got to the middle of the chorus, she heard something. She turned quickly, "Who dat!" Delia shouted. She looked for who or what had ruffled the bushes behind the trees off to her left.

"I know somebody there! Is that you, Charlie White? I'm done for the night, and I ain't giving you no special attention. I'm goin' go home! Besides, you ain't never got money," Delia called.

She was afraid, and she stood quietly as the waves from Taylor Creek lapped against the shoreline. Still frightened, Delia turned and walked once more.

Delia only sang a few more words to the song before being struck in the head from behind. She didn't remember falling to the ground, but she soon realized she was lying on the ground, looking through a small opening in the Spanish moss at the moon. Warm streams of blood trickled down her cheek and into her eyes, and the moon faded away as darkness overtook the light.

NO LIFEGUARD
ON DUTY
SWIM AT YOUR
OWN RISK

Chapter 1
The Secret Discovered

Agent Jaxson Locke entered the town of Beaufort, North Carolina, shortly before five o'clock in the afternoon and quickly found the sheriff's office. He parked in the visitors' parking lot and made his way inside. He wasn't sure if he would find anyone in the office so late in the day on a Friday. Once inside, Agent Locke was greeted by a tall, thin man in his twenties with a strong Southern accent.

"May I help you?" he asked.

Jaxson smiled. "I'm Agent Locke with the FBI, and I'm here to see Sheriff Maggie Turner. I believe she's expecting me."

"I'll go see if she's ready for you."

Jaxson waited in the lobby where he saw a wall dedicated to the deputies who had been killed in the line of duty. At the top was Sheriff Dwight Carter. Jaxson recognized the name from the one in the file he carried. He was reading the circumstances surrounding Carter's death when the side door next to the lobby opened.

"Sheriff Turner will see you now," the young man announced from the door.

Jaxson followed the man down a short hallway to the

office at the end. When he entered the office, Sheriff Turner was sitting at her desk. Upon seeing Agent Locke, she stood, walked around from behind her desk, and approached him while extending her hand.

"I'm Sheriff Turner," she stated professionally as she shook the agent's hand.

"I'm Agent Locke with the FBI," he replied while displaying his credentials.

"Please have a seat." She gestured toward the chair on the other side of her desk.

"I'm here to recover a car—"

"Yes, I know. The very popular and very collectible 1965 Shelby Mustang GT350 that belonged to Agent Nathan Emerson, which we now have in our impound lot," she said, interrupting him.

Jaxson nodded. "Right. I was hoping to look at it this evening."

"That won't be possible. My guys have already gone home for the evening, but you're more than welcome to look at it tomorrow. I have already scheduled one of the fellas to be there for you in the morning."

Jaxson's eyes widened. "Well, okay then. I guess I'll find a place to stay the night and—"

"I booked you a room at the Beaufort Bed and Breakfast. It's at two thirty-one Ann Street. The sheriff's office is picking up the tab for your stay this evening," Sheriff Turner explained.

The FBI agent nodded his head. "All right. Do you know where I can find—"

"The widow Mrs. Josephine Arrington and Mr. William Turner Junior?" she asked, interrupting once more.

"Yes," he answered with a confused look on his face.

"Josephine goes by Stormie, and William Turner Junior, my father, would rather be called Will," she stated and then stood. "They're both over at Mrs. Stormie's home on Taylor

Creek. You can follow me over there. Do you have any questions so far?" she asked as they walked out of the lobby and into the parking lot.

"Do you know where I can find Agent Nathan Emerson?" Jaxson asked comically.

The sheriff turned and gave him a disapproving glare. "No, but maybe you'll find him before you leave," she remarked as she got in her car. "Now, just follow me."

Jaxson did as he was instructed, and after a short drive, he pulled into a long driveway that led to a beautiful home on the water. When he got closer, he saw two people sitting on the porch. Jaxson parked beside Sheriff Turner, then got out of the car and followed her up the steps and onto the porch.

"Hi, Mrs. Stormie, Daddy," Sheriff Turner said politely to the two of them. "This is Agent Locke with the FBI, and he wanted to come and speak to the two of you."

Agent Locke reached out his hand and greeted the two of them. Mr. Turner was an elderly black man in his sixties who was well dressed and spoke with a deep voice. Mrs. Stormie was older, and based on the information in the file, Agent Locke knew she was eighty-three years old.

"Please have a seat," Stormie offered and gestured for Jaxson to sit in the chair across from them.

"I'm here to—"

"To recover Agent Emerson's car that the department of transportation road crew found on Wednesday, over where they're putting in the new highway," Will responded, interrupting Agent Locke.

Like father, like daughter. At least she comes by it naturally, Jaxson thought to himself.

"Yes, sir, I am," Jaxson replied.

"What can we help you with, Agent Locke?" Stormie asked.

"Is there anything you can tell me that's not in this file?" Jaxson asked, holding up a thick folder he had brought with him.

"No, I don't think there is," Stormie answered solemnly and then looked at Will.

"I agree. I don't think we left anything out when we spoke to the other agents who were here questioning everyone in nineteen sixty-five."

"I just thought maybe you could tell me why Agent Emerson left his car here, in the woods, instead of taking it with him," Jaxson asked, looking back and forth between the two of them and waiting for an answer or some type of observable behavior.

"I have no idea. He did leave in a hurry," Stormie answered and then slowly turned away toward the water.

"He came here to look into the deaths of those young girls, and the next thing we know, everything was turned upside down. Nathan got out of town as quickly as he could," Will explained when he noticed Stormie looking away.

Odd. Will Turner just referred to Agent Emerson by his first name, Jaxson thought to himself.

"Well, unless you have any further questions, I don't think they have anything to add, Agent Locke, but after you look at the car tomorrow and you find that you have other questions, then just reach out. We'll see if we can help," Sheriff Turner said as she stood, hinting to Agent Locke it was time for them to leave.

"No. I can't think of anything right now," Jaxson said as he stood. He knew the two had more information, but he also knew that now wasn't the time to pursue it.

He thanked them for their time and followed Sheriff Turner back to their cars. She gave him directions to the Beaufort Bed and Breakfast and to the county impound lot where he could find the car. Jaxson found the directions easy to follow, and before long, he pulled into the parking lot of the converted Victorian-style home and checked in with the owner.

After unpacking and cleaning up, he read over the file once

more. Jaxson asked his supervisor before leaving Charlotte as to why he was being sent to recover a car belonging to an FBI agent who disappeared in 1965. Jaxson's caseload usually involved unsolvable cases, cases where there were no leads, and cases that involved serial killers. Jaxson, unlike others, had a sense about him that most investigators did not. He had the natural ability to notice things that were out of place or that other people simply overlooked.

Jaxson was told that Agent Emerson was wanted for the murder of two, maybe three people. He had come to Beaufort on his own accord and conducted an unauthorized investigation into the deaths of three young girls of color in 1965. The current media attention surrounding the case has been centered on the discovery of his personal car, an original 1965 Shelby Mustang GT350. Car collectors had reached out to the FBI, wanting to know what was to become of the car once the FBI was finished with it. The town was full of media personnel waiting to get a photo of the rare vehicle.

Jaxson ordered pizza from a local pizzeria and sat at the small table in his room, reading over the file concerning Agent Emerson. He learned Agent Emerson had gone to the University of Oklahoma and played in the Orange Bowl in 1958. After graduation, he went to law school at Duke.

Interesting. Agent Emerson grew up in North Carolina, went to the University of Oklahoma, played in the Orange Bowl against Duke University, and came back to Duke to go to law school, Jaxson thought to himself.

He also learned Agent Emerson was involved in some highly publicized civil rights cases in the sixties. Jaxson sat back in his chair. The things Emerson was accused of and the things he was a part of in his short career weren't adding up. Jaxson then focused on reading the reports from the investigating FBI agents, the sheriff, and the coroner. Once more, things didn't add up. They were also very brief. They contained little information about the people Emerson had supposedly killed, the disappearance of Agent Emerson, and the deaths of the girls. One thing that the FBI agents' and the sheriff's reports had in common was the guilt of one person: Agent Nathan Emerson, who suddenly disappeared into thin air, leaving an expensive car in the woods.

Jaxson finally moved on to the few available photos that had not been destroyed or misplaced in the past fifty-plus years. He reviewed autopsy photos, crime scene photos, and photos of victims in the hospital. There were photos of young Stormie and Benjamin Arrington in the hospital, recovering from their extensive injuries. At about twelve-thirty, Jaxson finally decided to go to bed. After lying there for about thirty minutes thinking about the case, he fell asleep.

SATURDAY, JUNE 1

Jaxson woke up at about seven and quickly got in the shower. It was there where he was still trying to wake up when a thought occurred to him. He turned off the water and hustled toward the table with the files on it. He shuffled through the photos and finally found the right one. There it was, a detail in the image right in front for everyone to see, but it seemed no one ever had… until now.

Jaxson made it down to the impound lot and met with the man Sheriff Turner said would be there. His name was Tim, and he was overly helpful yet slightly hard to understand when he spoke. Jaxson had found him in the office sitting over a large portion of biscuits and gravy. Outside along the fence, were news vans and media people waiting to get a glimpse and a photo of the car. Tim led Jaxson through a door into the garage bay, where Jaxson got his first look at the 1965 Shelby GT350.

"I towed the car inside the shop out of view of the cameras until you got a chance to look it over," Tim explained.

"Thank you. Did you have a look inside it?" Jaxson asked.

"Nope, I just lifted the hood and made sure all the critters were out of it before I brought it inside."

"No critters?" Jaxson asked.

"Nope. The car was buttoned up pretty good. All the windows were up, the keys were in the ignition, and the doors were unlocked. I'm pretty sure the guys who found it went through it and took some photos. I found smudge marks in the dust inside from where people had climbed around before I got there."

"Well, thanks. I guess I'll take it from here," Jaxson said as the man walked out of the building.

Jaxson took photos of the outside of the car and then moved to the inside to take more. After an hour, he sat in the front seat to document and log the items he found in the glove box. He finally moved to the back seat, and under the passenger seat, he came across a journal written by William "Preacher" Turner.

Jaxson took the journal from the car and walked to an old chair sitting in the corner of the garage to read it. After about an hour, he realized he had discovered an amazing story, but he still had questions. Jaxson collected his things and made his way to his car. He placed the journal in the passenger seat and headed toward the two people he believed could answer those questions.

Once again, he drove down the driveway leading to the home on the water. On the porch, Stormie and Will sat, appearing as if they were waiting for his return. Jaxson walked onto the porch holding the tattered journal.

"My father couldn't let the truth die. He told me before he died that he'd written everything down. I just didn't know where he'd left it," Will admitted.

"Can I have the truth that goes with the journal?" Jaxson asked.

"I think you already know the truth," Stormie answered.

"I think I do. I found it this morning in this photo." Jaxson handed her a copy of one of the evidence photos. In his very brief investigation, Agent Jaxson Locke believed he had found the truth in the photo. The journal confirmed it, but still, there were unanswered questions.

Stormie looked at the red circle that Agent Locke had made. She smiled and then looked back up at Agent Locke. "Start reading, and Will and I can fill in the blanks."

Jaxson sat in a chair across the table from them. He opened the journal, took a deep breath, and read aloud from the beginning.

Chapter 2
The Past

Nathan Emerson
Thursday, July 1, 1965

FBI Agent Nathan Emerson was in Charlotte, North Carolina, sitting in the waiting room of the office of the special agent in charge, Nicolas Smith. Smith enjoyed a corner office on the second floor of the federal building, with views of the city. Special agent in charge was a difficult position to achieve in any city within the bureau, and it was usually reserved for hardworking, decorated, and committed agents of the FBI who were in their final years of service.

Emerson pondered how Smith had received the corner office and the title of special agent in charge since he was not and had not achieved anything close to those requirements in his short ten years of service. He had actually just transferred from Florida to North Carolina within the past month. This was the second meeting Emerson was going to have with Agent Smith.

Their first meeting had been brief and down in Florida, where Agent Smith had been overseeing the Federal Bureau of Narcotics. In Miami, where Agent Emerson had been sent on a temporary assignment, soon found himself working with five corrupt federal agents who were selling marijuana and pocketing the money. He also suspected they'd had a hand in killing three people. Two of the five agents were out of his own office in Charlotte on temporary assignment just like himself.

When Agent Emerson filed his report, the agents had been taken off the case and placed on desk duty—which included Agent Emerson—pending an investigation. The two agents from Charlotte and Emerson were also sent back to the Charlotte office. It was while he was on desk duty that the other two agents conspired against him and spread rumors within the bureau. Agent Emerson learned recently that the other agents had accused him of being the one who was corrupt in Miami. During the past few months, many people were reassigned, including Agent Smith. Many other agents distanced themselves from Agent Emerson and would not speak to him.

Agent Emerson didn't know what to expect from his second meeting with Agent Smith, who had somehow gotten himself assigned to the Charlotte office, even though he was in charge of the mess that occurred in Miami. The previous special agent in charge, with whom Agent Emerson had a better relationship with, had been transferred to Mississippi without an explanation to anyone. Agent Emerson was the one who had requested today's appointment with the new supervisor a week ago.

He was told this morning by Smith's secretary, Sharon Bunting, that he was being squeezed in between 9:00 and 9:15 a.m. Sharon had been with the bureau for a very long time. Rumors swirled that she had once dated the legendary leader of the FBI, J. Edgar Hoover himself. No one really knew for sure, and no one dared to ask her. Sharon was nice, very formal and businesslike. She was tall, thin, wore a lot of makeup to cover up her wrinkles, and smelled of smoke. It was believed that she was in her sixties, but once again, no one dared to ask unless they wanted to find themselves checking for communists at the North Pole.

It was the common belief that the men in the Bureau ran the office, but the agents in the office knew secretaries decided who would be assigned where and for how long. Sharon sat behind her desk most days running interference and making excuses for Agent Smith, just as she had done for the previous nine or ten other Agent Smiths before him.

In the waiting area, Sharon had directed Agent Emerson where to sit and then used the intercom to inform Agent Smith that his meeting had arrived. Sharon made no attempt at conversation nor pleasantries whatsoever toward Agent Emerson. She just pecked on her typewriter after announcing his arrival. Nathan sat there quietly, looking at the portraits of the various men on the wall. If an agent ever wanted to know where he was in the bureau food chain, he simply needed to look at that wall. At the top was President Johnson, at the bottom was Agent Smith, and somewhere much further down was Agent Emerson. *Not pictured, of course,* he thought to himself.

Smith's voice resonated from the intercom. "Send Agent Emerson in please, Sharon."

"Yes, sir." She looked up at Emerson. "You may go in now."

Emerson stood, walked to the door, and stopped to straighten his suit coat before walking into Smith's office. Inside, Smith was standing behind his desk looking out over the city with his back to the door. He was a small thin man with wire-rimmed glasses, and he wore an expensive three-piece suit.

"I don't care for this view much. I had a view of the ocean in Miami," Smith commented as he lit a cigarette before turning around to face Emerson.

"Nathan, I understand you're worried about some colored girls who have died over in Beaufort, North Carolina, and—"

"Killed," Emerson stated, interrupting.

"Yes. They're all dead, and those deaths have been ruled accidental," Smith responded, visibly irritated by the interruption.

"The local sheriff has investigated those deaths, and he has cleared them all as accidental. And now, from this memo you sent me, it seems a colored preacher by the name of Turner has contacted you and requested a formal investigation by the FBI."

"Yes, sir."

"Well, I understand you've only been here a short time, but still, I'd think that you would know the FBI is not some local radio station."

Smith's comment confused Nathan. "I don't understand, sir."

Smith huffed. "In other words, we don't do requests, especially from non-law-enforcement officials, Agent Emerson."

"But with all due respect, with everything that's happened in the past few years regarding civil rights violations, I thought Mr. Hoover wanted us looking into cases like this."

"Cases… There are no cases, nor one single case for that matter. These deaths have been cleared by the local law enforcement agency. They haven't even asked for our involvement."

"So, we're to do nothing?" Emerson asked disgruntledly.

"No." Smith exhaled the cigarette smoke from his lungs as he walked from behind the desk. "Shouldn't you be more concerned with the internal investigation you started?" he asked as he picked up a thick file off his desk.

"To my understanding, that investigation will be over soon, and I would be eligible for field assignment again," Emerson stated in his defense.

"Agent Emerson, it's never over in the FBI, especially if I'm in charge. You, after all, have made accusations against your fellow agents, all of whom happen to be very close to me."

"I saw corruption, and I reported it," Emerson said defensively once more. Other agents would have backed off by now, but Emerson never understood the meaning of the word tact when it came to saying what was on his mind, nor did he have a filter or a disposition of listening to nonsense.

"Yes, I know, but I also know you used your fancy law degree to help yourself in your defense throughout this investigation and—"

"Defense! Agent Smith, as I said before, I wasn't the subject of that investigation until those other agents conspired after I reported them!" Emerson stated loudly, interrupting Smith once more.

"In my opinion, any other agent would've already been out of a job. Possibly in prison by now. I've read the investigation, and I think you're dirty," Smith said and then sat on the corner of his desk, waiting to see if Emerson would take the bait.

Smith wanted Emerson to lose control so he could be done with him. He needed his men back to work in Miami, making him money, but Emerson had to go away first. All the accused agents worked for Smith. He needed Emerson gone before one of his men tried to avoid a lengthy prison sentence by cutting a deal for themselves. It had taken a lot of favors to get assigned to Charlotte, and he was determined to get rid of Emerson in one way or another.

Emerson stood without saying a word. He knew he was being lured into a losing argument that could have disastrous consequences.

"You know something, Emerson? Why don't you take some time and go on down to Beaufort and see what you can find," Smith suggested as he walked in the direction of the window once more.

"I don't understand. Are we opening an investigation or not?" Emerson asked aggravatedly as he moved toward the desk.

"No. Not at this time. I mean, we really don't have anything to go on, now do we?" Smith answered while continuing to look out the window.

"Then what am I supposed to do?" Emerson didn't understand the direction Smith was going with his indirect answers.

"I'll tell you what, Emerson. You go to Beaufort. Take your own car, and make it look like you're there on vacation. If you find something, then let me know. I'll give you forty-five days to find something."

Emerson stood there confused and then said, "I guess I'll send in weekly reports as usual."

"No, that won't be necessary. Just contact me if you find evidence. You know what that is, right? I mean evidence, not accusations—the kind of stuff that's used in a court of law to convict someone of a crime. I'm sure you learned about evidence in law school."

"Yes, sir. I believe I did," Emerson answered in frustration.

"Besides, forty-five days is the amount of leave you have saved up. That will give the bureau plenty of time to complete its investigation and me plenty of time to get you transferred out of here. I don't think I like you much, Agent Emerson. I really don't think you'll find anything in Beaufort, and at the end of your trip, one of two things will happen: I'll have you transferred out of here, or you'll find nothing in Beaufort, and I'll have you terminated for being incompetent. Either way, the bureau and I will be done with you."

"And if I find evidence?" Emerson asked before opening the door to leave.

"Then I'll transfer you somewhere else after the official investigation into whatever you find."

"So, I'm on my personal leave investigating this case?"

"You're not really investigating anything. You're burning forty-five vacation days. If you find something, then I'll give them back, but you'll still be transferred out. It'll be a win for both of us."

"It's a deal," Emerson reluctantly agreed as he walked out the door and slammed it shut behind him.

CHAPTER 3
STORMIE ARRINGTON

FRIDAY, JULY 2, 1965

Nathan spent the morning packing for the trip. At first, he put together a few suits, shirts, and ties, but then he decided to only bring one business suit. After all, he was supposed to be on vacation, and people on vacation usually didn't wear business suits near the ocean during summer. In the end, he decided on a few slacks, shorts, a few V-neck T-shirts, and a few short-sleeved camp shirts. All the shirts he packed were perfect for carrying his gun concealed while wearing shorts or with slacks. He also made room for one bathing suit, although he doubted he would get to use it.

After spending the day getting his things ready for the trip, he sat down over a hot pastrami sandwich and a nice cold beer and read over the file sent to him from the local sheriff's office. Nathan had requested the records from the sheriff's office before speaking to Smith, but after their hostile meeting, he decided there was no reason to tell him about it. The files included the victim's names, a map of where the bodies were found, and the coroner's report.

Sheriff Dwight Carter had been very brief in his reports, and as for the coroner's reports, they appeared to mimic the sheriff's. Apparently, one girl had drowned. She was in the water for so long, her body was infested with various marine life. The water scavengers mutilated it beyond recognition. Another girl was struck by a boat propeller after drowning, and a third had been attacked by an alligator after entering the water. In all the reports, two things were consistent: the girls had met their deaths while intoxicated, and all of them were found in or near Taylor Creek. Delia Snipes was last seen Saturday, April 17, 1965. Rose Melton was found on May 1, 1965, and no one knew when Ida Freeman was last seen.

Agent Emerson found a few other things that all the reports had in common, but it wasn't what was in the report where he found the commonality. It was what was not in the reports that piqued his interest. There were no photos of the deceased, nor were there any witnesses listed or information on next of kin.

Surely someone had found these girls other than the sheriff. In a small town, someone must have known them, Nathan thought to himself as he finished his sandwich.

Lastly, all three girls had immediately been cremated after the coroner completed his examination. "Why?" Nathan mumbled to himself.

He sat back on the couch, placed his feet on the coffee table, and finished off the beer. He had spent the better part of the evening looking over the file and had lost track of time. On the end table, the clock read twelve thirty, and next to the clock, he saw the picture of his parents.

He smiled for a moment, then missed them both. He missed the times he'd called his dad for advice or just sitting down with the two of them for dinner when he would come home from college during the holidays. Nathan remembered getting his college ring, which he still wore, the summer before his senior year was to start. The ring had been expensive, but they insisted he have it. He looked down at it on his finger and twisted it back and forth as he recalled other fond memories of his parents.

Nathan's parents were good people, and they were taken away from him way too soon. He contemplated whether he was doing what they would have wanted him to do in life. They had always supported him in his endeavors. *Would they be proud of me today?* Nathan asked himself as he walked his plate into the kitchen. He set the plate on the counter. *They'd be proud of me for anything I did.*

SATURDAY, JULY 3, 1965

The early morning sun was bright as it slowly made its way higher into the sky. It was a beautiful day for a drive toward the coast. Nathan rolled the window down and inhaled the fresh scents of nature, noticing that everything was green and blooming along the road. The Shelby 350 roared as he pressed the accelerator down and entered the oncoming lane to pass a slow-moving tractor being driven by a local farmer. The sports car was expensive and had been a spontaneous purchase after he sold the family farm earlier in the year. There were many attributes Nathan inherited from his parents. He had his mother's spontaneity and his father's need for cruising down the highway in a fast car with the radio blasting.

As he passed one farm after another, he allowed his childhood memories to consume his thoughts. One farm had a barn resembling the one his parents had on their peanut farm. It was red and brown with a high-pitched roof. He and his father had rebuilt a 1940 Ford pickup in that old barn of theirs, and the pickup had been Nathan's first introduction to independence and freedom. He drove it around the farm at the age of fourteen, scaring the chickens and geese. When he was seventeen, he drove it to his high school prom with Betty Lou Martin. Nathan smiled at the thought of Betty Lou, another first in his life.

The 350 had a powerful motor, and Nathan wondered if his father had ever driven a car so smooth and fast when he was running moonshine down the backroads of North Carolina during prohibition. Nathan never really knew if his father's stories of being a bootlegger were true or not. Maybe they were just stories—stories that kept a twelve-year-old boy's attention in the evenings during the summer after he broke his leg jumping out of a tree on a dare, just to impress Betty Lou Martin.

Nathan's attention was brought back to the present when he heard the announcer on the radio talking about the future of space and how it was just one month ago today when Edward Higgins White had made the first spacewalk. The announcer then introduced someone else to the show, and the two began a conversation about the Russians and what their next step might be. The space topic grew boring, and Nathan changed from station to station until he found one reporting baseball scores. He was disappointed to hear that the Pirates had beaten the Braves, as he was a Braves fan, so he once again searched the airwaves and finally stopped on the Rolling Stones singing *"I Can't Get No Satisfaction."* The song was all he needed to go faster with the radio blaring.

The drive from Charlotte to Beaufort usually took about six hours, but Nathan made it in just over five. After asking residents where 231 Ann Street was located, Nathan parked in front of an old Victorian that appeared to be built in the late 1800s. It was three stories and painted white, with a brick foundation and large windows. The building sat on the edge of Taylor Creek and provided easy walking access to most places in town. Nathan had booked the room earlier in the month after he received the letter from Pastor William Turner, or simply "Preacher" to his friends. Preacher was also the person who had recommended the Beaufort Bed and Breakfast. Walking up to the front door, Nathan noticed a sign that made him laugh.

WELCOME TO THE BEAUFORT BED AND BREAKFAST, WHERE YOU MAKE BOTH!

Nathan walked up the stairs, and on the door was another sign.

It's not locked. Turn the knob and come in! Once inside, ring the bell one time at the desk if I'm not there, then wait until I show up!

Nathan shook his head, but did as the sign instructed and waited at the front desk. A few seconds later, a thin, bald, and unshaven elderly man wearing a white button-down shirt, brown slacks, and house slippers came out of a door on the left side of the front desk.

"I'm Mr. Jackson, and I own the bed and breakfast." the elderly man stated as he reached down and grabbed a key from under the desk.

"I'm Nathan Emerson and I have a reservation."

"I know Everyone else with a reservation has already checked in."

"Can I get a room that overlooks the water and the street?"

"There's only one room left but lucky for you it has a view of both."

"It looks pretty busy here," Nathan remarked, trying to make conversation.

"It's always busy around the Fourth of July. Now, there are some things you need to know. I don't come into your room to clean. If you need something like a towel or extra blanket, then come down here and let me know before seven p.m. You can have visitors but don't have them coming in after seven p.m. Your room rate for the month is two hundred dollars. You pay by the week. I'll need fifty dollars now."

"Well, thank you," Nathan responded as he handed the man the money.

"You're welcome. I'll give you a receipt when you check out. Please sign the guest registration"

"All right."

"Your room is on the third floor, and the doors are marked. Your room is three oh one. You'll recognize it because it will have a sign that says three oh one," Mr. Jackson stated and walked back out through the same door he had entered.

Nathan shook his head once more and made his way up to his room. It was three flights of stairs and a hallway later where he stood in front of a door. He determined the room was one of six on the third floor. The door was stained dark cherry, like the rest of the wood trim in the home. In the center was a sign that read 301.

"This must be the place," he mumbled quietly. He reached down and unlocked the door and then turned the knob. Upon entering the room, he found it to be much better than what he thought it would be. He had based his opinion, before going upstairs, off his minimal engagement with the plain hotel proprietor. The bed was made and covered with a quilt that had designs of ships from the 1700s on it. There was a bathroom off to the left, and on the far wall were three large windows overlooking the street and Taylor Creek.

Nathan unpacked his suitcase and placed some clothes in the dresser, while others he hung in the closet. The bed was queen size, which he was happy to see rather than the usual smaller twin bed, which his six-foot-two, 205-pound frame didn't fit very well in. Next to the bed was a nightstand. On it was one lamp, an alarm clock, a bible, and a radio. Directly across from the bed was a dresser that held a small TV. The room had four pictures that were paintings of sailing ships.

Simple but comfortable, he thought.

The day was hot and humid. Nathan thought about taking a shower and finding a place to eat, but he wanted to speak to Sheriff Carter before it got too late. He decided against taking a shower but changed his sweat-dried T-shirt into a clean blue-and-white, short-sleeved camp shirt that concealed the .45 he carried in the small of his back.

Nathan left his room and walked back downstairs, passing other guests who were dressed in shorts and flip-flops, coming and going as they enjoyed their Fourth of July weekend. Mr. Jackson, who had at first appeared to be pestered by Nathan for ringing the bell once more, kindly gave him directions. At around four o'clock, Nathan stood in the lobby of the sheriff's office. The building was off Ann Street, just like the bed and breakfast, and it, too, was painted white. Inside was a small lobby area with a large counter separating the visitors from the offices and holding cells. Nathan was greeted by the receptionist, a heavy woman wearing a white-and-green dress. She also wore an ill-fitted wig atop her head that Nathan tried not to stare at. He didn't know what to expect from Sheriff Carter, but Preacher, during his phone calls with Nathan, had warned him not to get his hopes up.

Sheriff Carter came out into the waiting area from a side door. He was a large man, whom Nathan estimated was six foot four and weighed about three hundred pounds. He had gray hair and a large pot belly that hung over his duty belt.

"I'm Agent Emerson with the FB—"

"I know who you are, son," Carter said as he crossed his arms over his belly. "I don't appreciate the FBI coming into my county without an invitation. Pastor Turner told me he'd requested you boys."

"I'm sorry, Sheriff, and I don't mean to interfere or give anyone the feeling that the FBI is interfering with your investigation. We're just simply following up on the information that we received and—"

"And, the truth is, boy, no one cares or gives a damn about a few dead nigger whores who were known to have spread their legs for a couple of dollars," the sheriff stated loudly.

"Whores? That's odd. There was no mention in any of the reports that I have that identified the girls as prostitutes. Besides, Sheriff Carter, I'm here on vacation. To tell you the truth, there is no official investigation by the FBI. I was asked by my superior to see if I could be of any assistance to you while I was here. I'm simply following up on a complaint the FBI received concerning a possible violation of civil rights. Now, we're not saying there was a violation, but I'm sure you understand that based on everything that has happened in the past few years, we have to investigate some of the complaints we receive. With that said, you can rest assured, Sheriff, if I find anything to substantiate the complaint, then the FBI will do everything in its power to bring the wrongdoers to justice—with the full support of the local sheriff's office, I'm sure. After all, Sheriff, we're on the same team here. Our job is to ensure that people living within the United States, which includes our small-town communities, are safe no matter their color."

"I think you talk a lot, but I understand. Now you try to enjoy your vacation," Sheriff Carter suggested as he turned to walk back through the door.

"Oh, Sheriff… If you've got any additional information that wasn't sent to me before, could you get it to me, please?"

"I'll have everything ready for you on Monday."

Nathan nodded toward the receptionist, turned, and walked out the door.

It was about five o'clock in the evening when Nathan walked

around the town of Beaufort like the vacationer, he said he was. The town was small, but the number of people moving in and out of the local shops suggested otherwise. He discovered he enjoyed reading the history of Beaufort that he found in a local paper. He learned the town was first inhabited by the Coree Indians who were eventually forced farther inland by settlers. The coastal town became a significant fishing and whaling port until some time back. Now, Beaufort flourished as a vacation destination for beachgoers during the summer months.

The town's history also boasted the exploits of Edward Teach, more commonly known as Blackbeard, which interested Nathan the most. He read how the feared pirate had sailed the seas around the east coast and down into the Florida panhandle. He discovered the pirate had a lure of sorts to the small fishing port of Beaufort. The pirate's history could be found in most storefront windows that sold pirate costumes and other souvenirs. Nathan learned Blackbeard had captured a French ship and renamed it the Queen Anne's Revenge, and he later ran the ship aground on a sandbar near Beaufort, joining the town and the pirate forever in history.

Nathan wasn't paying much attention to the people around him until he spotted a woman who appeared to be taking photos of random vacationers. She was maybe five foot four with blonde hair she wore in a ponytail. She wore a blue peri-print pullover and blue Capri pants to match. She smiled at people passing by and spoke to everyone who approached her. Nathan presumed she was a local photographer due to the number of people who addressed her as they walked by. He also determined she was the most beautiful woman he had ever seen.

Stormie Arrington was busy taking photos of the Fourth of July weekend activities for the local newspaper, unaware she had captured the attention of a stranger in town. The day was busy, and people were everywhere. Near the entrance to Jack's House of Fresh Fish, she saw two toddlers holding hands, dressed in red-white-and-blue outfits waving small flags. She lifted her camera, quickly adjusted herself, and snapped the shot. She then adjusted her lens and placed the camera to her eye once more, and she spotted, through the viewfinder, the tall, handsome man across the way in front of what she believed was the worst seafood restaurant in town. She dropped her camera to her waist and looked at him directly. Stormie was always direct.

Nathan, not realizing he was staring at her until she looked right at him, immediately looked toward the menu in the window of the restaurant on his right. He stood there, pretending to browse the dinner choices for a few moments, and casually turned his head to the left to see if she was still there.

"I'm not over there anymore," Stormie whispered from behind the startled Nathan.

"Oh, hello. I wasn't—"

"I wasn't gonna eat here. Is that what you were about to say? I mean, I wouldn't eat here either. It's the worst place in town for seafood. And the worst part of it is it should be fresh because that's what the sign says. I mean, the damn creek that runs out into the Atlantic Ocean is sitting no more than a hundred yards away from their back door," she explained in her southern Alabama accent.

Nathan was fascinated, to say the least, at how upfront and friendly this beautiful woman with dark green eyes was toward a stranger. "Okay. Then where would a visitor like me eat dinner in this lovely town of yours?"

"Well, it ain't my town. I'm just visiting too, goin' on about ten years now. I think. Now, my husband, he may call it his town. Come to think of it, he probably thinks he owns it. But anyway, I'd eat over there, at Pirate's Cove and Fish House. It's fresh and tasty."

"Thanks for the information. I'm Nathan Emerson, by the way," Nathan greeted as he extended his right hand.

"Nice to meet you, Nathan Emerson. I'm Stormie, Stormie Arrington," she replied as she shook his hand.

"What brings you to Beaufort? Are you and your family here on vacation?"

"No. I don't have a family. I'm here just vacationing," he answered awkwardly.

"Well, ain't that the beans! You mean to tell me you came to Beaufort for the Fourth of July, and you don't have a family? No kids, wife... Maybe you're here with your brother or sister and their family?"

Nathan shook his head no as Stormie spoke.

"No, you're really here by yourself?"

"Yep, just me."

Stormie enjoyed quizzing the dark-haired, blue-eyed visitor. She thought he was an attractive man who appeared to be fit and friendly. But she was still suspicious about him being alone and on vacation. "Well, I guess everyone likes Beaufort on the Fourth of July, even a man who vacations alone."

"Maybe I like pirates. Now, you say Pirate Cove is the place for dinner over thar?" Nathan pointed across the park while emphasizing the word "thar," in his best attempt at sounding like a pirate.

"Yes, c'mon I'll walk you over and get you a seat. Normally, if you don't have a reservation this weekend at Pirate's Cove, you'd be out of luck. But, seeing that you're a pirate and all, I'm sure they can make room for one of their own."

Stormie continued to make small talk about the weather as she led Nathan toward the restaurant. She was sure she heard an accent when the stranger spoke. She wasn't sure if it was North or South, but one thing was evident; he was from the Carolinas.

Stormie took Nathan to the back of the restaurant, away

from the long line in front. She knocked on the back door, and a large man wearing an apron covered in blood and other seafood remains opened the door.

"Hi, Mrs. Stormie," the man said, greeting a regular guest of his.

"Hi, Freddy. Do you think you can get my close friend, Nathan here, a seat tonight? He came into town unexpectedly last night, and I've been telling him for years that this was the best seafood restaurant in town. And now, as you can imagine, I can't just let him leave without trying the red snapper you bake to perfection."

Nathan smiled at Freddy but never said a word or tried to interrupt Stormie as she laid it on thick.

"Absolutely, Mrs. Stormie. Give me a minute, and I'll set a place for him." Freddy closed the door and went back inside.

"Mrs. Arrington, could I show you my gratitude by asking you to join me for dinner tonight?"

"Why, Nathan Emerson, are you asking a married woman out on a date?" Stormie asked, looking as if she were appalled at such an idea.

"Uh, no…I was just…" Nathan stumbled, looking for the right words.

"I'm just teasing you, honey. Normally I'd jump at the chance to eat here, but I can't this evening. By the way, please call me Stormie."

"Okay then, but I'd prefer to be called Nathan."

"It's a deal," Stormie agreed just as the door opened.

"I got a place for him," Freddy said, interrupting.

"Enjoy your dinner, Nathan. And if you stick around town long enough, maybe I'll take you up on that offer," Stormie said flirtatiously.

"I look forward to it."

Stormie made her way back to her car, and before she knew it, she was heading back home. She always looked forward to getting out and meeting new people. Her husband, Ben, seldom ever wanted to go out for dinner, travel, or take her anywhere for that matter. He barely even spoke to her these days as it was. The idea of having dinner with a handsome man excited her a bit. She really wanted to say yes to dinner with the handsome stranger, but word would get out in the small town, as it always did, and it would just cause more trouble for her with Ben.

She and Ben had been married for almost ten years, and for the past five, she had felt neglected, mistreated, and, on a few occasions, physically abused by Ben. She wanted so many times in the past few years to run away. At times, she thought maybe she would go back to Alabama or move to California. The pictures she saw in magazines made it appear to be a lovely place with sunny beaches and palm trees that reached for the sky. But Ben would never leave North Carolina, and she had come to believe that he would never allow her to leave either.

Chapter 4
Ben Arrington

Nathan walked out of Pirate's Cove, satisfied with the red snapper dinner Stormie had suggested. He made his way down toward the waterfront and then in the direction of the bed and breakfast. As Nathan walked, he thought about Stormie Arrington. He thought how lucky a man had to be to have her by his side.

She's beautiful, witty, and, well, smart. Yeah, she's smart. I can tell just by talking to her, he thought to himself.

Nathan continued making his way down the sidewalk until he passed a late-night bar and grill. The sign in the window read "Judge's Revenge" in red letters.

Looking through the window, he saw the place was packed. Customers were crowded around tables. Some sat elbow to elbow, while others danced in the aisles to the music blasting from the jukebox. Nathan was about to continue on his way until he took another look and saw Sheriff Carter sitting at a table with three other men and an attractive brunette, who appeared to be quite comfortable with the well-dressed man sitting close to her.

Nathan thought about keeping to himself, but curiosity

took over, and he decided to enter the establishment to say hello once more to the town sheriff. Once inside, the smell of cigarette smoke was overwhelming, and from what he could tell, the booze flowed freely. Nathan thought some of the liquor he observed being consumed was illegal moonshine, which wasn't governed by the state or county.

No need to say anything about it. Besides, I'm on vacation, he thought. Nathan made his way past a few drunk patrons until he was standing next to the table directly across from Sheriff Carter.

"Evening, Sheriff," Nathan said loudly while looking at the inebriated, uniformed lawman.

"Evening yourself," Sheriff Carter slurred.

Nathan quickly looked around the bar. "This looks like the place to be tonight."

"It is if you're a local, but you're not a local, are you?" the sheriff replied, making sure Agent Emerson knew he was not welcome.

"Now, Sheriff Carter, don't go running our guest off," the well-dressed man sitting next to the woman said as he stood and shook Nathan's hand. "I'm Ben Arrington, town prosecutor, and to my left here is our own public defender, Jack Walters. Next to him is the Honorable Judge Thomas Jefferson Ridge. And I'm guessing you're that visiting FBI agent, Nathan Emerson."

"You're correct, sir," Nathan said as he leaned over and greeted everyone with a firm handshake.

"Pleased to meet each one of you," Nathan offered. He then turned toward the woman whose eyes he had noticed were uncomfortably locked on him.

Emma suddenly realized that she was staring. "Ben's the next governor of North Carolina," she said proudly and pointed at Ben Arrington.

"Well, maybe if I get enough votes and the support of some friends," Ben clarified and then turned to face Emma.

"This is Miss Emma Rodgers, my legal assistant," Ben said as he placed his foot on the chair and used his napkin to wipe a smudge mark off his expensive shoes.

"Ma'am," Nathan said as he extended his hand toward Emma. She was impressed with the FBI man standing in front of her, and she didn't hide that she was. She simply stood, extended her hand toward Nathan, and lightly gripped his hand.

"Welcome to Beaufort, Mr. Emerson, or is it Agent Emerson?" Emma asked with what Nathan guessed to be a rather poor attempt at a Southern accent. She was beautiful, thin, and wore too much makeup along with a tight dress that accentuated every one of her curves.

Somewhere from up north, maybe Philadelphia, Nathan thought. "Nathan is fine."

"How are you finding the likes of our town, Agent Emerson?" Judge Ridge asked and then sipped the remaining whiskey from his glass. Ridge appeared to be an older man, possibly in his sixties. He was bald and had a potbelly. His face and head were red, his eyes were bloodshot, and he spoke in a slow slurred speech.

"Very well. Thank you for asking."

"I'm glad," he said and then yelled for Dolly as he looked around for her. "Dolly, get your Black ass out here and fill my glass!"

A few minutes later, a young light-skinned Black girl walked up with a whiskey bottle and poured the contents into the judge's glass.

"Now, you keep close by in case I run dry again. You don't want me firing you for slouching on the job, do you?" He rubbed his hand against her buttocks.

"Nathan, what's your take on these dead colored girls?" Ben Arrington asked.

"I really don't know yet. I just arrived a few hours ago. I'll keep the sheriff updated if I find something." In the short time Nathan stood there conversing with the group, he had quickly assessed everyone.

He knew Ben was the leader, and everyone else at the table served a purpose for him. The sheriff was his muscle, who took care of problems. The judge was his endorsement and introduced him to influential people. The little guy, Jack Walters, who said nothing and hoped no one saw him, was a weasel who did whatever he was told. If something was going on in this town, these four men knew about it. As for Emma, she was nothing more than a pleasurable distraction for Ben Arrington. He would use her until she no longer served a purpose.

"I believe I met your wife earlier today," Nathan said, adding to the conversation.

"Oh! How'd that come to be?" Ben asked suspiciously.

"I was looking for a place to eat this evening, and she gave me a recommendation, and then she walked me over and helped get me a seat."

"That's my little woman. Always taking pictures and taking in strays," Ben said sarcastically. He laughed and looked around the table, unconsciously directing the others to laugh as well.

"Well, I imagine I'm a bit of a stray, but please do thank her again. Let her know I enjoyed the meal. It was nice meeting all of you. Good night," Nathan said, then turned and walked out.

Everyone at Ben's table watched and waited until the agent left the bar before speaking.

"I hope he's not going to be a problem," Walters said, finally breaking his silence.

"We don't need any new problems now. We have enough already," the judge said, reminding everyone.

Ben straightened his shirt. "You two relax. I think the sheriff will keep a good eye on him while he's here. Won't you, Sheriff?"

"You can count on it. But the judge is right. We already got problems, if you ain't noticed."

"Getting new girls?" Ben asked.

"Exactly, new girls. And let's not forget the old ones we still have who may talk to the FBI man, just in case any of you've forgotten why he's here. We damn sure don't need them nigger whores talking to anyone," the sheriff announced as he looked over at Dolly.

"You're correct, Sheriff. I think it's best if you get the word out to the other girls and anyone else we do business with. Maybe remind them that it's in everyone's best interest not to speak to the FBI man. And then get our old whores busy recruiting some new girls. Maybe some from another county would be a good idea. It shouldn't be that hard. These damn niggers breed like rabbits. Have them call their cousins and then have those cousins call their cousins. We need a bunch of girls for the big Gentlemen's Social we have coming up," Ben said in frustration.

"Good idea, Ben. Sheriff, don't fuck this up, because you can be replaced!" the drunken Judge said.

"Judge, I said I'll take care of it and I will. But let me remind everyone at this table that we're all in this together and I'd watch how you speak to me," the sheriff stated, leaning across the table toward the judge. "Don't even think about pulling out some bullshit about being the judge because it doesn't mean a damn thing to me. Your hands are just as dirty as mine. I allow all of you to get away with a lot of shit in my county, but none of you give me orders. Remember, a new broom sweeps clean, but an old broom knows where the dirt is."

"Dwight, the judge is just nervous like the rest of us. He didn't mean to sound ungrateful or threatening, and nor do I. We've all come too far to let something like this stop us now. I think we all know we're in this together. I just think it's best that we resolve all the loose ends before all our asses are hanging in the wind." Ben quickly interjected after seeing that things were getting heated between the two men.

"This is getting all messed up. We're so close to putting your ass in the governor's mansion, Ben, and the judge on the state supreme court, and dammit, I'm supposed to be the next state attorney general," Walters explained.

Judge Ridge dropped his glass onto the table. "Dammit, we all got plans for the future, Jack, and—"

"And y'all better keep to the plan. We all knew there would be bumps in the road along the way. Now, like I told my men in Korea, boot up and keep to the plan," the sheriff said.

"A few bumps! How about a fucking minefield in the road, soldier! We got a couple of dead nigger whores with the fucking FBI investigating!" Walters remarked loudly.

"Jack, keep your voice down! I think all y'all should just stop worrying and keep quiet. We're so close to finishing what we started. Jack, you will be the state attorney general. Judge, you'll get your appointment to the state supreme court, and, Sheriff, you'll get all the money you were promised once that little woman of mine is taken care of just as we've planned," Ben explained.

"That's on hold until Charlie gets back in town," the sheriff stated.

Ben looked at the sheriff pointedly. "Dwight, I think a lot's on hold until the FBI is out of town."

"Charlie will still want to be paid even though things are being put off. And he ain't gonna like sitting around, waiting."

"Then figure something else out. No one can die or disappear right now," Ben remarked, keeping his voice low.

"Damn it! I want her gone! I hate and despise that woman!" Emma burst.

"She will be in due time, my dear," Ben said, reassuring her as he patted her leg.

"I'll see if I can't find something for Charlie to do until we're ready."

"I think that's a good idea, Sheriff."

Nathan returned to his room and briefly looked over the case file once more to write down a few notes. He wrote about the four men he had met at the bar to whom he now referred to as "The Four Horsemen."

After he was done, he lay on the bed and thought about his life. He pondered what it could be like without the FBI in it. He thought about settling down with a beautiful woman, a woman whom he thought would keep him on his toes, never knowing what she was going to say or do at any moment. A woman like the one he met today.

He got up and walked across the room, and from the second-story window, he saw Taylor Creek and the Shackleford Banks. A small boat with two fishermen inside slowly drifted along with the current, under the full moon that glowed above.

How nice and peaceful, he thought.

Nathan was still watching the boat slowly drift farther and farther away when from the corner of his eye, he saw the dark figure of a large man underneath the streetlight. The man's cigarette glowed in the shadows with each puff. Nathan moved the curtain for a better look, but the cigarette glow disappeared as the man backed up, vanishing into the shadows of the trees behind him.

Nathan rushed across the room and turned the light off. He then went back to the window and looked for the shadow once more, but it was too late. He was gone. After a few minutes of looking into the night, Nathan walked to his door and made sure it was locked before lying down to go to sleep.

He lay there in the queen bed in the darkness, arranging his thoughts. Finally, he decided the only person who would have any interest in him right now would be Sheriff Carter.

Sheriff Carter was a large enough man to be the figure I saw in the shadows below. And if it were him, then Ben Arrington sent him to keep a close eye on me, he thought before drifting off to sleep.

Ben and Emma arrived at her front door after a short drive from Judge's Revenge. Ben unlocked it with his key, and the couple walked in. Emma's home was smaller than what she wanted, but it would do for now. Besides, she wasn't paying for it. She took some satisfaction knowing that Mrs. Stormie Arrington and her family's money kept her in the lifestyle she had grown accustomed to. Beaufort was a long way from Philadelphia and the people she'd had to run away from. For now, it was a safe place to be.

Inside, Emma turned on the radio while Ben shut and locked the door. She didn't say much to Ben in the car, but after tossing her purse onto the sofa, she put her hands on her hips and turned and faced him with pouty lips.

"What's wrong, my dear?" Ben asked.

"Everything is taking too long. I should be helping you through the mourning process by now!" she said and then turned away.

"You will, but right now, we have to be careful."

"Well, I still don't like it," she grumbled softly as she felt Ben come up behind her.

"Tell me, honey, how does it feel being in the arms of the next governor of North Carolina?" Ben asked as he pulled her closer.

She reached behind her back to unzip his pants. "It feels good. Really good. How does it feel to have the next first lady of North Carolina in your arms?"

"It feels really good," Ben whispered.

Emma heard Ben's breathing becoming heavy and faster as she caressed his excitement, which was growing between her fingers. Then she felt his strong hands on her shoulders, and without a word of warning, he forced her over the sofa. She made a slight gasping sound as if she were surprised by his aggressiveness, but if truth be told, she enjoyed being submissive to him. The pleasure in both their bodies built with each breath they took together. Ben ran both his hands along her large firm breasts.

"You want it, don't you, baby?" he whispered in her ear.

"Yes, oh, yes!"

He pulled at her blouse, which ripped the buttons off and sent them flying across the room.

"Take me, Ben, take me!" She begged between breaths as he cupped her breasts. Emma pushed back onto his groin and ground hard against it.

"All right, baby!" Ben whispered in her ear.

He violently tore away her bra, exposing her breast to the dimly lit room. Emma moaned as she gasped for air. Ben wanted and needed her. He reached down and ripped her skirt from the bottom of her ankles up to her waist.

"Yes, darling. Oh yes, take me!"

He ripped her panties off and entered her from behind. Ben moved slowly at first, holding her down with his right hand while he caressed up and down her backside.

"Faster, Ben. Faster!" Emma shouted.

Ben did not yield, and he pushed harder, faster, and deeper until they both could no longer hold out. Ben was first as he let out a sound of pure pleasure, followed by Emma screaming while she gripped the back of the sofa with both hands and pushed back against him.

As quickly as it had begun, it was over, and Ben slowed his movements while holding her hips. Emma continued to push backward. "Yes, oh, yes!" she said softly as Ben lightly kissed the back of her neck.

He expected Ben and Emma to arrive much later, as they had done previously. He barely got out of the house in time. He was inside lying on her bed with her pillow wrapped in his arms, where he could smell her scent. He allowed his thoughts to run wild in moments like those, and he cherished them. He imagined lying next to her and feeling her naked body against his. He longed for the feeling or the emotional touch of a woman wanting him as much as he wanted her. He was thinking about Emma when the car pulled into the driveway, forcing him to leave quickly out the back door.

Once again, he watched the two of them inside, but something was different this time. She was upset. Maybe she wouldn't be so willing to give in to his charm, and she would ignore his advances. He hated Ben Arrington and desired to take everything from him, just as Ben had done to him. He had nothing, but Ben Arrington had the love of two women.

Looking through the window, he stood, a dark figure masked by the shadows of trees. He watched as Emma once more gave herself to Ben. He longed desperately for the chance to be with her—or any woman who would have him for what he was—even if it was for a brief moment. He, like other men, longed for the touch and affection of a woman. For him, it would never be, because of Ben Arrington. One day, he would have his reckoning with him. One day soon.

He watched until the two of them disappeared into the bedroom where he could not see them anymore. Maybe one day, he would have her too. Maybe one day, he would surprise her. Maybe one day, she could feel the steel of his blade being thrust inside her.

Maybe… one day, he thought hungrily.

Sunday, July 4, 1965

Nathan allowed himself to sleep in a little. When he finally got up, he got dressed, ate a quick breakfast at a local diner, and then drove to the Beaufort Southern Baptist Community Church. The church was located at 1616 Water Street, in what people in town referred to as the colored area of Beaufort. The church was small with a large bell tower at the entrance. It was covered in a reddish brick at the bottom and had white siding. The entrance had a large wood double door entry.

Once inside, Nathan found the tall and thin Pastor Turner the same way he had left him in Birmingham: standing in front of a congregation, dressed in a black suit, and preaching the word of God. The pastor stood behind a thin, wooden, cross-shaped podium, delivering the Sunday sermon to his all-Black congregation. He was an enthusiastic pastor, to say the least. Nathan believed no one slept during his sermon.

"And, Lord, before we close this sermon on this beautiful day that you've once again bestowed upon us sinners, please let us remember Peter two sixteen. *Live as people who are free, not using your freedom as a cover-up for evil but living as servants of God,*" the pastor roared as he beat his fist on the pulpit. His voice echoed out the door and into the street.

"Amen!" many voices replied from the congregation.

Preacher looked over his flock and saw his old friend standing in the back, which brought a smile to his old weathered face.

"For he is God's servant for your good. But if you do wrong, be afraid, for he does not bear the sword in vain. For he is the servant of God, an avenger who carries out God's wrath on the wrongdoer."

Nathan smiled back at his old friend and shook his head. Preacher always had verses ready for every occasion.

"Now let us bow our heads once more in our final prayer. *Lord, as these people leave this place today, please continue to remind them to be submissive to rulers and authorities, to be obedient, to be ready for every good work, to speak evil of no one, to avoid quarreling, to be gentle, and to show perfect courtesy toward all people. For we ourselves were once foolish, disobedient, led astray, slaves to various passions and pleasures, passing our days in malice and envy, hated by others and hating one another… But when the goodness and loving kindness of God our Savior appeared, he saved us, not because of works done by us in righteousness but, according to his own mercy, by the washing of regeneration and renewal of the Holy Spirit. Amen."*

As Preacher and the rest of his congregation had their heads lowered, Nathan felt someone slide by next to him. He looked to his left just as two teenage boys quietly pushed past him and found seats in the last pew. They obviously had not dressed for church this morning, as they wore shorts and T-shirts. Nathan was sure he caught the smell of fish as they passed by.

The sermon appeared to have been a good one. Nathan wished he had not slept in this morning. He had sat through numerous sermons delivered by Preacher. The two of them had met in Birmingham, after the bombing of the 16th Street Baptist Church in September of 1963. He had forgotten how good Preacher was at delivering the message.

Chapter 5
Preacher

Nathan stood out of the way in the corner toward the back of the church. He watched quietly as Preacher shook hands and spoke to his flock as they exited. Soon the pews were empty, except where the two young latecomers had seated themselves. They sat there quietly, occasionally waving at other members as they passed. Preacher glared at the young men as he walked toward Nathan, where he happily shook his hand with a smile.

"I'm very pleased to see you again!"

"As am I, Preacher," Nathan replied.

The two young men started to get up and walk to the front of the church to make their way out through another entrance, hoping they wouldn't be noticed.

Preacher heard his sons trying to sneak away. He turned his attention from his old friend to them. "Just a minute, you two."

"How do you think it looks to the congregation when the pastor's sons can't get here on time? Don't you think it's important to hear the message?"

Willie, the taller and oldest son, dropped his arms to his

side and held his hands outward. "Yes, but, Pops, we both heard the message four times yesterday," he answered.

"Besides, you wanted us to catch some fresh fish for lunch today. We had to go out early this morning. We caught a mess of 'em, and Mr. Jake is fixin' to fry 'em up right now," the shorter and younger brother, Samuel, added to their defense.

Preacher closed his eyes and listened for a moment as his sons continued to plead their case. Finally, he raised his right hand, palm out, stopping them short from saying anything else. "You were supposed to catch the fish yesterday and put them in the refrigerator until this morning. And it doesn't matter if you heard the message ten times yesterday. The message can tell you something different each time you hear it!"

Willie spoke up. "But, Pops…"

"No Pops! Come over here. I want you two to meet a good friend of mine."

He introduced his sons to Nathan Emerson, whom they were told to address as Mr. Nathan. Preacher quickly sent his sons off to help with the Fourth of July luncheon the church had planned. The two old friends caught each other up on their lives before talking about why Preacher had asked for the FBI to come to Beaufort.

"You see, all three girls, Delia, Rose, and Ida, were working as prostitutes. They were half white and half black. They were murdered, and their bodies were found around Taylor Creek," Preacher explained.

Nathan shook his head from side to side. "I can't say murdered yet. I've got nothin' to go on. The sheriff's report and the coroner's report both indicate they all died accidentally."

Preacher huffed. "They weren't accidents, Nathan. I think Sheriff Carter is hiding something."

"I agree he's bad people, along with a few others I met last night, but I need more. I'd like to speak to the family or someone who knows more about the girls."

"I'll see what I can do, but colored folks around here are afraid to talk to strangers, especially strangers who are lawmen, like you."

"Well, after meeting Sheriff Carter, I can understand why."

"Exactly. That son of a b—son of a person is just bad!" Preacher quickly stopped himself before using profanity in the house of the Lord.

Nathan grinned. "That was close, Preacher," he said.

Preacher lifted his hand and pointed upward with his index finger. "Judge not, that ye be not judged," he replied.

"You're right. Now, I'm staying at the bed and breakfast you told me about. If you hear anything, you can contact me there."

Nathan left the church just after the noon hour and went back to his room to change out of his suit and into something more like a vacationer. After he left the church, he noticed there was a police car following him, just not too close. He figured it was the sheriff, who was keeping his distance.

Sheriff Carter didn't try to conceal the fact he was there; he wanted the FBI agent to know he was being watched.

Nathan made his way back into town, where he found it even busier than the day before. He found a vendor selling hot dogs and hamburgers from a cart near Taylor Creek and decided to enjoy the traditional Fourth of July favorite as he walked along Front Street. Occasionally, he stopped and looked toward the water at the many boats that pulled close to the shore and anchored. It seemed everyone had come to Beaufort for the annual fireworks display planned for later in the evening. The people in the boats on Taylor Creek looked to have the best seats for the show.

Nathan continued to walk around the park. Occasionally, he found people to speak with who seemed eager to converse with him about the town and their plans for the evening. Nathan knew he needed to blend in and make others believe he really was there for a vacation and that any investigation he was doing came in second. Besides, he had noticed Sheriff Carter standing at the other side of the park, still following him. The sheriff kept his distance. Sheriff Carter made sure he was always on the opposite side of the park from the agent, but he let the agent know he was still there.

Nathan was about to cut the day short and head back to his room when he saw her. Stormie walked through the park and spoke to everyone in between taking photos of what Nathan believed to be everything in sight.

There's something about her. She's beautiful… I know that, but there's something else, he thought to himself.

She was wearing a sleeveless white summer dress that had strawberries and flowers in bloom printed on it. She wore a pearl choker to accent the outfit. Nathan looked up and noticed she was looking at him. *Turnabout is fair play,* he mused to himself.

Stormie had arrived at the park early. She took photos of the vendors setting up for the day and then turned to the vacationers. She knew that only a few of the hundred-plus photos she took between yesterday and today would be printed in the newspaper next weekend, but she wanted to have a lot to choose from. She was never paid for the photos, but the money didn't matter to her.

Taking photos was something for her to do between gardening, helping Sissy take care of the house, and speaking to her husband for about thirty minutes a day. She tried pretending she didn't notice the stranger from the other day. He stood watching her from across the park. She looked for him in the crowd without trying to make it obvious. She saw some boys running around, throwing sidewalk poppers at girls who screamed and ran away. She then turned and looked for the agent once more.

"I'm not over there anymore," he whispered from behind her.

Stormie was caught off guard. "I was—"

Nathan stepped in front of her and smiled. "'I was about to take a picture of that elderly couple dressed as a US flag.' Was that what you were about to say?" He asked.

"Why, yes it was," she replied. Stormie raised her camera and took a picture of the couple she had photographed earlier, but that was a little fact she decided to keep to herself. She looked at Nathan and decided she approved of the light khaki pants and tan shoes with the form-fitting royal-blue camp shirt. She liked how the shirt complemented his muscular arms.

"It certainly is a nice day for the Independence celebration," he offered.

"Beaufort is always nice on the Fourth of July."

Nathan didn't know what else to say, but he wanted to keep talking with her. He was robbed of words for the moment, but then he thought of something. "I believe I met your husband yesterday," he blurted.

"Oh, and where might have you run into him?" she replied unenthusiastically.

"Judge's Revenge."

Stormie placed her right hand over her heart. "Bless your heart. I wouldn't have guessed you would associate with the likes of the people who go into that place."

"I don't normally, but I was walking back to where I'm staying, and I saw Sheriff Carter there, whom I had met earlier in the day. I thought I'd drop in and say hello to him."

"I guess my husband's evening meeting with the judge and the town's public defender was over supper and drinks, no less."

"Yes, I believe they were all sitting with your husband and drinking."

Stormie smiled. "Well, that takes the cake! Who'd believe your luck meeting all the men who think they're important in this town in one spot. Surely, you've met more than those four ne'er-do-wells since you arrived."

"Well yes, I met a woman with them as well," he answered and wished he could take the words back upon seeing Stormie's surprised expression.

"Well, do tell."

Nathan cleared his throat. "I think her name was Emma."

Stormie's mood quickly changed. "I imagine it was. Wherever the four of them are, she is surely gonna be close-by. With one hand o'er heart and the other, well…"

"I'm sorry. I didn't mean to—"

"No. It's okay. I'm sorry. Please excuse my poor choice of words. She's my husband's receptionist, secretary, or whatever Ben needs her to be," she replied as her mood changed again.

Nathan heard the change in her voice. He'd discovered the topic of Ben and Emma upset her, and he would remember to avoid it in the future at all costs. Apparently, he was right about Emma Rodgers and Ben Arrington.

"I guess I'll let you get back to what you were doing before I came along and obviously ruined your day," Nathan said.

"Oh, don't run off, Nathan. You should stay and enjoy everything Beaufort has to offer on the Fourth of July. My issues are mine. Please stay. Besides, after some people get enough to drink around here, things get really exciting. Someone may even get naked and run off into Taylor Creek."

Nathan laughed. "I doubt that happens," he replied.

"Oh, it happens. I've got a picture of our mayor doing it last year."

"I don't know if that's something I'd want to see. Besides, I may be on vacation, but I've got some work to do as well. Thank you anyway," Nathan explained as he began to walk away.

"Maybe you may not want to see it, but if it does happen and you miss it, I'm gonna get a picture of it to show you later!" she yelled.

"I'm sure you will," Nathan said and turned around and walked away. He wanted to talk with her more, but he felt he had ruined any good conversation they could have had, after her embarrassing comments and her reaction to the subject of her husband and his secretary.

Monday, July 5, 1965

Charlie White turned right, flipped his headlights off, and made his way down the road until he was in front of the church. His friends were all crowded in the bed of his truck, with their faces covered. They had everything planned, and they were going to be quick about it. The truck was loaded with their supplies, and everyone waited for Charlie to give the word. Every man had a job to do, and each one knew what he was responsible for. All of them had plenty of practice with this type of job. They were all drunk. They had been in town earlier for the fireworks show, drinking and harassing the town's vacationers before heading to complete the job they were hired to do.

"Go," Charlie whispered.

Eight men jumped from the truck. Three of them ran to the entrance and forced the doors open. The other five grabbed the cross and quickly ran to the front of the lawn. One man used a post-hole digger and rapidly removed the soil. With the help of the other men, he hoisted the cross into place and then held it there while the other four anchored it to the ground at the four corners.

Charlie walked toward the men hoisting the cross as he lit a cigarette. He was a small man with an evil reputation. He wore faded blue jeans, a short-sleeve shirt, and boots. On his hip hung a large knife with his initials CW on the end of it. He had notches in the handle, in remembrance of his seven victims. Charlie was the only one who did not cover his face with a sack. He knew no witnesses or victims would ever testify against him.

Charlie waited for the other three to exit the church before he used his lighter and ignited the already-fuel-soaked cross. Flames erupted toward the sky, and all the men ran back to the truck and sped away.

Charlie paid each of them ten dollars and one gallon of mountain shine for their help. The sheriff had called him and explained the situation with the visiting FBI agent. The sheriff had asked Charlie to send a message, to remind certain people in town that the Klan was watching them and anyone else they talked to.

Charlie White was just the man to send that kind of message.

Nathan had made it back to his room by six the previous night. He had eaten a sandwich and chips, which he had picked up from a local deli. He watched the fireworks from his bedroom window and later fell asleep to the sounds of fireworks going off in the distance.

His alarm clock went off at seven o'clock. He dressed in casual attire and ventured out for the day. He ate breakfast at the same deli he had stopped at the night before. He enjoyed a sausage-and-egg biscuit with a glass of orange juice before driving to the sheriff's office.

At around nine, he entered the sheriff's office, where he found Sheriff Carter waiting for him in the lobby, holding a cup of coffee.

"This should be everything you need," Carter said as he handed Nathan a thick package.

"Thank you," Nathan said as he started to look through it.

"I know you think I'm an asshole, but I don't give a damn what anyone thinks of me, and that includes anyone from the FBI. I'm the law in this town. Like it or not, I'm demanding you keep me informed. Do we understand each other?"

Nathan stopped looking through the package and looked at Sheriff Carter. "I think we understand each other more than you know. And I mean it, from one asshole to another." The agent looked the sheriff directly in the eye and smiled.

Carter smiled back and then sipped from his mug. Nathan looked back down at the package and flipped through the pages inside one by one.

Sheriff Carter just stared at the agent for a few minutes. "So, why did the FBI only send one agent down here to investigate these killings?" He finally asked.

Nathan stopped once more. He heard Carter say something that piqued his interest. He glared at Sheriff Carter. "Killings? I thought these were unfortunate accidents?"

Sheriff Carter became visibly uncomfortable. "Either way, the girls are dead, and it's my professional opinion that their deaths are by accident. So once again, why only you?" Sheriff Carter asked more directly and then placed his coffee cup on the counter.

"I guess they thought the opinion of two assholes was better than one. Like I said, Sheriff Carter, we understand each other," Nathan offered and then turned to walk out.

"Every investigation I've seen you boys involved in seemed to have a few of you fellas in tow," the sheriff explained as he picked up his coffee cup again.

Nathan stopped at the door and turned to look at the sheriff. "Maybe they think the way you do."

"And what do I think, Agent Emerson?"

"You told me when I got here."

Sheriff Carter lifted his right eyebrow. "What did I tell you?"

"That no one gives a good damn about a few dead nigger whores," Nathan answered sarcastically before walking out.

The sheriff slammed his fist on the counter, spilling his coffee on his shirt. "Well, that's one thing you got right so far!" He shouted before the door closed.

Emma Rodgers sat at the front desk, filing her nails, when the front door quickly opened. It startled her at first, and she dropped her file. Emma reached for the drawer and pulled it open slightly before seeing Sheriff Carter standing there. She had grown a bit jumpy since leaving Philadelphia. The sheriff appeared to be upset and looked as though he was about to have a heart attack. But, to her, he always looked like he was about to have a heart attack.

"Damn! Can't you knock?" she complained as she closed the drawer hiding the .38 revolver she kept inside.

The sheriff angrily stepped across the room. "Is Ben in?"

"Yes," she answered, just as Ben opened the door to his office.

Ben saw the expression on the sheriff's face. He knew there was a problem. "Come on in," the prosecutor offered.

Sheriff Carter walked in and took a seat in front of Ben's desk. He then used his handkerchief to wipe the sweat off his forehead. "That son of a bitch came to my office today for the case files."

Ben sat down across from Carter. "I guess we're talking about Agent Emerson. What did you do?"

The sheriff took a deep breath. "I gave him the files."

Ben nodded. "Is there anything in those files that could hurt us?"

"Hell no! Do you think I'm stupid? I gave him what he needed, which is nothin'. And he can go out and talk to anybody he wants, but he ain't got nothin' in those files and ain't nobody talking to him."

"I hope you're right, but I think I'll make some calls to Charlotte and see what I can learn about Nathan Emerson in the meantime," Ben stated.

"That's a good idea, but I'll keep watching him like I've been doing for all our sakes."

Ben nodded in agreement. "Good. Remember what you said the other night. We're all in this together. We have a plan, and if this FBI agent doesn't get in the way, then there's nothing to stop us, which reminds me… Do you have everything ready to move forward when the time comes regarding my wife?"

Carter pressed his lips and thought before speaking. "Charlie will be ready to move forward when we let him know. He's got a plan on how to make it look like an accident."

"Good, but I want it to be quick."

"I know. By the way, Mrs. Stormie was talking to Agent Emerson in town again yesterday."

"Really?"

"Really," Sheriff Carter repeated as he stood to leave.

Emma walked in, carrying two glasses of iced tea. "It's so hot outside. I thought you boys would like something to drink."

"Thank you, darlin," Sheriff Carter said after grabbing one of the glasses and drinking the contents at once.

"I'll keep you informed, but in the meantime, maybe you should talk to your wife about speaking to strangers."

Ben's nostrils flared. "I'll take care of her. You just keep an eye on him."

Sheriff Carter nodded, handed the empty glass to Emma, and walked out.

Rose's Story

SATURDAY, MAY 1, 1965

Rose was tired, but she continued walking on the road toward town. The bright full moon was descending in the night sky above, and soon the sun would rise. The Gentlemen's Social at the Old Klan House was exhausting, and she had stayed longer than she had expected with the hope of making more money.

Unfortunately, the white men she had spent time with were not in the mood to spend money, and she had left the Old Klan House short of her financial goal for the evening. Rose set a financial goal every night. Some of the money she gave to her father, and the rest she kept for herself. She had plans, after all, and she needed money for those plans.

But now, all she wanted to do was climb into her bed at home and fall asleep. Her home was not much to speak of regarding comfort, but still, it was home, where she lived with her father. As she continued walking toward town, she became increasingly upset and angry with her father, Clyde, who had once again forgotten to pick her up. Usually, he found his way to her no matter how much he had to drink, but not tonight.

Rose decided nothing could be done about it now, so she turned her thoughts to California and what she would do when she got there. Hollywood was Rose's plan and was calling for women like her. She dreamed of being the next Dorothy Dandridge. She believed she favored the actress with her light skin and beauty. Rose, like many of the other girls at the Gentlemen's Social, was biracial, with a black mother and white father.

Rose's mother had run away from her father and her when Rose was five years old, and her father never got over it. Rose believed it was what had driven her father to drink. Clyde knew some people in town talked about him and his "mulatto" daughter, but he didn't care. She knew her father loved her no matter how people looked at them.

Rose was imagining herself in the lead role of a Hollywood movie when she saw the lights of a car approaching from behind.

"A ride!" she said out loud and moved off the road. She stood in the dirt and waited for the car to pull alongside.

She placed her hand out, making a fist with her thumb in the air. The car came to a stop next to her, and the driver leaned over and opened the passenger door.

"Hey, baby. Didn't I see you at the Gentlemen's Social?" Rose asked as she got in and sat down.

The driver pressed the accelerator, and the two headed toward town. The driver looked at Rose and smiled. Rose knew what he was thinking, so she slid closer to him. She placed her hand on his thigh and rubbed it.

"You got any money you want to spend?" she asked.

The driver reached into his pocket, pulled out a twenty-dollar bill, and handed it to her.

"Why don't you pull over somewhere private, and I can give you what you want."

Once the car was off the main road and down a dark back road, the driver stopped, placed the vehicle in park, and turned the motor off. Rose thought he looked nervous, so she leaned over to caress his chest and kiss his neck. He closed his eyes and turned toward her. Rose leaned back and pulled her dress down, exposing her ample breasts.

"For twenty dollars, you can pretty much do anything you want with me," she said as she pulled her dress up over her waist and leaned toward him. He placed his right hand on her shoulder, held the back of her neck, and pulled her into him for a kiss.

"No, baby. I don't kiss on the lips," she whispered and tried to pull away.

He increased his grip, overpowering her as he pulled her closer to him while she struggled to release herself from his grasp.

"No! I don't do that!" She snapped as she pushed against his chest with both of her hands. "Why are you doing this?"

He pulled out his knife and held it in his left hand for her to see it shine in the light of the full moon.

"No, please don't!" She pleaded right before he plunged the knife deep into her abdomen, just below her breast. He looked into her eyes, pulled her into him, and kissed her lips, and as she gasped for her last breath, he pushed the knife upward, deep into her heart.

Rose's body went limp, and he laid her back in the passenger seat. He held her up with his right arm while he caressed and kissed her breasts. He was mesmerized by her delicate features and womanly figure. He cupped her buttocks with his left hand and drew her closer, then kissed her lips once more.

On the main road, a car drove up and then back down the highway. Clyde Melton was driving along the dark road, looking for his daughter, Rose. He was sure he would find her walking along the highway somewhere, just as he had done the other times. Clyde knew he had messed up by not being at the end of the driveway when she left the social, but he had passed out earlier in the evening, and when he finally woke, he was already late. He knew he would have hell to pay when he found her, but right now, all he wanted to do was find his Rose. She was his life and the only person who really cared about what happened to him.

Chapter 6
Judge's Revenge

Nathan drove to the Beaufort Southern Baptist Community Church once he left the sheriff's office. As he sped along the back country roads, he occasionally parked in the woods and waited to see if anyone was following him before continuing toward the church.

When he arrived, he noticed a burned cross in the front yard. He walked in through the front door and announced himself. Looking around, he saw the church had been vandalized. There were broken windows, and the walls had racist slurs and markings on them.

"Nathan!" Preacher yelled from the back.

"You okay?" Nathan asked as he walked toward him.

"Yes," Preacher answered as he carried two cans of paint to the sanctuary, followed by an army of church members who also carried paint cans and brushes.

Nathan looked around. "What happened?"

"The Fourth of July, I imagine."

"The Fourth of July?" Nathan asked, confused.

"Yeah, in the past, some drunk Klan members have come by on the evening of the Fourth to remind us that the Fourth of

July is their celebration. They haven't done this in about four years though. I guess they figured it was time to remind us."

"I don't think that's the message they were delivering. Look," Nathan said as he pointed at one of the writings on the wall.

Don't talk to strangers nigger!

The pastor glared at the words. "Let's talk outside," Preacher suggested.

Outside in front of the church, Nathan turned and faced his old friend. "There's something I need to tell you," he said in a low voice.

"What is it, Nathan?"

The agent looked around before answering. "I'm here alone. The FBI is not investigating this yet. I'll need a lot more information about the girls, and some evidence before anyone else gets involved."

Preacher nodded his head and dropped his shoulders. "I understand. We're used to it," he stated as his sons walked up.

"You've got two fine-looking young men here," Nathan said.

"I believe they are but getting them to do their chores during these long summer days is getting to be difficult. I think they spend more time fishing and scouring Taylor Creek for treasure than anything else."

Nathan gave the boys a curious expression. "Treasure!?" he commented.

Preacher's eyes widened. "Yes, legend has it that Blackbeard buried treasure around these parts, and my boys spend a lot of their time looking for it."

"We'll find it one day too," Samuel announced.

"Well, why don't you two start by looking for it inside those paint cans while you help the others."

"Okay, Pops," Willie said as he and Samuel walked inside the church.

"Were you able to contact any of the girls' families?" Nathan asked.

"Yes, I convinced Iris Snipes, Delia's mother, to meet you at the church after services on Wednesday. Rose's father, Clyde Melton, killed himself after Rose's body was found."

"What about Ida Freeman?"

"After last night, everyone's afraid. You gotta understand that after this is all over, you'll leave and everyone else stays, including friends of the person who is responsible for the killings. And besides, I think someone may have gotten to folks before I did."

"Can you try to convince them to speak with me anyway?"

"I'll try."

"In the meantime, do you think you can help me find anyone who found the bodies? There's no mention of anyone in the reports the sheriff gave me, but someone had to find them."

"Yes, you mean George Butler and Otis Bettis. They found Rose Melton."

"Do you know them?"

"Small town, Agent Emerson. Both of those men are members of this congregation, even if I only see them on Christmas and Easter. They both work for Rhett Jenkins at his dock, where they unload fishing boats for him."

"Do you think they'll speak to me?"

"Probably not if you just showed up. I'll get word to them that it's okay to speak to you. I'll let you know when I hear from them."

Nathan waited before saying anything else as two members of the church walked by carrying more cleaning supplies. "Do you know who found Ida? Sheriff Carter said in his report that it was an anonymous caller who made his office aware of a body floating in Harlowe Creek."

Preacher shook his head. "No, ain't nobody said anything about who found Ida, as far as I know, but I'll ask some folks."

"Okay. I'll check around too. I'll see you later," Nathan said as he headed back toward his car.

"Yeah, see you later," Preacher said, as he began to have second thoughts about contacting the FBI. He shook his head and walked back inside to help clean up the mess.

Stormie was on her hands and knees, pouring dirt and mulch into a pot for new flowers, which she planned to hang from the porch. If she wasn't taking pictures, she was planting flowers, and if she wasn't planting flowers, she was taking pictures of flowers.

"You workin' yourself to death on those flowers, Mrs. Stormie. C'mon up here and eat somethin'," Sissy said as she walked out of the house carrying a tray with a glass of sweet tea and a ham sandwich. Sissy was the closest person Stormie had to family. She practically raised Stormie after her mother had passed away. Sissy was the one person Stormie could count on. Sissy always made sure her Stormie was taken care of, no matter the cost.

"Hard work is good for the soul," Stormie declared.

"I don't know about that, but hard work is hard work, and you'd be lucky to get anything to grow in this sea-salted soil around here."

"Sissy, in the immortal words of Thomas Jefferson, *I'm a great believer in luck, and I find the harder I work, the more I have of it.*"

"Well, I don't know much about Mr. Jefferson, but I ain't found no work that led to luck. I've been working hard at it, but no luck, especially when it comes to finding a man."

"Well, havin' a man ain't all that great. I'm here to tell you," Stormie replied.

"That reminds me. Will Mr. Arrington be joining you for dinner tonight?"

"I don't know. Would you be a dear and call his office and ask Ms. Emma Rodgers if my husband is planning on havin' dinner at home with his wife or in town with his whore?"

"Surely, I will not! I guarantee you I'll never ask her such a thing. Your daddy always told me I need to keep my mouth shut if I ain't got nothin' nice to say."

"Well, you can ask her any way you like, but please make the call for me because I'm sure I wouldn't be as delicate as you."

"If he decides to eat here, what shall I make for dinner?"

"Fried fish with hush puppies and collard greens sounds wonderful," Stormie answered as she rubbed her stomach.

"Mr. Arrington hates fried fish and collard greens."

Stormie poured more dirt into a pot. "Yes, I know that."

"Mrs. Stormie, I don't know about you sometimes."

It was four thirty when Preacher called Nathan and told him he had contacted George and Otis and that they had agreed to speak to him. He also told him he couldn't find anyone who knew anything about Ida Freeman. He did, however, provide him with Ida's home address. After the phone call, Nathan rushed to the docks but discovered the two men had already left for the day. Instead of going back to his room, Nathan made his way to Bo's Diner. He found a booth next to the window that gave him a view of the courthouse across the street.

From the window, Nathan saw Judge Ridge, the sheriff, and Walters talking in front of the courthouse. How nice it would be to know what they were talking about, he thought to himself. The sheriff appeared to do most of the talking, until a large colored man walked up and stood behind the judge.

"Now listen to me, Amos. I do not, I repeat, I do not, want to find any dirt in the corners of my chambers anymore where you've been sweeping it. My job in the courthouse is to sit on the bench and make very important decisions, and your job in the courthouse is to sweep the damn floors. Now, I do my job with a sense of pride every damn day, and I want you to do your job the same way, with pride! The job does not matter; it's how one does it. Do you understand me, boy?" Judge Ridge lectured to the large man standing in front of him. Amos was the courthouse custodian, and Judge Ridge took every opportunity to belittle him and berate him, especially when there was an audience.

"Yes, sir, I do. It be a better job from now on," Amos answered. Amos always did what he was told, never talked back, and kept to his own.

"With pride."

"With pride," Amos repeated.

"Well go on, boy. Get your ass in there and get it done. I ain't got all day to be telling you how to do your job."

Amos quickly jogged back into the courthouse as Judge Ridge turned his attention to the sheriff.

The sheriff laughed. "That big nigger doesn't understand a damn word you said. He doesn't know anything about pride or much of anything else," Sheriff Carter stated.

"He understands. Now tell me what that FBI man was up to today," Judge Ridge said.

"I don't know what he did this morning, but later, he went by the docks to speak to George and Otis. He was surprised to find they'd already left for the day. I made sure of it. Now he's over at the diner there, eating his dinner," Sheriff Carter explained and nodded in the direction of the diner.

"Do those two boys know anything?" Ridge asked.

"They found the Melton girl and called it in. All they know is that."

"Still, you better keep an eye on him and them."

"I will, but for now, I'm going home to eat."

"All right. Well then, Jack, you keep an eye on him until he goes to bed."

Jack huffed. "I have plans," he complained.

"I don't give a damn what you've planned. You do as I tell you. Understand? Besides, it's just one night," the judge explained.

The angry attorney threw his hands in the air. "Fine," he said as he walked away.

Nathan watched as the men talked for a few minutes and then walked away in separate directions. He ate his dinner and made his way back to his room. In his room, Nathan read over the case files the sheriff had given him. The files contained nothing more than what he already had. His eyes began to get heavy as he turned his attention to the television to watch Johnny Carson.

After a few minutes, he turned off both the television and the light. He then slowly made his way to the window. Looking outside, he saw Jack Walters standing under the light pole. He had caught Jack following him from the diner earlier and decided Jack knew nothing about tailing someone. Jack stood there for about twenty more minutes before leaving the area. Nathan moved across the room and checked the door lock before lying down for the night. He turned the radio on and listened to the song "Hold me, Thrill me, Kiss me" as he fell asleep thinking of Stormie Arrington.

Tuesday, July 6, 1965

Stormie was sitting at the breakfast table when Ben came downstairs to join her. He sat and read the paper while sipping the coffee Sissy had poured for him.

"Will you be home for dinner tonight? It would be nice to know so Sissy can put something out that you like. It did not appear you enjoyed your dinner last night."

Ben looked at his wife with a pained expression. "Well, I'm sure I've voiced my dislike for fried fish and collard greens in the past to you and Sissy, but somehow it still makes its way to my plate. It does give the impression there was a conspiracy of sorts amidst."

Stormie grinned. "Well, my dear husband, you so seldom make it home that Sissy and I don't know when you're gonna grace us with your presence for supper. Sissy did call your receptionist and asked her if you would be home, but she said she didn't know. So, I took it upon myself to have Sissy make one of my favorite meals for supper. Maybe we can avoid this in the future if you could give us a little advanced notice on whether you'll be coming home or not."

"That's a wonderful idea, but in my line of work, I sometimes don't know if I'm gonna make it home in time for supper."

Stormie slapped her hands down on the table. "Well, shut my mouth, I was unaware of the crime spree that has apparently overtaken Beaufort. Is there a gang of robbers and thieves running rampant? There must be. Why else would the town sheriff, the public defender, the judge, the county prosecutor, and the prosecutor's secretary be working through dinner these nights? Tell me, Ben, is it safe to go out at night?" Stormie sat straight up in her chair, looking around in all directions. "Sissy, make sure you lock up the house whenever you leave. We wouldn't want to be one of the many victims to the apparent crime spree overtaking Beaufort!" Stormie said loudly in a sarcastic tone.

Sissy did not answer, and she knew to stay in the kitchen, minding her own business, even if she did enjoy Stormie's performance. After all, Ben didn't care much for Sissy, and he viewed her as nothing more than Stormie's colored replacement mother whom he had the misfortune of inheriting when he married Stormie.

"If I didn't know better, I'd think you'd someone watching me," Ben said as he laid the paper down.

"No, dear, I simply made conversation with a handsome stranger who is visiting our town, who, by the way, ran into you and the other scoundrels at the Judge's place the other evening."

"Well, what did you and the FBI agent talk about?"

"FBI? I didn't know he was an FBI agent. I think we discussed the weather, I do believe."

"Anything else?" Ben questioned in an irritated tone.

"Nothin'… Oh, wait… I think we agreed it was hot that day. After all, what could a lonely housewife like me tell a good-lookin' FBI man like him anyway? You seem nervous, Ben. You got something to be nervous about?"

Ben stood to leave. "Not at all, my dear. And you're right; you've got nothin' to tell him. Unless he asks you about pictures and flowers of course," he answered sarcastically.

"That's right, Ben, but if I did have something to tell him, you can be sure I would."

Ben's demeanor changed. "Just stay away from him. I don't want anything to do with his business here in town."

"Don't worry, I won't go looking for him, but if he should find me, I'll surely extend the customary Southern hospitality that any true Southern woman would offer."

"I mean what I said," Ben replied as he walked out and slammed the screen door behind him.

"I do too, dear!" Stormie yelled back.

Stormie stood and watched Ben climb into his car.

I won't be told what to do anymore, she thought to herself.

Sissy came out of the kitchen. "Well, ain't that the berries. Stormie, don't go causin' no trouble. I knows you, and ain't nobody telling you what to do, especially that man," Sissy said as she watched Stormie stand there looking out the screen door. Sissy had seen that look on Stormie's face before, so she knew she was up to something. After all, she was called Stormie for a reason.

Agent Nathan Emerson makes him nervous, and I want to know why, Stormie thought.

Nathan had coffee at the deli and then got in his car and headed to speak to George and Otis. He drove along the waterfront in the direction of the docks, making sure he obeyed the traffic laws because Sheriff Carter had already found his way behind him.

Follow me all you want, Sheriff; it doesn't matter now. You're way too concerned about me being here. That tells me you're worried about what I might find, Nathan thought as he looked in the rearview mirror at the sheriff's car.

Nathan pulled into the parking lot and quickly found a place to park. As he got out, he noticed the sheriff pulling up to the curb across the street. Walking toward the front door, Nathan detected the unmistakable smell of dead fish. There were a few boats tied to the dock on the side of the building, where workers were unloading the most recent catch from the Atlantic. He watched for a moment as the men tossed large fish from their boat onto the pier and then into large blue containers on wheels, where other men rolled them into the building to be processed.

Nathan didn't make it into the building before being

stopped by a large, white, middle-aged man. He wore a blue T-shirt and blue jeans that were tucked into calf-high rubber boots.

"Can I help you?" the man asked.

"I'm looking for George Butler and Otis Bettis," Nathan replied as he pulled his identification out.

The man looked over Nathan's shoulder, in the direction of Sheriff Carter. "I'm Rhett Jenkins. I own this place. I know why you're here, and I think it's a good thing that you are, but I cannot help you and neither can they," he explained and pointed back toward Nathan's car in the parking lot.

"I just want to speak to them for a few minutes," Nathan pleaded.

"I know. George and Otis ain't got nothin' to say to you!" Rhett shouted and continued to point at the parking lot.

"Now turn around to leave," Rhett said quietly. He placed his hand on Nathan's shoulder and gently turned him toward the parking lot. Nathan was about to object when he felt the man slide something into his front shirt pocket, carefully out of the view of Sheriff Carter.

"I understand," Nathan said as he started back toward his car.

"Don't come back here either. Them boys ain't got nothin' to say to you!" Rhett yelled and then looked back and nodded at the sheriff before going back inside.

Nathan pulled out of the parking lot and looked at Sheriff Carter, who was still parked along the curb. Sheriff Carter smirked and placed his hand on his head in a lazy salute to the unwanted FBI man.

Nathan drove back to the bed and breakfast but sat in his car. He looked around to make sure the sheriff wasn't anywhere close by before he retrieved the item from his front pocket. It was a sheet of paper, and when he unfolded it, he read the message:

The word is out about you. Everyone has been warned about talking to you. George and Otis will meet you at 11:00 tonight at Bay View Cemetery. It's off of 20th St. right before Piggotts Bridge. Make sure you're not followed and come alone. Most people here are good folks, but the bad ones have a lot of power. People are afraid. Tread lightly.

Ben was sitting behind his desk and speaking on the phone when Sheriff Carter arrived. Emma let him in, and Ben nodded for the sheriff to sit down.

"Frank, thanks for the information, and I do hope you'll be at our next Gentlemen's Social. Yes, it will be on Saturday the seventeenth. Yes, I'll make sure Bessie is there. I know, and she enjoys your company as well. I'll see you then." Ben hung up the phone and shook his head in disbelief. "Where is the FBI man today, Dwight?"

"Right now, he's eating lunch over at Maud's."

"You've decided not to watch him anymore?"

Sheriff Carter shook his head. "No, I just figured I'd let him be for a bit. Besides, they ran him off over at the docks. Folks know not to talk to him. He's probably trying to figure out what to do next."

"Good. I just got off the phone with Deputy DA Frank Jackson over in Charlotte, and he told me a lot about Agent Nathan Emerson."

Emma Rodgers returned to the office and walked in carrying a bag of food. She opened it and took out some sandwiches for her and Ben.

"Sorry, Sheriff Carter, I didn't know we'd be havin' company or I'd have brought you something too."

"I ate earlier," Sheriff Carter replied. "You were saying that Frank Jackson told you something."

"Yes. Apparently, Agent Emerson is from right here in North Carolina. He played football in high school near here and was a star linebacker who went on to play middle linebacker for the Oklahoma Sooners."

The sheriff had a bewildered look on his face. "No shit," he said as he leaned forward in his chair.

"No shit is right. The son of a bitch played in the Orange Bowl against our own North Carolina Blue Devils in nineteen fifty-eight, where he helped them beat us forty-eight to twenty-one."

"I remember that game. Amazing!"

Ben held his hand up. "Wait, it gets better. After football, he went on to law school."

"He's got a law degree?"

"Yes, from Duke. He came back here and got his degree from Duke."

"I'll be damned."

"Didn't you go to Duke, Ben?" Emma asked between bites of her roast beef sandwich.

"Yes, darlin'. I did." Ben said and then took a bite of his food.

"Did he ever practice law?" the sheriff asked.

Ben quickly swallowed. "No. He, however, did pass the bar and then applied to be an FBI agent in nineteen sixty-one."

"He's only been an agent for four years?"

"Yes, sir. And you know what else?" Ben asked enthusiastically.

"No, what?" the sheriff asked.

"He worked in Washington until nineteen sixty-three. Then he moved around investigating cases involving civil rights violations."

"Really? Well, that explains all the talk about civil rights the first day I met him."

"Really is right. He helped on the Medgar Evers Investigation in Jackson, Mississippi, the Sixteenth Street Baptist Church bombing in Birmingham, Alabama, and up until March of this year, he was back in Mississippi for the murders of those three civil rights workers. Then he went to Miami."

The sheriff took a minute to allow Ben to eat. "How did he get back to North Carolina?"

Ben took a drink to wash his food down before answering. "Frank doesn't know for sure, but he thinks Agent Emerson was involved in some situation in Miami where he ratted on a few other agents who were involved in some type of corruption. It didn't sound like he's very well liked within the bureau right now."

"That's good to know. Is that all?" the Sheriff asked as he stood to leave.

"Yes, for now," Ben answered.

"The man could be trouble, but if something needs to be done, it will get done. I ain't lettin' nothin' interfere with my retirement plans," Sheriff Carter said before walking out.

Chapter 7
George and Otis

Nathan spent the afternoon trying to make himself look busy, as he had the feeling he was still being watched by someone. He had returned to the Beaufort Bed and Breakfast after eating a late dinner and did everything he could to make himself visible through the window. He'd left the light on and made various passes by it between commercial breaks while he watched an episode of Gilligan's Island and a few reruns of other sitcoms.

At ten o'clock, he turned the television and room lights off to give the impression he was going to bed. After a few minutes, he crawled across the floor where he made his way to the window and peered out the side of the curtain. He watched as his babysitter tried to conceal himself along the tree line, out of the glow of the streetlight. The sitter was careful not to show his face like Jack Walters had done. At first, he thought the tail was Sheriff Carter, who had followed him earlier in the day, but the person outside was smaller than the sheriff.

Nathan waited quietly and was motionless as he knelt and peered out the window until he saw the figure walk into the woods behind him. He heard a car door shut and the sound of an engine starting. A few seconds later, while keeping low and still watching the area, Nathan saw a truck pull out of the parking lot on the other side of the woods. The truck entered the street, where the driver turned on his headlights and made his way down the road.

Not wasting any time, Nathan walked across the room and out the door, then shut it quietly. He walked down the hall to the staircase and made sure to avoid the creaking steps he had already identified. Downstairs in the lobby, Nathan peered out the side door window of the house. He looked down both sides of the street before opening the door and running to his car.

Nathan had used the map he had of the area and found the cemetery. He arrived early and found a place to stand under a tree, where he had a clear view of anyone entering the cemetery. Headstones silhouetted in the darkness, and he guessed there were a few hundred people buried in the cemetery. He retrieved his flashlight from his pocket and checked the middle of his back for his .45.

Quietly, he scanned the area for any movement or sound. Suddenly, there were footsteps off to his right. Nathan stood motionless, listening as he gripped the handle of his .45, ready to draw it if he needed. Many thoughts ran through his mind.

It's a trap! he thought to himself. He crouched to a knee and gripped his gun tighter.

"FBI man, are you here? It's George Butler and Otis Bettis," said a whispered voice.

"Over here," Nathan whispered back as he cautiously stood and walked out of the shadows, still gripping his pistol.

George and Otis slowly approached the man. "I'm George, and this is Otis. You the FBI man who wants to speak to us about Rose?" George asked.

"Yes, I am," Nathan answered.

"I don't like this," Otis said, looking around nervously. They'll kill us for talking to you."

"No one is gonna kill you. I won't let that happen. Now, you're the two who found Rose Melton, correct?"

"Yes, sir," George answered.

"We found what was left of her anyway," Otis said.

"I understand you found her near Taylor Creek and you think she was attacked by an alligator."

"Ain't no damn alligator eat that poor girl," Otis said as he looked around once more.

Nathan looked at the man unblinking. "How do you know? The sheriff said she fell in the creek, where she drowned and was later partially eaten by a large alligator."

"My cousin Ronny and me went to Pensacola, Florida a few years back to work bailing hay. One day, we went fishing and Ronny got his line all tangled in some logs. He went in the water and was attacked by an alligator. That alligator tore him up something bad before I was able to get him away from it. His entire belly was covered in teeth marks. The skin on his arm was torn away, but he lived, and his cuts didn't look anything like Rose's cuts."

"Rose's injuries weren't the same as your cousin's? What I mean to say is that she wasn't torn open or anything like that?"

"No. Ronny had bite marks like a V on his belly and back. Rose was stuck kind of all over. And she had parts that were missing."

Nathan looked at the man quizzically. "What do you mean by missing parts?"

"Her titties were cut off," Otis answered flatly.

"How do you know her breasts were missing and cut off? Did Sheriff Carter remove her clothes before the coroner arrived?"

"No, she was already naked when we found her." George answered.

"Was there anything else you noticed?"

Otis and George looked at each other suspiciously in the

darkness. They had more information but were afraid to talk to anyone about it.

"She was cut up really bad down there," George said as he pointed toward his groin.

Nathan took a moment to think about what George had just said. "What kind of cuts did she have?"

Otis took a deep breath. "Like something stabbed her a whole bunch down there and around her thighs. I think it's why the sheriff thinks she was eaten by an alligator. But that won't no alligator bite!"

"Is there anything else the two of you can tell me?"

The men looked at each other once more and then toward the ground. They had more, and Nathan needed the information.

"What are you not telling me?" Nathan asked.

"You should speak to Warren Prater. He's the one who found Delia Snipes," George said.

"Have you two spoken to him? Has he said anything to the two of you about what he saw?"

"Yeah. Warren was out in his boat, and he had engine trouble, so he went to shore, and that's when he found Delia and..."

"And?" Nathan said, encouraging George to finish.

"And she was cut up too," he said and looked at Otis.

"Go ahead, tell the rest."

"What else is there?" Nathan asked quickly.

Suddenly there was a crack of a branch in the distance, and all three men ducked and looked toward the direction of the noise. Nathan again reached for his pistol, but this time, he pulled it from his back and held it at his side. George and Otis were scared and looking around. Nathan held George by his shirt in one hand and his gun in the other while all three of them surveyed the darkness around them.

"Tell me the rest!" Nathan ordered.

"Warren stole a camera from a car that belonged to some people passing through some time back. He had it with him that day and told us he took pictures of Delia," George answered excitedly.

"Did he give the camera to Sheriff Carter?"

"Hell no, that fat son of a bitch would have arrested him!"

"Where is Warren now?"

Another sound in the distance startled the men.

"I think people are watching us. We gotta go," Otis said impatiently.

"He's over in New Bern at his uncle's house near the marine base. Everyone there knows his uncle, Thurman. But they call him Hoot.'"

"Let's go!" Otis said, grabbing and pulling George while standing up.

Suddenly, a gunshot echoed through the night air. The round struck the tree behind the three men. Nathan released George and fired three shots at a tombstone marker from where he'd seen the muzzle flash, giving his two witnesses time to disappear into the darkness on the other side of the road.

Nathan stood and fired once more at the tombstone and then sprinted across the cemetery at a forty-five-degree angle toward a statue of Michael, the archangel, with his wings spread wide. From behind Michael's shield, he fired four more rounds at the target and then squatted as four shots whizzed by him and splintered one of Michael's wings. Nathan pulled a fresh magazine from his pocket, dropped the empty one from the pistol, and quickly reloaded.

He waited for a few seconds and then took a deep breath, stood, and fired two more rounds as he sprinted in the direction of the tombstone, firing periodically until he reached it. He leaped into the air over the marker and landed hard on his right shoulder but still managed to fire his .45 once more, hitting the marker square.

Using his flashlight, he lit the back of the tombstone but discovered the assassin had escaped. He quickly turned the flashlight off and peered into the darkness around him while remaining on his stomach for about ten minutes. Using the cover of darkness and being cautious, Nathan made it back to his car and drove back to his room.

Nathan returned to the bed and breakfast and soundlessly walked up the stairs. He used his key to gently unlock his room door. Still being vigilant, he entered the room in a crouched position, holding his pistol painfully at eye level, and surveyed the room. His shoulder still ached with the slightest movement. After walking around in the dark and believing he was alone, he locked the door, and placed an empty cola bottle in front of it. Nathan then slowly walked into the bathroom and shut the door. He put a towel under the crack at the bottom and turned on the light. His eyes took a minute to adjust, but soon the spots vanished, and he saw himself clearly in the mirror.

Nathan had dirt on his face and clothes, and his shoulder was scuffed up and bruising. He removed his clothes and turned on the shower. For about twenty minutes, he allowed the cold water to run down his back and along his injured shoulder.

You've had worse. Besides, it's gonna hurt a lot more in the morning, so don't start feeling sorry for yourself yet. Clean yourself up and get in bed, he thought to himself as he shut the water off.

Carefully, he exited the bathroom and gently lay on the bed, with his .45 by his side and the cola bottle still upright by the door.

He had followed George and Otis to the cemetery and thought about killing them before they could talk to the agent. He had heard George and Otis talking about meeting the FBI man when they were eating supper at the diner. After he thought about it for a little while, he decided against it and watched them instead. The two of them didn't really know anything anyway. All they did was find Rose's body. It wasn't like they knew it was him who had killed her.

Why was that idiot shooting at them? I should have killed him, he thought to himself before falling asleep.

Wednesday, July 7, 1965

Stormie glanced at the clock that was visible from the small amount of light that entered from the bathroom window. It was almost one o'clock in the morning when Ben finally returned home. Once again, she caught the smell of honey as he slid into bed next to her. She did not move or say a word. Stormie believed Ben knew she was awake. She lay there waiting for something from him but was unsure of what that something was. Maybe she wanted an apology or an admission of guilt, but as the clock ticked the minutes away, she received nothing. She was angry. She wanted to roll over and scream at him.

It was about a year and a half ago when Ben started having the lingering smell of honey on him. It was nearly eight months ago when Stormie was shopping in Raleigh where she picked up a bottle of Y perfume and found the same honey smell. It was six months ago when she saw the Y perfume bottle sitting on Emma's desk at Ben's office. At first, she told herself they just worked closely together, and her perfume was sprayed into the air at the office. Then Ben started spending a lot more time with Emma. Their time together included overnight meetings in Raleigh, Charlotte, and Durham, for trials Ben was working on with other prosecutors.

In March, Ben had gone to Durham for a month for a legal conference for state prosecutors. Emma had stayed in Beaufort for the first two weeks of Ben's trip, answering calls and setting appointments for Ben's return. At the beginning of the third week, Stormie received a call from Emma, who said her mother in Mississippi was sick and she needed to go home for a couple of weeks to take care of her.

Emma explained she had already spoken to Ben and told him. Ben wanted Stormie to come in and watch the office each day, until he or Emma returned.

Stormie had her suspicions at that time, as most wives would, but she could not prove anything until a month ago, when she took Ben's car to be detailed. The man cleaning the car handed her a roll of film he had found under the front passenger seat while he was vacuuming. The film was not the brand Stormie used for her photography. When she got it home, she went into her darkroom and developed it herself. The images that appeared made her nauseated.

The photos were of Ben and Emma sitting on some beach next to Jack Walters and another woman whom Stormie did not recognize. The other photos were of a naked Emma alone on a bed, posing seductively. The mirror behind the bed showed the reflection of an equally naked Ben taking the pictures.

Ben and Emma naked were the last images Stormie had right before she fell asleep.

Nathan awoke to a very sore shoulder, just as he thought he would. He did not mean to sleep in, but he'd had trouble falling asleep after the shooting at the cemetery. When he did fall asleep, he dreamed of the cola bottle falling over as an unknown assailant entered his room and emptied a gun into his body.

After getting dressed, Nathan walked downstairs and across the street for an early lunch. He ordered a club sandwich with potato salad. While he ate, he thought about what he should do next. Maybe he should report the incident to the sheriff, but the shooter could have been the sheriff, or perhaps he had arranged the shooting.

If Carter wasn't the shooter, he would want to know what I was doing at the cemetery. I certainly couldn't tell him that, Nathan thought.

Maybe I should report the shooting back to the bureau office and let Agent Smith know about it, but somehow Smith would use it to get rid of me, and he'd stop the investigation. The headlines would read *"Vacationing FBI Agent Shoots up Cemetery!"*

Right now, the killer or killers think they've nothin' to fear from me looking into their actions, he thought.

By the time he had finished his meal, he'd decided to keep the evening's events to himself for now.

Stormie awoke and found the bed empty next to her. She heard the front door close, the sound of Ben's car starting, and finally, him driving away. A tear dropped from the bridge of her nose onto the pillow. She looked at the wedding photo on the dresser, and more tears began to form. She reflected and asked herself how she'd come to this place with this man. Next to the wedding photo was a picture of her mother, and for the first time in years, she remembered the note. Stormie walked over to her dresser and took out the note she kept in a keepsake box. Her mother had written it to her right before she died. Stormie read it to herself.

Stormie,

Each person's life is a precious journey, but to really experience life and to enjoy it, you must make sure that the people you allow into it accept your love unconditionally and are worthy of it. Love is what makes the journey precious, and without love, the journey isn't worth the effort. Trust me, my dear sweet child, the journey is better and more precious when those you love, love you back.

You're right, Stormie thought as she placed the note back in the box and wiped tears from her eyes. She picked up her wedding photo and dropped it into the trash can in the bathroom.

Today is the first day of my new journey, she thought proudly.

Nathan left the bed and breakfast at around eight o'clock. He started toward the diner and was on Ann Street when he noticed Sheriff Carter behind him.

"Sorry, Sheriff Carter, but I can't have you tailing me today," he said to himself as he looked in the rearview mirror.

He pulled his powerful mustang along the curb in front of the deli. Nathan waited for Carter to pass by. As he did, he looked over at Nathan, smiled, and once more gave him his half salute. Nathan smiled back, returned the salute, punched the accelerator, spun the car around, and raced back down the road.

Sheriff Carter heard the squealing tires, looked in his rearview mirror, and saw nothing more than a cloud of smoke behind him.

Nathan drove to the cemetery after losing Sheriff Carter. The thought of Sheriff Carter driving around looking for him put a smile on Nathan's face. He parked in the same spot as the previous night and walked to the tree that had been struck by the would-be assassin's bullet. Using his pocketknife, he carefully pried it out. He determined it was a .38-caliber bullet.

He placed it in his pocket and walked to the tombstone the shooter used for cover. He knelt in front of it.

* Howard Worthy Hughes
January 3, 1801 – January 2, 1870
Beloved Husband, Father, and Grandfather *

Just below the writing on the tombstone and on the ground was what appeared to be dried blood.

I must have hit him last night. How bad? I need to find him. Hopefully, his injury will force him out. I think I'll go visit the sheriff first and see how he's feeling this morning, Nathan thought.

Sissy was at the kitchen sink when she heard Stormie coming down the stairs. A few seconds later, she burst into the kitchen.

"How do I look?" Stormie asked as she spun around in her white summer dress.

"You looks as beautiful as always, baby. What's the matter with you this morning?" she asked as she dried her hands on her apron.

"Nothing's the matter. I just decided that today is the first day of my new journey, and I've decided to take you with me," Stormie called as she grabbed Sissy's hands and danced and spun the two of them around in circles.

"Stormie, have you been drinking this morning? It ain't ladylike to be drinking this early. I think yous done chugged full!"

"No, I haven't been drinking, but I might," Stormie

declared. She grabbed Sissy's hands once more and started dancing again.

"Stormie, if'n you ain't drunk, then surely you must be touched."

Stormie laughed. "No crazy here, my dearest and closest friend. Today we're going into town and havin' lunch and then…"

"And then what, Mrs. Stormie?" Sissy asked with excitement, allowing herself to get caught in the moment.

"And then…" Stormie looked around the room and saw the magazine on the table. "And then we're gonna go and buy this!" Stormie proclaimed.

"Oh no, baby, you done gone hog-wild. Mr. Ben will be fit to be tied when he finds out."

"I don't give a damn about anything that man has to say anymore," Stormie declared as she pulled the apron from around Sissy's waist. She turned Sissy around toward the stairs and then popped her in the rear with the apron.

"Hurry and go change your clothes, and get ready to have some fun today," Stormie ordered as she looked at the advertisement once more.

Sheriff Carter was sitting in his office drinking coffee when Charlie White came in and sat in the chair across from him. The sheriff just looked at him, saying nothing. He watched as Charlie took his hat off and placed it on the desk. He also noticed Charlie's arm was bandaged.

"What the hell happened to you?" Sheriff Carter asked.

"That damn FBI agent is what," Charlie answered as he rubbed his arm below the bandage.

The sheriff's eyes widened. "What did you do now, Charlie?"

"I did what you told me to do last night."

"You watched the FBI agent?"

Charlie twisted in the chair. "Yes, I stayed there watching his room until it looked like he was in for the night," he answered.

"When did you leave?" Sheriff Carter inquired.

"I left right after you," he answered.

Sheriff Carter huffed. "I told you to stay there until one in the morning to make sure he was staying in for the night."

"I was tired, and he turned out all the lights after you left. For all I knew, he was done for the night," Charlie said in his defense.

The sheriff grew more and more agitated. "What happened? You're not telling me something!"

Charlie paused before answering. "After I drove away, I noticed I left my jug in the woods, so I went back to get it. That's when I saw him pulling out of the parking lot."

"And?"

"And I followed him in that hotrod of his over to the cemetery, where he met George Butler and his friend Otis."

"What happened?" Dwight suspiciously asked.

"You didn't want him talking to anyone. That's what you told me anyway. So I tried to scare them off."

"How, Charlie? How?"

"I pulled out my .38 and shot a couple o' rounds over their way."

Sheriff Carter quickly stood, forcing his chair back against the wall. "You did what? You stupid son of a—"

"Oh, big deal. I shot at them, and you know what? That FBI man shot back and hit me in my damn arm!"

"Did they see you?"

"Hell no, it was dark. And I'm okay, by the way, thanks for asking."

"I don't give a damn about you!" Sheriff Carter clarified before sitting back down.

"No shit! Anyway, I got out of there quickly and patched myself up. The bullet went straight through, and it hurt like hell."

"If you don't beat all. You're a damn fool."

"Yeah, but I'm a fool you need," Charlie said, reminding him.

For now, Carter thought to himself. "I'll be the judge of that. Did you make the delivery to Ben's?" the sheriff asked.

"Yeah, it's done. By the way, this is gonna cost you fellas extra."

"I imagined it would. You just keep an eye on the FBI man and don't try to do anything on your own. I'll let you know if and when we need you to do something more drastic."

"I want to do it when the time comes. I mean, I owe that son of a bitch," Charlie declared, then got up and walked out of the office.

Sheriff Carter made a call and set up an appointment to meet with Ben and Jack at his office. At fifteen minutes before four, both men arrived. Jack appeared to be nervous, but Ben was calm as usual. Both men sat across the desk from Carter.

"What did our FBI man do last night?" Ben asked.

"Well, I followed him most of the day and then I had Charlie meet me across from his room last night. I paid Charlie what was owed so far and decided to have Charlie watch our visitor since we're not ready for Charlie to complete the other job yet. Besides, I can't watch the agent twenty-four hours a day."

Ben nodded. "The other job is on hold, as we discussed. My wife can't be harmed until Agent Emerson is long gone. It would look way too suspicious," he clarified as he looked at both men.

"Charlie will keep an eye on Agent Emerson, and if needed, he will make him go away. Anyway, Charlie kept an eye on him after I left last night."

"That's good for now. Just watch him. We need to make sure we wait before we do anything extreme. By the way, did Charlie make the delivery to the Arrington House?"

"Yeah, a hundred gallons of West Virginia moonshine was delivered to the cellar of your family's home, but... Charlie already did something extreme and a little messy last night."

Jack beat his fist on the chair arm. "Oh, shit. What did he do?" He asked. He then rubbed his forehead just as he always did when he was anxious or nervous.

"Shut up and relax, Jack," Ben ordered. "Messy how, Sheriff?"

The office door suddenly opened, and Nathan Emerson walked in.

"Afternoon, gentlemen!"

CHAPTER 8
CHARLIE WHITE

"**M**a'am, are you sure this is the car you want to drive?" the salesman asked as he pressed the accelerator, making the engine roar.

"No, it's the one I want to buy," Stormie stated.

"Mrs. Stormie, maybe you should think about this for a bit," Sissy pleaded.

"Ma'am, we just got this car this past weekend," the man said, getting out of the car. "It's brand new to the market. We only got one, and some dealerships didn't get any. Maybe you should listen to your girl. This car is a Corvette with a big-block, three-hundred-ninety-six-cubic-inch engine that's pushing four hundred twenty-five horsepower. It has a four-speed transmission. Do you know what that is? It's a whole lot of car! That's what it is."

"Yes, it means I need to make sure the clutch is in before I shift gears. I grew up on a farm and drove many trucks with manual transmissions. I'm sure I can drive this one. I'm very aware of how powerful it is, and her name is Sissy. Please call her by her name."

The man smiled and looked at both women. "Yes, ma'am,

I understand. Ms. Sissy, I apologize. But in all due respect, ma'am, I don't think any of those trucks on your farm could deliver four hundred twenty-five horsepower as quickly as this car."

Stormie glared at the salesman. "How much is it?"

"It's a lot. Maybe you'd like to bring your husband by, get his opinion and let him drive it around to see how he likes it."

Hearing the word *'husband'* angered Stormie. "Mr. Davis, I'm sure I can find another salesman who is willing to sell me this car if you're reluctant to do so. I don't see how my husband's opinion matters one iota concerning my car. Or the fact that Mr. Thomas, the bank manager in Beaufort, has already given me a lot of cash to pay for it," Stormie said as Sissy pulled out a stack of hundred-dollar bills from her purse and waved them in front of the salesman.

The salesman's attitude quickly changed upon seeing the money wrapped in a band that read "$5,000." "You're absolutely right. What's his opinion matter anyway? Like you said, it's your car."

"Now, don't forget to subtract the eight hundred dollars from the price," Stormie said.

The salesman chuckled. "Why would I do that?" he asked.

Stormie turned and pointed to her car. "Because that's how much I want for my old car over there."

The man placed his hands on his hips. "Well, I don't know if I can give you eight hundred dollars for your old car. I mean, we haven't even looked at it," he replied, like any good car salesman would.

"Very well. I'll just drive to Raleigh and get my car there. I'm sure they will give me eight hundred or even a thousand for my old car," Stormie said and started to walk away.

"No! There's no need for that. I'll give you the eight hundred for your old car," the salesman said in frustration.

"Fine then, we have a deal."

"I believe we do," the beaten man said. He shook her hand, turned, and walked back toward the main office to complete the paperwork.

"I sure hope you know what's you doin', baby," Sissy said from the side of the car.

Stormie smiled at Sissy, opened the car door, and sat in the driver's seat of the convertible. The car was still running, so she placed her foot on the accelerator and pressed it. The motor roared once more as the car came alive and shook violently in place. She could feel the power and freedom the car was going to provide. The car wanted to go fast, run down the highway, and leave the past in the dust, just like its new owner wanted to do.

My, my, my... she thought.

Nathan walked into the office without knocking, surprising the three men. The sheriff was startled and stood quickly as Ben and Jack turned to look at the agent. Nathan had been standing outside the door. He had been trying to listen to what was being said inside, but the door was too thick. When he heard the receptionist coming back to her desk, he decided to just walk into the office.

"I'm sorry to startle you fellas, but no one was out front," Nathan said innocently enough, as he used his thumb pointing back toward the receptionist's desk.

"People normally knock around here instead of just barging in," the sheriff said in a displeasing tone.

"Agent Emerson, how is one of Mr. Hoover's most trusted men?" Ben smiled as he stood and offered his hand, to which Nathan reciprocated the gesture by painfully raising his arm and slightly grimacing as Ben shook it aggressively.

Nathan grinned through the pain. "I'm fine, and you?"

"I'm doing just fine as well. I'm glad you stopped by. You know, I heard a rumor the other day that you played football for the Sooners."

The agent looked at Carter then Jack, and back at Ben. "I'm surprised rumors about me would even spread. I've only been in town for a few days, and I really don't know anyone. It sounds more like someone has been checking up on me," Nathan remarked with a smile.

"I admit, I thought your name sounded familiar when we met, but I couldn't for the life of me remember where I had heard it before. So, I made some calls and discovered you played in the Orange Bowl of 1958 against our own Duke Blue Devils."

"I'll be. I remember that game," Jack stated.

"You should. Nathan Emerson sacked our quarterback three times, helping his team defeat our Blue Devils forty-eight to twenty-one."

"You know, you didn't need to call anyone. I'd have been happy to tell you everything you'd like to know about me."

"Normally I would've, Agent Emerson, but you see, I thought it would be impolite to pry, since you're a stranger and all."

"Don't let that stop you. I'm happy to answer any questions you may have. You just go ahead and ask whenever you'd like," Nathan said and smiled once more.

"Well, thank you for the invitation, and if I decide to do that, I'll surely find you and ask."

The two men stood there, sizing one another up in an uncomfortable silence. Nathan estimated that the prosecutor was slightly shorter than he was but with the same build. He also guessed Ben was senior to him by about eight to ten years.

"You need something, Agent Emerson? You did come by for a reason, right?" Sheriff Carter asked, breaking the silence.

"Not really. I was just stopping by to say hello and to say thank you for the file you got for me yesterday. But it looks like you gentlemen are busy, so I'll be on my way," Nathan said as he and Ben continued to lock eyes for a few moments longer. Nathan then smiled and turned to walk out.

"By the way, you find anything yet?" Ben asked.

Nathan turned around and looked at Ben. "Nothin' useful. It's as quiet as a cemetery around here. But hey, the day isn't over."

"Agent Emerson. How about you drive in accordance with the traffic laws while you're in town from now on… Doing burnouts in the middle of the road isn't something we allow," Sheriff Carter said.

"I'll be sure to do that. I think my foot slipped. It's a newer car, and I'm still getting used to it," Nathan said and walked out.

The three men waited for the FBI agent to walk out of the building before carrying on with their conversation.

Ben sat back down and was the first to speak. "Well, it's clear he's doing whatever the hell he wants to in our town."

"That ain't my fault. And that cemetery comment was a bunch of horseshit!"

"What are you talking about?" Ben asked.

"Before he barged in, I was about to tell you that Charlie followed him to the cemetery last night. And, well, he got a little carried away when he saw the agent meeting with George and Otis."

"So?"

"So he fired a few shots at them."

Ben stood once more. "What in the hell does Charlie think he's doing?!"

"He said he was just trying to scare them a little. It worked. I went by their place earlier and found out they left town early this morning."

"Did they have time to tell him anything?"

"I don't know. Agent Emerson shot back and hit Charlie."

"How bad?" Jack asked.

"Not bad, he'll be fine."

"That's too bad," Jack mumbled.

"We may not like Charlie, but he gets the dirty work done for us," Ben said, directing his comment to Jack.

"I know, but there ain't much we can do about Agent Emerson until he's ready to leave," Jack explained to the men.

"There is something we can do," Ben stated.

"What's that?" Sheriff Carter asked, looking at Ben questionably.

"Help him."

"The hell you say?!" Sheriff Carter yelled.

"Listen. If he starts reporting back that you're not cooperating and he suddenly comes up missing or he's found dead, it's gonna be a big problem. We want to be the ones who report it and appear as though we're more concerned about him than anyone else around here. Or we'll be the ones the FBI is investigating," Ben explained.

"Okay, but what do we do if we decide to kill him? The FBI won't stop until they get the killer or killers," Jack said.

Ben looked back and forth between the two men. "Then maybe we give them their killer."

"Who do you plan on giving to the FBI?" Jack asked, worried that it could be him who the others were willing to sacrifice for the good of the group.

Ben gave Jack a vacant stare. "Not you, so stop worrying. It's simple. I think old Charlie White has served his purpose and worn out his welcome, and I think he'll fit the bill just fine. He's becoming more of a problem every day he's alive. Besides, he did have a shootout with an FBI agent and has the wound to prove it. He's also been seen with all the dead girls."

"I agree. Charlie ain't nothin' but a loose end who can bury us all if he wants. He needs to be taken care of after all of this is done," the sheriff explained.

Ben nodded. "I think we all know he's gonna be a problem in the future."

The sheriff quickly nodded his head. "Ben, I agree Charlie will blackmail us forever after we all get where we want."

Ben looked over at Jack. "How about it, Jack? You agree?"

"I agree, but I don't like it. More and more people are getting in the way."

"Jack, it'll be fine. Can you handle it, Sheriff Carter, when the time comes?"

"I ain't never liked Charlie. I'll think of something and take care of it."

"Then we're agreed. I'll tell the judge," Ben said.

"So what's the plan?" Jack asked.

"Dammit, Jack. Charlie will take care of the FBI agent and my wife, and the sheriff here will take care of Charlie."

"That still leaves us one real problem that none of us has got a hold on yet," Jack said.

"I'm working on solving that. And when I do, I'll take care of it too," the sheriff declared.

Nathan waited outside the church for everyone to leave before going in. Preacher was waiting with Iris Snipes near the front. She was a thin but strong woman who appeared older than she was. She was wearing a black dress, and she looked as though she had been crying. Nathan calmly sat next to her and before he could ask a question she began to speak about Delia.

"Delia was a beautiful girl, and she only did what she did to help feed us when I got sick," she said and paused to look at Nathan with wet eyes.

Nathan nodded at her and said he understood.

"She was raped when she was sixteen and ended up pregnant. She lost the baby two months in. When she was in the hospital, the sheriff came by with some woman from the North Carolina Eugenics Board and told me the best thing for me to do was to sign the papers so Delia could be sent to Mecklenburg County and made so she couldn't have no more babies."

"Really? Did you sign it?" Nathan asked.

"Yes. The sheriff said if I didn't that I could be arrested for putting my child in danger because Delia was retarded and couldn't take care of herself. The lady said Delia could be raped again and again, and the court may see it as my fault and have me arrested for not looking after her."

"They said Delia was mentally retarded and this was the best thing for her? How did they know she was mentally retarded?" Nathan asked.

"They had a test score or something, and it showed she wasn't right in her mind, and then they said she could be taken away and locked in a home somewhere if I didn't sign. They told me she would not be harmed from the surgery, so I signed. I mean, I just didn't wants to lose my baby. Pastor Turner, I know what it is to be touched, but I never felt like Delia was touched. They were gonna take her away. I didn't know what else to do!" she cried.

"It's all right, Iris," Preacher said as he sat next to her and held her in his arms.

"Can you tell me the rest, Mrs. Iris?" Nathan asked.

"When Delia came back, she had some money and told me it was given to her by the woman and sheriff for havin' the surgery. The next thing I knows is Delia is going out at night and coming home late. I told her she should find a job, and she told me she had one, and that's when I knew," Iris said and cried more. "I knew it was wrong, but Delia kept saying it's only for a little longer, until she got enough money to move us away from here. We were gonna move away right after that night, but she never came home."

"Do you know where she was that night?" Nathan asked.

"No, but it was a party. Delia went to some party once or twice a month, but I don't know where."

"Was Delia ever arrested for doing what she was doing?"

"No!"

Nathan sat there a little longer, listening to Iris share the good memories she had about Delia. Eventually, Preacher escorted her out of the church and came back to speak to Nathan.

"I need to go out and see where these girls were found," Nathan said. "If the sheriff did anything right, it was marking the locations on a map of where the girls' bodies were found."

"Do you know how to get to those places on the map?" Preacher asked.

"I think so, but I'm worried about the sheriff following me."

"Leave your room and walk out toward Taylor Creek on Friday at nine, and I'll have my boys pick you up in their boat. They'll take you out on the water. You can get to all the locations by traveling on the water. It'll be difficult for anyone to follow you if you're on a boat."

"Are you sure?"

"After hearing Iris, I am. You just keep an eye on my boys."

"I will," Nathan assured him.

The night was warm. Nathan opened his bedroom window and lay on the bed with a bag of ice on his shoulder. He watched the Wednesday night movie on NBC, *Fear Strikes Out.* It was the true story of the life of Jimmy Piersall, who battled mental illness to achieve stardom in Major League Baseball. No one knew that the strong independent FBI agent was a sucker for underdog stories—no one but his mother anyway.

When the show ended, he got up and turned off the television, then sat back on the bed and turned the lamp off before lying down. After about two hours of not falling asleep, he walked to the window and peered out the side of the curtain. The dark figure of a man stood in the shadows once again. It wasn't the sheriff, and it wasn't Walters. He assumed it was the same person who had watched him the night of the shooting at the cemetery.

Maybe he was the shooter. Perhaps I should go down and introduce myself. No, not yet. There's still too much to do, he thought to himself.

He placed a chair in front of the door, wedging it under the knob. He figured it would buy him more time than the cola bottle in case someone tried to come in while he was asleep. He lay back down and thought about the case again, and many of the same questions that he didn't have answers to kept coming up.

Who was the new tail? Is he the shooter? Why was Delia sent to Mecklenburg County for the sterilization surgery? How do the Four Horsemen fit into the girls' deaths?

Stormie was sitting in the living room, flipping through the owner's manual of her new car, when she heard Ben pull into the driveway. He didn't come in right away, so Stormie assumed he was looking over her latest purchase parked out front. She had prepared for his arrival and had already sent Sissy upstairs and told her not to come out when he got home. Stormie decided that any discussion they were going to have tonight was not going to be so one-sided. Benjamin Arrington would hear what she had to say.

Ben entered through the front door and set his briefcase on the floor. He turned around and was momentarily startled to find Stormie sitting there.

"I guess someone decided to buy herself a new car," he said.

"Somebody did decide to buy herself a new car."

"What was wrong with the old one?"

"You just said it; it was old."

"I meant—"

"I know what you meant. As a matter of fact, I know a lot. And because of all I know, I've decided to get rid of a lot of old stuff and start new," Stormie said as she sat the owner's manual on the table beside her.

"I find it hard to believe that you would go and spend my money on a new car without discussing it with me first," Ben said as he walked toward her.

His money! Stormie thought to herself, getting upset. "Your money? I believe I am the one with all the money, and according to the bank, I still am. I put my money into my account every month and then I put some of that money into our account," she said flatly as she stood and brushed past Ben.

"That's not how I see it. According to the laws of North Carolina, I'm entitled to half of the money. So what was once all of yours is now half mine," he explained.

"All the money we have is 'mine'! All the money 'you' have is mine, as well! I had it when I met you! It was left to 'me' by my parents, and if 'you' think that you're gonna take it, 'you' are sadly mistaken! If you remember, I intentionally left 'my money' in the bank in Alabama, and on occasions, I have some of 'my' money put into 'our' account here in North Carolina. So when it comes to 'my' money, it's better you keep your mouth shut and seem a fool than to open it and remove all doubt," Stormie announced defiantly.

"You stupid fucking country girl! Do you think you're smarter than me? I'll take all the money if I decide to do so, and there's not a damned thing you can do about it!" Ben yelled.

"You son of a bitch! No judge in Alabama would ever allow it!" Stormie shouted and started toward him.

Ben stepped forward into her approach and backhanded her across the face, which sent her over the chair. He then grabbed her by the shirt, lifted her, and drew his hand into a fist as he prepared to hit her again.

"Stop right there, or I'll blow your head clean off!" Sissy yelled from the bottom of the stairs.

Ben slowly turned around and found Sissy standing there at the smart end of a shotgun. He glared at her and let Stormie go.

"From now on, we'll discuss what you can buy. You can keep the car for now. Besides, I may like to drive it on one of my trips," he explained as he walked out the door, laughing.

Stormie sat on the floor and held her face until she heard him pull out of the driveway. Sissy helped her up. She looked Sissy in the eye once she was on her feet.

"I'm leaving him," she declared.

THURSDAY, JULY 8, 1965

Nathan woke at around seven in the morning. He had decided late last night to drive the five and a half hours to Charlotte to find out where Delia had had the surgery. If anything, he could go by and speak to someone with the Eugenics Board.

The roads leading from Beaufort to Charlotte had very little traffic to contend with, so Nathan enjoyed the drive as he sped down the highway. The GT350 with its Wimbledon-white and Guardsman-blue rocker stripes were but a blur to pedestrians along the roadway. He waited until he was closer to Charlotte before really pushing the Mustang. After all, he had to finally lose his shadow that was having trouble keeping up with him. He decided he had toyed with him long enough, and it was time to say good-bye.

As he climbed a small hill, he immediately turned off onto a side road at the top and sped out of view from the main road. He took a few back roads he was familiar with, and before long, he was in Charlotte. He passed his office and thought about going inside, but he decided against it. Agent Smith would question him about the unofficial investigation, and Nathan was sure he wouldn't be happy with anything he had to say.

Nathan soon found the Mecklenburg County Courthouse and the office of the Eugenics Board of North Carolina located inside. Nathan was familiar with the Eugenics Board of North Carolina and how they came to be. The board had been formed in July of 1933, and they handled cases in North Carolina relating to the sterilization of people deemed mentally defective. Nathan felt most of the people who were judged by the board to be mentally defective were people from black communities. Eventually, people who were viewed as criminals or had a lack of moral character were processed through the Eugenics Board as well.

Nathan introduced himself to the receptionist, and she told him someone would be with him in a few minutes. While he waited, he walked around the waiting area and observed the many photos hanging on the wall. Suddenly, he stopped at one in particular. He saw someone he recognized in one of the pictures. Judge Ridge was standing there with a group of men receiving an award. Nathan looked closer at the photo and saw

Ben Arrington standing in the background, behind the men getting the awards. The picture was dated January 1960, with an inscription below the date:

District Attorney Thomas Jefferson Ridge is recognized for 10 years of service as a member of the Eugenics Board of North Carolina.

A short time later, a woman came out and greeted Nathan. She was polite and spoke to Nathan at great lengths about the board. She even provided information regarding people whom the board had deemed necessary for sterilization in the past five years. Nathan thanked her for her time and excused himself.

He rushed past the receptionist into the main hallway and located the bathroom. He hurried inside and found an empty stall where he quickly looked over the list. After a few minutes, he dropped the list to his side and allowed himself a chance to really breathe. All three girls' names were on the list.

Finally, a lead! he thought to himself.

Nathan walked out of the bathroom and left the courthouse. On the sidewalk, he looked around for a moment and saw a diner across the way. He decided to go inside for lunch. He was satisfied with the discovery of another piece of the puzzle.

The diner was crowded. Nathan thought everyone appeared to be either a witness, a defendant, a lawyer, or a judge. Either way, he assumed they all had business at the courthouse. At some of the tables, attorneys, in their uncomfortably warm suits, reviewed court briefs with other lawyers over burgers and fries, while other lawyers discussed plea deals and defense strategies with their clients. Nathan sat at a table that had not yet been cleared off. He waited patiently before being greeted by a waitress, who apparently was overworked and in a hurry.

"Let me clear these dishes for you, honey," she said as she wiped her forehead with her arm and cleared the table.

"Thank you."

"We don't have a lunch menu because we're so busy this

time of day. You can have pretty much any cold meat sandwich or a burger from the grill. All of them come with a side of fries. We have various sodas and of course tea. Now, you think about what you want, and I'll be back in a minute to get your order," she said and walked away.

"Why, hello, Nathan!"

Nathan looked up and saw Stormie Arrington standing next to his table. She wore a light-blue summer dress with white gloves and shoes and was holding a matching purse.

The clothes, the way she moves, the way she somehow commands a room full of people to stop what they were doing and take notice is like that of Jacqueline Kennedy, he thought.

"Hello, Mrs. Arrington," he said as he stood and clumsily bumped the table when he reached out to shake her hand. "Does your husband have a case at the courthouse today?" he asked curiously.

"No. I'm in Charlotte by myself today on a personal matter," she said directly, as she was bumped into by another patron who was rushing to an empty table.

"Is your lady friend gonna be joinin' you?" the waitress asked upon her return, holding a small pad of paper in one hand and a pen in the other.

"Well, I don't know. Um, would you like to join me for lunch, Mrs. Arrington?" Nathan asked.

"If it's no bother, I'd be delighted. I'm a bit hungry, and it looks like I better take advantage of such a wonderful offer if I plan on eating today." She pulled the chair out that was directly across from him and sat down.

"I believe you can tell her what we have for lunch today," the waitress said as she pointed toward Stormie with her pen.

"Yes, I'll take care of it," he replied with a slight smile.

Charlie White was driving around Charlotte, looking for Agent Emerson. He was angry with himself for losing him earlier on the road, but his old truck couldn't keep up with the agent's car. He stopped at a red light and took the opportunity to light a cigarette.

Damn fool! I should've been closer to that son of a bitch. Where'd he go? Charlie asked himself as he took a long drag.

He looked all over for the agent, to no avail. He figured the FBI man would be going to the FBI office, but he didn't see his car there when he drove by.

Charlie was trying to decide where he would go next when a car pulled up next to him. He watched and listened as the driver, a young blonde girl, sang along to the radio. The girl looked over and caught Charlie staring at her. She looked uncomfortable but smiled at him. Charlie returned the smile, bearing his crooked, yellow-stained teeth.

The light turned green, and the girl turned right. Charlie thought for a moment, and when the car behind him honked their horn, he whipped the steering wheel to the right. He turned down the same road as the girl and followed her.

No sense in wasting my day looking for that FBI son of a bitch, Charlie thought.

Chapter 9
Table for Two

Nathan went over the menu options with his lunch guest. Stormie, after careful deliberation, decided on a burger and fries. If she told the truth, she really didn't care about what she was going to eat. She was more focused on learning about the man she was eating it with.

"Would you like sweet tea or just plain tea with your burger?" the waitress asked as she held her pen over the pad of paper, impatiently waiting for an answer.

"Well, sweet of course," Stormie answered matter-of-factly.

The waitress, not particularly liking Stormie's tone, placed her hands on her hips and parted her lips to say something.

"I'll have the same," Nathan said, quickly recognizing the uncomfortable situation about to unfold.

"Sure, honey," the annoyed waitress replied. She turned, threw her hip to the side in Stormie's direction, and walked away.

Stormie leaned across the table toward Nathan. "I do believe that woman is a Yankee."

"Why do you say that?"

"No woman who was born and raised in the South would

ever ask another Southerner if they wanted sweet tea or plain tea. Tea should always be sweet," she said as if the sweetness of tea was common knowledge to women born South of the Mason-Dixon Line.

Nathan discovered Stormie to be direct and without filter, like himself. He also found her amusing, beautiful, and intriguing. He felt drawn to her, and he had a strong desire to know more about Stormie Arrington.

Nathan looked upward, trying to recall his memories. "Now that you say that, I can't think of any time my own mother ever made anything but sweet tea in our home when I was growing up."

"Well, that speaks highly of your mother, Agent Emerson."

"Agent Emerson?" Nathan asked.

"Yes. A little bird told me that you, my new friend, were none other than one of J. Edgar Hoover's boys. Actually, I believe the bird was more like a large ugly vulture. You know… the kind you see on the highway eating three-day-old roadkill."

"I know the bird, Mrs. Arrington," he replied with a smile, as he believed she was describing one of the Four Horsemen— most likely her husband.

"If I recall, I asked that you call me Stormie. I mean, everyone else calls me Stormie. Besides, Mrs. Arrington was my husband's mother. Mrs. Arrington was a bit of an atrocious woman, so when I hear the words 'Mrs. Arrington,' I just cringe," Stormie explained and then shivered for added effect.

"Then Stormie it is, but you were supposed to call me Nathan, if I remember correctly."

"Yes, I do recall. Nathan. And you know what? You look like a Nathan."

"I do? What if my name was Michael?"

"No. You're not a Michael," she answered as she placed her hands into her lap and looked him over with a smile.

"Really?"

"Really. In my experience, I've come to believe there are certain things that we see in others, and we subconsciously connect those things with our past experiences, especially when we meet someone new and hear their name for the first time."

"Really, please explain," Nathan said. He leaned back in the chair and crossed his arms.

"Well, take the name Nick."

"I know a Nick," he said, thinking of his supervisor.

"Really? Well, to me, anyone named Nick is an ass simply because I knew a Nick in grade school, and he was the meanest child to ever walk the face of God's green earth."

"I'd have to agree with that analogy. That's the Nick I know to the letter. I mean, the part about being a child and just mean."

"Now, other names like Michael, Benjamin, and Stephen are names I've come to associate with people like Nick. In my experience, they are either complete asses, adulterous, or self-absorbed S-O-Bs. And names like Nathan are for people I've determined to be kind, polite, well mannered, and handsome," she explained, just as the waitress returned and placed two glasses of sweet tea on the table.

"Thank you," Nathan said, looking up at the waitress.

She smiled and then once more threw her hip out toward Stormie as she turned and walked away. Stormie watched the woman and then smiled at Nathan in amusement.

"Lord have mercy, I do believe her feathers are done ruffled up a bit," she said, still smiling before lifting her glass and taking a drink. She made a sour face and put the glass back on the table. "Yep, Northerner."

Nathan laughed as he stared at the woman sitting across from him.

"It might as well be plain tea; I don't think there is a grain of sugar in this glass. If there is, she probably stirred it in with her old sour-ass finger."

"Will you be able to drink it, or should we grab our pitchforks and torches?"

"Nathan Emerson, with a comment like that, I might believe that you could very well be a Michael in a Nathan disguise," she said and laughed out loud.

She had a wonderful laugh and smile. It was a smile a man could get used to seeing every day. As he sat there with her, he found himself noticing the smallest details of her hair, her eyes, her lips, and her smell. He noticed she tilted her head upward when she spoke about something serious but downward ever so slightly when she was not. When she flirted, she tilted her head to the side and smiled as she brushed her hair back with her hand.

Wait, is she flirting? Wait... Is she flirting with me? Am I flirting with her? Nathan asked himself. "Speaking of people named Michael, Stephen, and Benjamin, I do recall your husband is a Benjamin."

"He most certainly is. How else could I have ever become such an expert about asses, adulterers, and self-absorbed S-O-Bs?"

Charlie made sure to keep two to three cars between himself and the girl as he followed her for about four miles through downtown Charlotte. He then followed her for about another mile through some neighborhood side streets until she finally pulled into the driveway of a small blue house.

He was sure the girl did not see him during their drive, nor did she notice him drive past her and park a few houses down. He placed the truck in park and adjusted the rearview mirror so he could have a better view of the girl exiting her car. He slouched in the driver's seat and looked around to make sure no one was watching him.

The mirror provided the perfect view for Charlie to watch the girl as she climbed out of her car and walked to the front door. The first thing he noticed about her was how white her skin was. She was tall and thin. Her revealing outfit consisted of a white, low-cut V-neck T-shirt, along with a red miniskirt and red shoes.

Charlie allowed a fantasy to consume his thoughts, and before long, he felt himself getting excited. He couldn't resist, so he looked around the area once more before slowly stroking himself over his jeans.

Charlie watched as she knocked on the front door, where she was greeted by another woman dressed in the same fashion. The two girls innocently embraced each other and disappeared into the house. Charlie, still aroused, closed his eyes and sat there rubbing himself faster as he fantasized about what the two girls were surely doing inside.

He imagined himself going up to the front door and finding it slightly open. There, he had a view of the two women embracing each other passionately. He would stand at the door and watch as the two women ran their hands over each other's naked bodies.

"Hey, you sick son of a bitch! What are you doing in there?!" a man shouted from the sidewalk near the passenger side of Charlie's truck. "We got kids in this neighborhood! What's your name?!" The man approached the window.

The surprised Charlie quickly put the truck in drive and pulled away from the curb. "Fuck you!" he yelled out the window as he raced away with his left arm out the driver's side window and his middle finger in the air.

Neither of them wanted the conversation to end. The food

arrived, and they both took their time eating it. They each even ordered a scoop of "North Carolina's Award-Winning Home-Churned Vanilla Ice-Cream."

"Would either of you like a dinner menu?" The waitress had a sarcastic tone to her voice. She had grown tired of waiting on the couple who had decided not to leave her section. Nathan looked at his watch and back at the waitress.

"No, I think we're done," he said as he pulled out his wallet.

"Nathan, I'd be very pleased if you would allow me to pay for our lunch. After all, it was me who intruded on you," Stormie explained as she opened her purse to take out her own wallet.

"There is no way I'd ever allow you to buy lunch," he explained and handed the waitress a ten-dollar bill.

"Nathan Emerson, I demand you allow me to buy lunch."

"No. I could not allow that. My mother surely would turn over in her grave if I allowed a beautiful woman such as yourself to pay for lunch."

"Well, thank you for the compliment, and with that, I'll allow you to buy my lunch, but only if you promise to allow me to return the courtesy in the very near future."

"Agreed."

The two of them walked out of the restaurant around three o'clock. Nathan asked Stormie where she had parked, and she pointed toward a new red convertible down the street. She slipped on a pair of white gloves and placed her purse on her arm.

"I'll walk you to your car if you would like."

"That would be nice, thank you."

The couple started up the street at a meandering pace. Stormie pretended to be interested in the merchandise on display in the windows of the stores that lined the sidewalk and occasionally stopped to look inside.

Nathan didn't believe she was interested in the new television or portable radio being advertised in the windows.

He thought she was more interested in looking for a way to extend their time together, just like he was doing. That was what he hoped she was doing anyway.

Wait. What am I doing? What am I thinking? She's a married woman! Nathan thought as he walked next to her.

"This is a really nice car," Nathan said, admiring the new Corvette. "I imagine that on hot days like this, you put the top down and enjoy the ride down the interstate as the wind whips all around you."

"You know, Nathan, I think I'd like to do that, but for the life of me, I can't figure out how to get the top down. Do you know how to get the top down?" she asked flirtatiously as she smiled and opened her car door.

"I think together we can figure it out. Why don't you get in the driver's seat, and I'll get in the passenger seat, and we'll see if we can get it down."

Stormie agreed and quickly sat in the seat. She reached over and unlocked the passenger door for him. Once inside and sitting next to her, he caught the scent of her perfume again. It was a plethora of carnations. . For a moment, he took it all in.

"Did you hear me?" Stormie asked.

"What?" he asked. He knew she had said something about the car, but his mind was preoccupied with other thoughts.

"I said, I just got the car the other day, and the salesman wasn't very helpful in explaining how things worked," she lied.

She'd had the top down when she arrived in Charlotte hours ago and put it up when she went into the divorce attorney's office. She had learned early on in life that men enjoyed helping women whom they believed were helpless.

"I was in Mississippi a while ago, and another agent owned a convertible. I borrowed it one night, and he showed me how to put the top down," Nathan explained as he reached up and pulled on the lever where the windshield and roof met on the passenger side.

"Oh, I see mine here." She reached up and tried to pull the lever down, without success.

"Sometimes in a new car, the levers need to be broken in a little bit before they're easier to use." He reached across her body with his right arm and balanced himself on her seat with his left.

The lever was stuck, so it was more difficult to get it to release than the one on the passenger side of the car. Nathan pulled hard and the lever swiftly released, and Nathan fell on the surprised Stormie. His right hand came to rest on her left breast, and Nathan was visually embarrassed. He quickly removed his hand and sat back in the passenger seat.

"What's your next move?"

"What?" he asked uncomfortably.

"The next move in getting my top down," she said, smiling and continuing to flirt. She was enjoying his embarrassment.

"Oh, yes! There should be a lever you can hold down under the dash. It should be just above your left knee."

Stormie used her left hand and pretended to find it for the first time.

The sound of the hydraulics and the warmth from the sun distracted the couple. A much-needed cool breeze blew across Nathan.

"This is gonna be a wonderful drive home," Stormie declared.

"Maybe your husband can help you get it back up when you get back home," he said and regretted mentioning her husband when her smile quickly disappeared.

"Nathan, do you think we can keep our lunch date between the two of us?" she asked while looking into his blue eyes. "I don't see why we have to share our delightful lunch date with anyone else. I don't mean to be secretive, but I—" She stopped and looked away.

"There is nothin' to explain. I understand completely. I

enjoyed havin' lunch with you today," he said awkwardly as he opened the passenger door and got out of the car.

He stood on the sidewalk and waited for her to pull away, but she just sat there, with both hands on the steering wheel, looking down the road.

He leaned forward and placed both hands on the passenger door. "Is something wrong?"

At first, she didn't say anything, nor did she take her eyes off the road in front of her.

"Stormie—"

She turned and placed her hand on top of his. "Nathan, I don't think we've done anything wrong today or that we should be ashamed of anything. I also don't think we need to hide it from anyone. It's just that my husband, Ben, doesn't know I came to Charlotte today," she told him and retrieved a facial tissue from her purse to dry the corners of her eyes.

Nathan placed his right hand over her left and squeezed it a bit. He gave her a moment to collect herself. "Stormie, I know we don't know each other that well, but if you need someone to talk to, I'd be more than happy to listen."

"Nathan, I came to Charlotte today to speak to a divorce attorney," she blurted. "I can't believe I said that to someone I hardly know. I'm so embarrassed," she said, continuing to dry her eyes with the tissue.

"There's nothin' to be embarrassed about," he assured her.

"Thank you. But it's just—"

"It's just nothin'. I'm gonna be in town for a while, and I think we should have lunch again," he said.

Then he thought to himself, *What did I just say? Did I just ask this beautiful woman out? This married woman!?*

"I think I'd like that."

"I'll be on Taylor Creek tomorrow with Pastor Turner's sons, but maybe later, we can meet and talk some more."

"You'll be on Taylor Creek tomorrow with Willie and Sam?"

"You know the Turner boys?"

"Of course, everyone knows them. They've helped me in the yard in the past. What are you doing with them? Surely those two adventurers didn't convince one of J. Edgar Hoover's finest to go looking for Blackbeard's treasure, did they? I think treasure-hunting and fishing is all those two ever do on Taylor Creek," she said as she put the tissue back in her purse.

"No, nothin' like that," he replied as he stood from the car.

"Although, treasure-hunting or even fishing sounds a lot better than what I'm gonna be doing tomorrow."

"Agent Emerson, do you mean to tell me you're gonna have those two young boys working on Taylor Creek all day tomorrow?"

"Well, I don't know about all day, but yes, I'll be with those two young men for a better part of the day."

"Well, that's settled then. I expect all three of you to be at my dock at precisely noon for sandwiches and snacks."

"I don't know what to say…"

"There's nothin' to say. It's come to my understanding that the FBI is in Beaufort on official business, and as a citizen of Beaufort, it is my duty, along with Willie's and Sam's, to assist the FBI. Willie and Sam know how to get to my place. I'll see you tomorrow," she said, then pulled away from the curb before he could object.

Stormie sat at the last traffic light before leaving downtown Charlotte and getting back on the road, the very road that would take her back home and back to her life. A home and a life that she now considered absent of love. A home filled with a husband's lies and abuse.

For a moment, she thought about escaping that home and

life. All she had to do was turn the car in the other direction and go back to Alabama—back to her childhood home. She still owned the home, but more importantly, it was the home where she was once loved and felt safe.

I could do it. What about Sissy? I could send for her later. Ben wouldn't hurt her. Would he? How could I have been so foolish to allow a man like Ben Arrington into my life so many years ago? Why couldn't he be like Nathan Emerson? Who is Nathan Emerson? Why did I follow him into the restaurant when I saw him crossing the street? Why did I share so much with a man I barely knew? Well, he was a good listener, polite, and handsome. Oh, my! What am I thinking? What are you doing, Josephine? Yep, that's precisely what Momma would say right now if she knew what I was thinking, Stormie thought.

For some, it may have been only an afternoon, but for Stormie, it was an afternoon escape with a man she felt attracted to. Deep down, Stormie knew it was not an appropriate situation she should allow herself to fall into, but it was a situation that made her feel free and excited at the same time. She imagined his deep blue eyes, perfectly combed black hair, and his rugged yet handsome face, not to mention his laugh that seemed to fill the room. He also put out an air of confidence.

Stormie allowed her thoughts to escape once more. The horn honking from the motorist behind her told her she had failed to notice the light had changed to green. She politely waved at the other driver and then moved through the intersection and onto the interstate back toward Beaufort. Once she was on the open road, she turned the volume up on the radio and sang along to Petula's Clark's hit *Downtown*.

The impatient driver who had honked at her decided to go around her in his beat-up truck. Stormie paid him no attention and turned the radio up even louder as the Corvette roared and the wind whipped around her.

It was a good day! she thought.

The drive back to Beaufort was beautiful. Nathan estimated he would be back in town and in his room by nine o'clock. He pulled down the visor and then leaned over and took his sunglasses out of the glove box. In all, he had decided his trip to Charlotte was a lucrative one.

As he drove, he thought about the case and presumed the relationship between Judge Ridge and Ben Arrington went back to Charlotte, when Arrington was getting started as an attorney. That was around about the same time Judge Ridge sat on the eugenics board, the same board that had approved all the girls' sterilization surgeries.

There were still a lot of things he had questions about, so he ran over each one in his mind.

Who was my new tail?

What's the connection between the Horsemen, the girls, and the eugenics board?

What was their interest in the girls?

How does Sheriff Carter and Jack Walter fit into all of this?

Damn it! How is everyone connected?

Did one of the men kill the girls? Which one and why?

And, then there's Stormie Arrington…

What if she was setting me up?

Did I really lose the tail this morning?

Was she sent to the diner to speak to me?

Is she part of all this?

No, she can't be… But wait, her husband is Ben Arrington. What about the divorce attorney she went to see, and the crying? She couldn't be part of this.

I know that Ridge, Arrington, Walter, and Carter are bad people because I've seen bad people, and all four of them fit the mold.

"Stormie isn't like them. She's a good person and genuine.

I know it," he said as if he were trying to convince someone in the empty passenger seat.

As the sky grew darker and he got closer to Beaufort, he tried to think about the case and the questions he had. Stormie was all he could think about, and that was all he could see as he cruised closer to the familiar convertible in front of him.

Stormie looked in her rearview mirror and saw the white car with the blue stripe on the hood getting closer, and at first, she was concerned. Within seconds, the other car was so close to her, she could no longer see its bumper. However, she did recognize the driver, and he made her smile.

Nathan questioned whether she would or would not do it. Once the oncoming lane was empty, he entered it and punched the accelerator. When he caught up, he looked over at her and saw a grin on her face that said: *Let's do it.*

Stormie pressed her foot hard on the accelerator, and the powerful car's front end lifted slightly and then it pulled away from the Shelby 350. She laughed and gripped the steering wheel tightly. Approaching the curve, Nathan saw a sedan barreling toward him. He eased off the gas, pressed the brake, and got behind her once again. She raised her hand in the air, signaling her victory.

The race ain't over! he thought to himself.

Nathan shifted to a lower gear and applied the brake as he entered the curve. Coming out of the curve, Nathan saw his chance, and once another car passed in the opposite lane, he pressed the accelerator hard and passed Stormie on the left.

Nathan determined she was unfamiliar with the mechanics of decelerating going into curves and accelerating out of them at the right moment. He got in front of her and waved.

"Dang it!" she called. "I got one more shot before we get to town," she said to herself.

Once out of the curve, she checked the oncoming lane,

and when it was clear, she moved into it, downshifted, and hit the accelerator. The front end rose even more than last time, and Stormie's heart raced as her big block started to gain on the pony car. Nathan saw her coming up on the side, and he saw the truck in front of him. He took his foot off the gas pedal and let her fly by him and then the truck.

"You can have the win," he said quietly as he, too, entered the other lane and passed the truck. Nathan smiled the rest of the way back to town. He liked her determination and spirit.

Chapter 10
My Protector

Charlie stood in the phone booth and used a large knife to sharpen a twig into a toothpick. He ran his thumb against the tip and placed the knife back into his boot. With the sharpened twig between his lips, he retrieved a dime from his pocket, looked around the area, and slid the coin into the slot. He had written the phone number onto a piece of paper earlier. While he waited for the phone to be answered, he leaned against the booth and used the makeshift toothpick to get the remainder of a roast beef sandwich from between his teeth.

"Hello," Emma said on the other end of the line.

"Let me speak to Ben," Charlie ordered.

"Just a minute, please."

"Hello, this is Ben Arrington."

"It's me."

"What took you so long to call?"

"It wasn't my fault. The son of a bitch drove to Charlotte."

"Why?"

"How am I supposed to know that?"

"Because you were following him, that's how, you ignorant bastard," Ben said. His patience with Charlie was wearing thin.

"Well, I lost him before we got to Charlotte."

"So we know nothing! Because you're incompetent! Is that what you've called to tell me?"

"No! You best watch how you talk to me! I called because I thought you might want to know who I saw in Charlotte."

"And who may that have been?" Ben asked sarcastically.

"Your wife," Charlie announced proudly.

"Where did you see my wife? She wasn't with him, was she?" Ben asked quickly.

"I don't know."

"What do you mean you don't know?"

"Well, I didn't see her until I was heading back to Beaufort. You see, I got to a traffic light, and there was this brand-new red convertible with some blonde in it sitting in front of me. She wasn't paying attention. I had to honk to get her to move when the light changed. When I got on the highway, I decided to pass her, and that's when I recognized her," Charlie explained proudly and continued to pick his teeth.

Ben thought about what Charlie had just told him. "Where did she go when she got back to Beaufort?"

"I don't know. But there is something else."

"What's that?"

"When I got closer to town, guess who came flying by me like I wasn't even moving?"

"Who?"

"Your wife."

"So?"

"So, the next thing I see is your FBI man passing me too. I think they were racing each other back to town. Odd, ain't it? Your wife is in Charlotte at the same time as the FBI man? Maybe they doin' the same thing you and Emma doin' right now," Charlie stated and hung up the phone without another word.

Ben heard the phone go dead, but he stood there holding

the receiver to his ear, looking out the front window of Emma's house.

"What was Stormie and Agent Emerson doing in Charlotte?" he asked quietly and hung up the phone.

Emma came up behind him and wrapped her arms around his waist. "What did you say?"

"Nothing. I better get going."

"I was hoping you could stay the night again," she said as she reached down the front of his boxers.

"I can't tonight." Ben turned to face Emma and kissed her full red lips while slowly opening her silk robe.

"Oh, but tomorrow, we'll go to Charlotte for some business and then we're off to Savannah. You and I'll have many fun-filled days together. And I've got a surprise for you," Ben said. He caressed and kissed her breasts before pulling himself away.

"What surprise, Ben? What are you planning, you devil?" Emma asked with excitement. She followed Ben to the chair, where he had left his clothes.

"I'm taking you to a party."

"What kind of party?" Emma pulled her robe further apart and rubbed her body against his naked back.

"A fun one," Ben answered, turning to face her.

"Really?" Emma was skeptical because she knew about the parties Ben liked to go to.

The night was growing shorter, but he could not pull himself away from the home of Emma Rodgers. He had found himself here more and more often, hiding in the shadows, watching the lovers enjoying each other night after night.

Once again, he longed to hold a beautiful woman in his arms and have her want him as much as he wanted her. It was almost midnight when Ben Arrington pulled out of Emma's driveway.

He remained in the shadows out of sight, until he could no longer see the lights of Ben's car.

"I'll wait a bit longer for her to go to bed and fall asleep," he said quietly as he pulled the knife from his boot and ran his thumb along its sharp edge.

Stormie lay awake in bed, thinking about her afternoon with Nathan Emerson while the ceiling fan spun overhead. More than once in the past few days, she'd imagined a life away from Beaufort with a man like Nathan. For the life of her, she could not get this man out of her mind. She dreamed of a life far away from this one, but where?

Maybe Hawaii, she thought.

After all, the *Life* magazine she had received in the mail earlier in the week depicted a life of sunny days and beach living for the locals there. She allowed her mind to escape to blue waters and the beaches with a man she believed was out of her reach—a man she could never be with. It was the sound and lights of Ben's car pulling up near the house that brought her back to the reality of her sad and lonely life.

She didn't move, pretending to be asleep when he entered the room. She waited for him to lie next to her, but he never did. Stormie kept her eyes shut until she felt Ben standing over her. The familiar smell of Emma's perfume lingered in the air.

Here goes nothing, she thought to herself. She opened her eyes lazily, as if she had been in a deep sleep for some time.

"Ben!" she yelled upon finding her husband standing over her with his fist clutching an electrical cord.

"Where did you go today?" he asked as Stormie scooted across to the other side of the bed.

"What are you going to do with that?" she asked.

"See, now that's the reason I think you're one Stupid bitch!" he yelled as he grabbed at her legs and pulled her toward him.

Tears ran down her face. "No, Ben, don't!" she cried.

"Why were you in Charlotte today?" Ben reached backward with the cord and started forward with it, taking aim at Stormie's bare legs.

"No, you don't!" Sissy shouted. She rushed into the room and knocked Ben over the nightstand. At first, he was bewildered and confused, but he quickly got to his feet. He swung the cord at Sissy over and over again across her backside. Sissy retreated to the corner of the room, where she cowered, with Ben right behind her.

Stormie rushed to the lamp that had fallen to the floor. She picked it up and ran toward Ben, screaming madly. Ben spun around, with his right hand clutched in a fist, and caught Stormie on the left side of her head. She picked herself up from the hardwood floor and tried to balance herself upright, but her vision grew dark, and she fell to the floor unconscious.

Stormie awoke lying in her bed, next to Sissy. Using her elbows, she lifted herself and cautiously looked around the room. Once she determined Ben was gone, she turned her attention to Sissy, who was sleeping on her stomach. The early morning light shined through the window, and Stormie felt pain on the left side of her head. She looked over and saw that Sissy's gown was blood-stained from the lashes Ben had delivered. Stormie cried as she reached over and held her protector, who had taken the brunt of Ben's anger.

"Sissy, are you awake?" Stormie asked as she lovingly caressed and lightly kissed her guardian's head.

"I's awake."

"Where is he?" Stormie whispered.

"He's gone. He left after you went unconscious," Sissy answered. She lifted herself from the bed, wincing slightly.

"Do you know where he went? Is he coming back?"

"He packed his bags and ran out the house. He said he's going out of town and won't be back until Friday and that you best have some answers for him when he gets back," Sissy answered as she stood and looked at Stormie's face.

"Oh, my Lord, Stormie! Your face is—"

Stormie stood, steadied herself, and slowly walked into the bathroom. She placed her hands on the sink to balance herself while briefly shutting her eyes.

Sissy followed her, making sure her head injury wasn't worse than she thought. Stormie took a deep breath and then opened her eyes.

Stormie gasped as she looked at her reflection in the mirror. Her eye was severely swollen, the white of her eye was bloodshot red, and the skin around it was turning black and blue.

"It'll be fine in no time at all," Sissy said.

Stormie ran her hand over the lump. "I imagine it will, but not before lunch."

"Why you worried about lunch, baby?"

"We have guests for lunch."

"Guests? Who you got comin' over here today?" Sissy asked, surprised.

"I'll tell you all about it after we have a look at your back," Stormie said. She turned Sissy around and untied the top of her nightgown. She started to cry again as the wounds were uncovered. She wiped the tears away and took out some bandages and peroxide from the medicine cabinet.

Stormie pulled Sissy close to her and kissed her head. "This may sting a little, my protector."

He sat there naked, running his knife's blade along the whetstone in the comfort and safety of his home. He thought about how the previous night had almost been ruined. After all, he had waited patiently in the darkness of the shadows of Emma Rodgers's home until Ben Arrington left. Then he waited and watched as Emma, in her thin silk robe, moved from one room to another, singing and dancing along to the sounds of the Temptations as they sang *My Girl.*

It was another hour before Emma turned the lights off and went to bed. He waited another thirty minutes before making his way to the front door, where he used his knife to quietly pry it open.

It was the lights from a speeding car coming down the street that forced him back into the shadows. He'd have to wait a few more minutes before enjoying Emma. From under a large white oak, hidden among the mature azalea bushes, he heard the car slow, and then to his surprise, he watched it turn into the driveway. He recognized the car and cursed under his breath as he watched Ben Arrington walk up to the front door and use his key to go inside.

Ben surprised Emma, who awoke to the light coming on in her room. She jumped from her bed and embraced her late-night visitor.

Once they turned the lights back off, it was too late to play, so he decided to give up on Emma Rogers and call it a night.

He cautiously made his way back to where he had parked his car, and he climbed inside. Sitting in the driver's seat, he thought about Ben Arrington and how he had once more screwed everything up.

He pulled the long-bladed knife out and stabbed the seat next to him as he pictured Ben and Emma in each other's arms. His anger and frustration escalated, and he stabbed the passenger seat faster. He gripped the steering wheel with his left hand and screamed in frustration as he plunged the blade into the cushion.

It finally found the metal underneath it, causing the knife to stop in place and his hand to slide against its sharp edge.

He retrieved a handkerchief from the glove box and applied pressure to the wound. Once he calmed, he pulled the knife from the seat and placed it on the dashboard. Then he removed the cloth and looked at the wound.

Good, it's not that bad, he thought as he covered the cut once more.

He closed his eyes and lay his head back on the seat. It was the sound of people in the distance that made him look up. There, at the entrance underneath the sign to Joe's Tavern, he saw Bessie Jones attempting to persuade Glenn Caruthers into spending some money on her.

He watched as she ran her hand along the top of his trousers and kissed his ear. Caruthers, who might have been interested inside the bar, was no longer in the mood. He pushed her away and called her a cheap whore. The drunken Caruthers stumbled toward his car.

"Well, fuck you! You old bastard!" Bessie yelled as she walked in the other direction down the alley next to the bar.

She's drunk, and no one is around. It would be easy, he thought to himself as he started the car and pulled onto the street.

Bessie stumbled and fell once, but she tried to walk straight. He slowly pulled the car up next to her and stopped. At first, she thought it was Caruthers.

"I knew you couldn't stay away," she said as she turned and faced him. She leaned over into the driver's open window. "Oh, shit. I thought you was somebody else. You want to have some fun, baby?" She reached in and ran her index finger along his chest. He reciprocated by reaching out and placing his hand onto her left breast. He pulled the top of her dress down, exposing her nipple without saying a word.

"All right, you can have a feel, but if you want more, it's

gonna cost you," she said softly as he continued to rub her breast. "All right, baby, that's enough." She pushed his hand away and pulled her dress back up. She smiled at him. "Are you willing to pay for it, baby?"

Without a sound, he reached for her breast once more, but she pulled away.

"Look, if you want more, you gonna have to pay for it," she explained in frustration. "Do you want more?" She stood up and backed away from the car.

He just looked at her and imagined her lying in his room, tied to his bed.

"Well, fuck you then!" she shouted and started to walk away.

He opened the door and got out, not wanting to pass up the opportunity. He stood behind her eagerly and waited for her to turn and face him.

"What's it gonna be? You want this or not?" she asked as she turned and pulled the top of her dress down, baring both of her breasts to him.

He ran his hand over his mouth and looked up and down the alley.

"Well, shit, what's it gonna be?" she asked impatiently, just as he drove his fist into her face.

The impact knocked her down, and she lay there unconscious. He quickly looked around, opened his back door, and picked her limp body up from the ground. He placed her into the back seat and hurriedly drove away.

At his house, he played with Bessie for the better part of the morning. She passed out from too much playing, but he played some more.

It's ready, he thought to himself as he ran his thumb over the warm, whetted steel blade. He'd spent an hour sharpening it while Bessie slept. He ran the knife along her stomach, slightly tickling her, which woke her up.

Bessie tasted the blood in her mouth. "Wait! Please don't do this!"

Her cut and battered body lay naked on the bed next to him. Her left eye was swollen shut. Bessie's ankles and wrists ached as she pulled at the bindings constraining her.

"Please let me go, I won't tell nobody!"

He danced the edge of the knife along her thighs and plunged it deep into her abdomen. She screamed slightly as she tried to catch a breath between each round of pain. He cut his way across her stomach, eviscerating the young girl. She continued to pull at her restraints to no avail.

He placed his hand over her eyes and kissed her lips as she quietly passed from life to death. He enjoyed having the power of life and death over his victims. He had never really had anything like that, but now he did.

It was he who determined who lived and who died. That power belonged to him and him alone. The power of life and death was a replacement for the things he could not do as a man.

Chapter 11
Alligators

It was about nine o'clock in the morning when Nathan arrived at the intersection of Moore Street and Front Street. He was able to be up and out of bed at about seven, which was just enough time for him to shower, dress, and make it to Mini's Bakery to get some much-needed coffee and donuts. Sam and Willie were already there, patiently waiting for him. Both welcomed him with smiles once they recognized the familiar Mini's Bakery donut box.

"I hope you two like glazed donuts, but if you don't, I think you'll be able to find something in this box to fit your fancy," he said as he approached them.

"You bet we like glazed donuts," Willie said as he reached for the box.

Sam took one glazed and one chocolate-covered donut out of the box. "We likes any type of donut!"

After a quick but thorough discussion about different types of donuts, the three headed toward their skiff sitting next to the dock. The skiff was in better condition than Nathan thought it would be. It was white with a pirate flag painted on the side and was approximately fifteen feet in length. The boat was powered by a small outboard motor. There were fishing rods that extended along both sides of the boat and tackle boxes under the flat wooden seats. In the back of the boat was a red can that held additional fuel, along with three orange life preservers.

Nathan sat in the middle as Willie got in and started the motor. Sam waited for it to start before untying them from the dock. Once he heard it turn over and saw the familiar white smoke, he untied the line and jumped in the front of the boat.

"Where to?" Willie asked over the sound of the motor.

"We need to head for Gallant Point. Do you know where that is?"

"Yeah. Ain't no good fishin' there. But we knows where it is," Sam answered.

The trip was a little longer than Nathan imagined, but they finally made it to Gallant Point. Sam found a sandy place to beach the boat and pointed toward it. Willie aimed the bow toward the spot and revved the throttle. Once the boat hit the soft sand, Sam jumped out and pulled the boat farther onshore.

"How long we gonna be here?" Willie asked.

"Why, you in a hurry?" Nathan asked in return.

"Nope. I just thought I'd do some fishin' while we waited."

"I thought there weren't any fish over here."

"It won't hurt none to try, and it beats sitting here listening to Sam's radio."

"I think you've got time to fish. I'll be back in a little while."

"Good," Willie said eagerly. He retrieved his fishing pole from the boat and ran down the beach in the opposite direction.

Sissy cut the tomatoes she got from the garden and carefully laid them out on a serving platter. She then cut the fresh onion that she had to run out to buy earlier in the morning, along with the pickles, the cold cuts, the mustard, the potato chips, and of course, all the ingredients to make potato salad.

She bent over and took the lettuce from the refrigerator. The stinging in her back reminded her of the events that had transpired the previous night. At times during the morning, the pain had been intense. More than once, she had to stop what she was doing to catch her breath.

The one question that kept running through her mind was: *Why didn't I just shoot the son of a bitch when I had the chance?*

She would have been convicted of murder for sure in North Carolina, but it would have been worth it if it set her Stormie free. In her eyes, Stormie was the light of day, the child she never had. She raised Stormie after the girl's mother died. Sissy knew everything about Stormie just as any other mother would. Like any mother, she had resolved herself to die before allowing anything to happen to her Stormie.

"I think the potatoes and everything else are ready to be added together for the potato salad," Stormie said as she entered the kitchen.

"The mayonnaise is in the refrigerator," Sissy said as she walked toward it.

"We will be making potato salad the way Daddy liked it," Stormie stated.

"Why?"

"Well, it's just a guess, but yesterday, Nathan ordered his burger without mayonnaise at the restaurant. By the way, our waitress was meaner than a snake with a head on both ends. Anyway, I don't believe he likes mayonnaise. Therefore, I think we should make it with mustard like Daddy used to like it." Stormie began mixing the potatoes with mustard.

"Good Lord, Stormie! Even mustard potato salad has some mayonnaise in it. We just never told your daddy. Now move over and let me make it before you use up all that mustard. As a matter of fact, go on and get out of my kitchen. Go upstairs and get yourself fixed up." Sissy took the jar of mustard away from Stormie and scooted her toward the door.

"Sissy, what about my face?" Stormie held her hand to her face and teared up. "What will I say?"

"Don't start crying! We'll have lunch outside. That way, you can wear one of your big hats and those big round sunglasses you bought last month. You know, the ones that make you look like a bug?"

"Do you think it will cover my eye?"

"Well, I really don't know, but there ain't nothin' we can do about it now. So go on and get ready. I'll take care of all this in the kitchen."

Nathan spent the better part of an hour looking and walking around Gallant Point. He didn't know what he was looking for, but he was desperate for anything. Anything was better than what he had, which was nothing. He looked toward the tall grass that ran along the shore for alligator footprints. It was the tall grass he was looking at when he heard someone or something behind him. He turned quickly and placed his hand on his gun that he had behind his back. Willie and Sam froze a few feet away.

"What're you looking for?" Willie asked.

"An alligator."

His answer caused the boys to turn and look at each other in a bewildered yet amused fashion, which was followed by uncontrollable laughter.

"I don't see the joke," Nathan replied as he released the handle of his gun and pulled his shirt back down over his waist.

Sam stopped laughing for a second. "Mr. Nathan, who told you there was alligators out here?"

"There ain't no alligators around here. There some farther down near the marshes and swamps, but there ain't none around here," Willie explained.

"The two of you know for certain that there aren't any alligators here?" he asked, feeling as though he were the butt of some joke.

"Yes, sir. We swim and fish in these waters all the time, and we ain't never seen no alligator," Willie answered as he tried to control his laughter, unlike Sam, who stood there snickering and holding his fishing pole.

"No, Mr. Nathan. There ain't no alligators around here," Sam said.

"But if you want to see some alligators, Sam and I'll take you to Catfish Lake, which is up around Havelock."

Nathan looked around once more for what he gathered was the sheriff's imaginary alligator he had written about in the police report. "No. I don't think that's necessary," he said.

If two local boys know there aren't any alligators in the area, then why did Sheriff Carter write Delia Snipes off as a drunk who drowned, who was later partially eaten by an alligator? he asked himself as he followed his two tour guides back toward the boat.

"I'm hungry. We got some cold fried chicken Momma made last night if you want some for lunch," Willie said as he led the way.

"Now don't get me wrong, fellas. I like fried chicken like anybody else, but the three of us have been invited to lunch," he explained as they loaded into the boat.

"Out here? Where?" Willie asked suspiciously.

"Well, I don't really know how to get there, but I'd bet the two of you do."

Sam smiled and shook his head up and down quickly. "That's a bet you'd win because we know where everything is out here," he declared.

"Well, all right then, do either of you know where Stormie Arrington's home is?"

"We most certainly do. Ms. Sissy makes real good peach cobbler," Willie said as Sam pushed the boat off the shore and jumped in.

True to their word, the treasure hunters knew precisely where to go. They were soon securing the boat to a long wooden pier that led to a lush, green, perfectly manicured lawn. At the end of the pier sat a nicely arranged set of lawn furniture. The furniture was black wrought iron and consisted of five chairs that circled a table covered in a white tablecloth.

The table itself was adorned with a bountiful selection of meats, vegetables, and other side dishes. In the center was a white rose bouquet, carefully arranged in a crystal vase. Behind the table and up a slight hill was a large, white, plantation-style home. When Nathan stepped out of the boat, he noticed a beautiful dark-mahogany, wooden motorboat docked on the opposite side of the pier with the words *"Stormie Forecast"* painted on the back.

The home off in the distance was reminiscent of the many spectacular plantation homes found throughout the South. Nathan Emerson marveled at the Arrington home. The sight brought out an old childhood memory of the summer when he had turned ten. That summer was spent with his grandmother at her home in Williamsburg, Virginia. Mini, his grandmother, and he had spent long hot days touring the many plantation homes along the James River.

In the car driving from one plantation home to the next, she'd shared the history and the local folklore of each one. It was later in bed before he fell asleep when she'd quiz him on all the homes they visited that day. He remembered waking each morning to the smell of pancakes and sausage. It was one of his most cherished memories.

"How y'all doin?" Stormie yelled from under the front porch, where she carried a pitcher of what had to be sweet tea.

"Good, and you?" Nathen answered as he walked toward her.

Once again, she reminded him of Jaqueline Kennedy. She wore a sophisticated white summer dress, complemented with a large white hat protecting her shoulders from the afternoon sun. The only thing that looked out of place was the pair of large sunglasses that hid her beautiful green eyes.

"I'm just fine. And how are you two duly sworn G-men doing today?" Stormie asked Sam and Willie, who were more concerned about the peach cobbler sitting on the table next to them.

"Boys! Mrs. Stormie is talken' at ya!" Sissy said, getting the two's attention.

"Mrs. Stormie, we're fine. We'd like to thank you for putting this out for us today," Willie answered. He removed his ball cap and then reached over and removed Sam's for him.

"Yes'm, we's just fine," Sam said and took his hat back from Willie.

"Please, everyone, sit down. Willie, if you would be so kind and offer a blessing for this meal, I'd surely appreciate it," Stormie said as she placed the pitcher of tea down and slid into a seat.

Nathan listened to Willie give the blessing but did not close his eyes as customary. He wanted to look at the beautiful woman on his right. She bowed her head along with everyone else, but he couldn't tell if she had her eyes closed because they were hidden behind her dark sunglasses.

Does she see me looking at her? he thought to himself.

It was right before he heard Willie say, "Amen," when he

noticed what appeared to be a bruise in the corner of Stormie's left eye. He tried to get a better look, but everyone lifted their heads, and the table erupted into a flurry of conversations, mostly from Sam and Willie, who asked questions about the long pier and whether or not Sissy or Stormie had ever caught any fish off of it.

Nathan was fascinated with Stormie. He admired how she maneuvered the conversation with Sam and Willie from fishing along Taylor Creek to hunting for Blackbeard's hidden treasure. She made the boys feel welcome at her dinner table. He didn't know what it was, but he found himself at a loss for words, which was unusual for him. He wanted to hear her voice and her laughter and see her smile. She was, indeed, the most beautiful woman he had ever seen in his life.

Once more, Stormie switched gears and moved the conversation in Nathan's direction, to what he and his two fellow crime fighters had been doing all morning. The two ladies enjoyed a long laugh as Willie, with some commentary from Sam, detailed Mr. Nathan's hopeless search for alligators that he thought lurked in the dark waters and tall grass along the shores of Beaufort. The lunch date seemed to fly by as his previous lunch with her had done. He wished once more that he could prolong the day and found himself thinking of somehow doing just that.

The ladies refused to allow their guests to help with clearing the dishes. The two G-men were ordered to the pier, where they were to use their fishing poles to capture and identify all fish trespassing the area. Nathan sat on the pier and watched the fishermen for a little while before taking a walk down the shoreline.

"Where is he?" Ben asked as he stood in front of the courthouse with a delighted Emma. She was smiling and standing next to Ben, eagerly waiting to go on their trip.

Emma checked her makeup in the small compact mirror. "He knew you were coming, didn't he?"

"Hell yes. He's the one who called your place this morning and told me to be here at one thirty. If it weren't for him, we could've been in the hotel in Savannah by now," Ben explained as he angrily looked up and down the street. "And where in the hell is Amos? I was hoping that son of a bitch would be here to wash the car before we left."

"That lazy good for nothin' is probably drunk somewhere. He'll come by Monday morning, asking the judge to forgive him like he always does," Emma said as she closed her compact and placed it back in her purse.

"Finally, here he comes," Ben said when he saw the car cruising down the road toward them with its unmistakable blue light on top. The couple stood on the sidewalk impatiently as Sheriff Carter parked along the curb in front of them and got out.

"It's about time, Dwight! We have been here for thirty damn minutes!" Ben said angrily as Sheriff Carter walked around the front of the car and stepped onto the sidewalk next to them.

"Well, I'm sorry, but Charlie White called this morning, and he said he had something to do and couldn't watch that nosey FBI man today."

"Who's watchin' him then?" Ben asked.

"I was, until he got in a boat with Pastor Turner's boys around nine this morning. The three of them took off up Taylor Creek."

"What in the hell is he doing with them?"

The sheriff removed his hat and rubbed the sweat from his forehead with his handkerchief. "I don't know. He just climbed into their boat, and off they went."

"Well, shit! Where's Amos?" Ben asked as he looked back toward the courthouse.

"He called the office late this morning and left a message with my deputy, saying he was sick."

"My ass, he's sick! More like hungover," Ben remarked in disgust, looking at his watch. "We gotta go. Dwight, you make sure everything is ready for the Gentlemen's Social next week. I'm inviting a lot of very important people to it, and I don't want anything screwing it up."

"What do you want me to do?" Sheriff Carter asked as Ben and Emma got into the car.

"I don't know, Sheriff, but maybe you could do what you're paid to do, like finding out what happened to those girls before the FBI does. I mean, do you really think the governors, the state attorney generals, and any other wealthy campaign supporters I've invited to my Gentlemen's Social are gonna show up if we or our town are associated with a bunch of murdered whores? Use your damn head."

"I'm working on it, and I've been working on it! You just do what you need to do to get elected. I'll take care of the other stuff," Sheriff Carter said loudly as Ben and Emma sped away from the curb.

Fuck him! Dwight thought as he went back to his car.

As Nathan walked down the shoreline, he occasionally found a smooth flat stone in the sand that he would pick up and attempt to skip across Taylor Creek. While he searched for the next stone, he thought about the murdered girls.

Well, I think they were murdered anyway, he thought to himself. But why did Sheriff Carter write them off as accidents? What was his connection to this?

"You seem deep in thought," Stormie said as she quietly walked up behind him. She had taken off her shoes, but she was still wearing her hat and the large sunglasses that hid her beautiful eyes.

"I've found myself deep in thought many times since I arrived here," Nathan replied.

"Maybe it would help to talk to someone. It helped me yesterday," she said as she moved closer to him.

He smelled the aroma of her perfume, and it made him want her. He knew it was wrong, but he had an urge to pull her against him and kiss her madly. He felt she had the same urges but also knew it was wrong.

"Maybe talking to someone could help," he said.

"You know, I've been told I'm a pretty good listener," she said as she looked up at him from behind the dark sunglasses.

He thought about the investigation and knew that sharing any information about it with her was probably not a good idea, but what else was there to talk about? "What would you like me to tell you?"

"You can talk about anything you'd like," she answered.

"What if I told you, you remind me of Jacqueline Kennedy?"

"And exactly how would you know what Jacqueline Kennedy is like? I mean, does my outfit remind you of one you've seen her wearing in a magazine or something?" she asked as she spun around, allowing the bottom of her dress to fly up slightly.

"No. I really don't read a lot of magazines these days."

Stormie gave him a wide-eyed expression. "Then how would you know?" She asked and then moved closer to the shoreline and looked over the water. She held her hands behind her back and swayed slightly as if she were dancing to the sound of music only she could hear.

"Because I was part of her protection team for a little while when I first came to the bureau," he answered and moved closer beside her.

"I thought the president and the first lady were protected by the secret service."

"They are, most of the time, but when the first family goes to visit other places, the FBI sends agents ahead of them to make sure everything is ready. You know, there are more FBI agents than secret service agents working in the federal government. When you've had a president who was as popular as President Kennedy was, it could get pretty busy for everyone."

"Did you ever talk to her?"

"A little, but nothin' like you would expect."

"Like what? What did you say to her?" Stormie asked excitedly.

"Oh, I don't know, let me think," he said and looked to the sky and thought for a minute. "I think I once asked, 'Mrs. Kennedy, will you run away with me?'" Nathan said, making light of the Dallas incident and the actual conversation from when he had spoken to the former first lady.

"Oh, Nathan, you did not ask her that!" Stormie reached over and jokingly hit his arm with her fist. "You never met Jaqueline Kennedy, did you?"

"Actually, I did. But the only thing I really said to her was, 'Can I get you anything?'"

Stormie's eyes widened. "Really?"

"Yes, really."

"And… Did you ever get her anything?"

"Just a glass of water." Nathan still didn't feel the need to share the other details of his few memorable minutes with Mrs. Kennedy.

"What was she like?"

Before Nathan thought of something to say, he heard someone running toward them. He turned and saw Sam standing near the pier, holding his pole in one hand and a fish in the other.

"Mrs. Stormie, I gots one of those trespassers for ya."

"That's great, Sam. Make sure you take him home with you!" Stormie yelled back.

"Mr. Nathan, we need to be a-goin'. Our daddy wants us back a little early to help clean the church. If we leave now, we'll have time to drop you off at your place before gettin' home."

Emma sat close to Ben as they sped down the highway toward Savannah. She used her left hand to rub the back of his neck as he sat there, driving the car without saying anything. He had not said anything to her since they left the courthouse.

Their conversations during their long road trips usually consisted of making plans for their future together. The two of them shared their deepest fantasies and how they imagined their life together in the governor's mansion would be. Emma thought about the many parties she would host there and the many other parties she would be going to where she would be introduced to people as North Carolina's First Lady Mrs. Benjamin Arrington.

"Who else will be at the party tomorrow night?" she asked.

"I don't know. It's just a small dinner with my old friend Johnny," Ben answered. He glanced over and placed his arm around Emma to pull her closer.

Emma stared out the window for a moment before speaking again. "You said it was a party. I thought there would be lots of people."

"Did you?"

"Will he be alone?" Emma asked.

Ben rubbed her shoulder. "I don't know."

"I mean, is it gonna be a real dinner, or is it one like the things we've done in the past?"

"It could be like that. Is that all right?"

"I guess. But…"

"But what, Emma? You seemed to enjoy yourself last time."

"I know, but are you planning on sharing me with Johnny, or is it just gonna be the two of us? You know some of your friends hurt me."

"Emma, I won't let anyone hurt you this time."

"That's what you've said before, but—"

Ben pulled her closer and kissed her head. "But nothing. You agreed you would do anything and everything to help us get elected. That's what we're trying to do, right, honey?"

"Yes, but—"

"No buts, Emma. We both must make sacrifices. It hurts me too when I see you with other men. The men I share you with are very powerful, wealthy, and influential. We need their support for the election. The best way to get their support is to have power over them.

"I know, but I just want to make sure that—"

"Hey, no more of this. Nothin' will happen to you. I'll be there the entire time. You're my gal. Right?" Ben once again pulled her closer but kissed her red pouty lips this time. He knew how to comfort her while controlling her at the same time.

"Yes, but tell me more about how it will be for the two of us after you're Governor Arrington."

"All right."

Emma closed her eyes and laid her head in Ben's lap as he talked about the types of parties that a governor's wife, like she would be one day, held at the governor's mansion.

He told her the two of them would be invited to the White House one day, where they would meet the president and first lady. Emma fell asleep, daydreaming of how people would one day soon admire her.

She believed people would finally listen to what she had

to say. She, in her own right, would be respected, but more importantly, Emma Rodgers would prove to her mother that she was wrong about her. She would make something of herself.

Damn the others she left in Philadelphia.

Chapter 12
Old Blue

Sam, Willie, and Nathan were offered the use of the Arringtons' bathroom before climbing back into the boat for a long ride back to the bed and breakfast. Nathan waited on the porch for his turn in the guest bathroom, where he took advantage of the few precious minutes he had left to speak with Stormie.

It was there, on her large wraparound porch, where she told him how she and Ben had decided to build their home here on Taylor Creek after they were married. She told him she'd always admired and loved the look of these types of homes and decided she would build this one here.

"Ben and I could've moved into his family's 1890 plantation-style home near Galant Point, but it would've required Ben's mother, who was still alive at the time, and I to live under the same roof. Living under the same roof as that woman was something I couldn't possibly stomach," Stormie explained right before Willie walked out onto the porch.

"Sam and I'll wait for you in the boat, Mr. Nathan. Thank you for lunch, Mrs. Stormie," Willie said as he leaped off the porch and ran toward the pier.

"I had Sissy pack the rest of that pie for you and your brother!" Stormie yelled.

"Thanks."

Nathan waited for a moment, looking at her before going inside. It didn't matter that the sun was slowly going down in the west or that she was on the covered porch. Stormie kept the hat and sunglasses on, covering her eyes. He desperately wanted to know how she had come to such a place like this in life. He was aware he barely knew her, but he wanted to know more.

"I'll only be a minute," he said before he opened the screen door and walked inside the home.

"Take as long as you need."

The Arrington home was as beautiful on the inside as it was on the outside. The floor was a dark, honey-glazed hardwood that ran wall to wall, where it was met with six-inch white baseboards below an elegant blue-and-white wallpaper. He determined that everything in the home, from the wallpaper design to the couch, to the chairs, and even the doilies on the tables were specifically picked out by the woman of the house. He thought certain things in life fit everyone's personality, and it was those things that told others about who people were individually. He felt Stormie's home told visitors they were welcome there.

Nathan didn't spend much time in the bathroom, and he was soon back out on the porch, where he found Stormie sitting in a chair that overlooked her front yard and Taylor Creek. Her hair blew in the afternoon breeze. She was waving to Sam and Willie, who were quickly disappearing in the distance as their boat bounced along the waves.

It was the sound of a car starting up that made Nathan turn toward the side of the house. Sissy drove by and waved at the two of them. He politely waved back and then watched as the black Buick made its way onto the main road. Nathan turned back toward Stormie and realized her dark sunglasses and hat were now lying on the table. He walked over and looked at her bruised and swollen eye. Nathan thought about asking her what had happened, but it would have been a question they both already knew the answer to. He did, however, wonder how long the abuse had been going on.

"Is it that bad?" she asked.

"No. You can hardly notice," he answered unconvincingly.

"Yeah, right. I look like I went one round with Muhammad Ali."

"Really, it's not that bad. Trust me, I've seen worse."

"You're kind. I still don't believe you, but I'll pretend I do."

"Where did everybody go?" he asked.

"The boys didn't want to get into trouble with their daddy for being late, so I told them I'd drive you back to where you were staying. Sissy visits with her man friend over in New Bern every second Friday of the month, so I guess all you've got left for company is me. I hope you don't mind," Stormie explained as she turned toward him and smiled.

"No... I don't mind as long as your husband doesn't mind me being here when he gets home," Nathan said. He looked back down the driveway, half-expecting to see Ben Arrington's car pulling in.

"My husband is gone, away on business until late next week," Stormie said as she stood, walked off the porch, and headed toward the pier.

Nathan watched her walk away. She moved across the lawn gracefully. She appeared to float in the air as she walked.

"Are you coming?" she asked without turning back toward him. He quickly found himself lost for an answer. It was another first in his life, and he didn't know what to do or say, so he did what felt right and stepped off the porch.

"Yeah, I'm right behind you."

Before he knew it, Nathan was sitting quietly next to

Stormie on the pier. He mimicked her by removing his shoes. Their bare feet dangled close to the surface of Taylor Creek. In the distance, the sun also hung closer to the water's surface as the evening hours approached. All he wanted to do at that moment was slow it down for a little bit longer. He desired to stop the present before it was nothing but a memory of the past.

"You're not scared, are you?" she asked, breaking the silence.

"Scared? Scared of what?" he asked in surprise and turned to face her.

"Havin' your bare feet so close to the water. I mean, an alligator could just come out of the darkness below and swallow you all up," she said and then laughed out loud.

Her laugh was contagious, and he soon found himself laughing right along with her until their stomachs ached.

"I'm not from around here. How was I supposed to know alligators were uncommon here?"

Stormie shook her head side to side. "You're not. But, honey, I couldn't pass that up!"

"You know, it's funny you mentioned how an alligator could come up here and get us right off this very pier."

"Why's that?" she asked curiously.

Nathan took a deep breath. "Well, about a year ago, a woman was sitting on her pier when she saw this huge gator swimming dangerously close."

"Did it eat her? It ate her, didn't it?" Stormie asked as she pulled her legs up, away from the water.

"Well, you see, the lady began feeding this monster-sized alligator large fish and whole chickens she got from the local grocery store. Every day like clockwork, she would throw all this uncooked meat into the water and then she'd watch as the gator tore through it."

"Did she fall in one day?" Stormie asked excitedly.

Nathan quickly turned to face her. "Wait, it gets better," he said, purposely putting her off as he built up the excitement. "You see, this lady went out one day, and the gator wasn't there."

"Where did it go? Was it onshore? Was it behind her?" Stormie asked, interrupting once more.

"No, no, nothin' like that. Listen. When she didn't see Old Blue—"

"Old Blue! She named it Old Blue? My heavens, it was her pet!"

"Yes. I didn't say that before?"

"No, no, you didn't. You can't leave stuff like that out of a story you're telling."

"Well, yeah, she named him Old Blue because he had one eye that was injured from a fight with another gator, and it left one eye all discolored with a blue film over it. Anyway, when the lady didn't see Old Blue, she sat on the pier and let her legs dangle over the dark water with all that uncooked chicken sitting right next to her. She sat on that pier for a while, swinging her feet back and forth, waiting for Old Blue to come swimming over."

"That's scary," Stormie said.

"What she didn't know was Old Blue was right there under the pier."

"Old Blue was right under her? Oh my!"

"Yep, and before long, Old Blue caught sight of those dangling feet moving back and forth right above him, and he didn't waste any time. He lunged for the surface, and in a flash, he had her foot in his powerful jaws."

"Oh, my! What on earth did she do?" Stormie asked and placed her hand over her mouth.

"Well, she held onto the pier until Old Blue got what he wanted and swam away."

"He got her foot?"

"Yep, he sure did."

"What did the lady do?"

"She had some family near the water, and they rushed her to the hospital."

"Did she live?"

"Oh, yes. She's a waitress over in Raleigh."

"Waitress! How can a one-footed woman work as a waitress?" Stormie asked suspiciously.

"You don't believe me? Okay, just go down to Frank's Diner in Raleigh and ask for Eileen."

"Eileen?"

"Yes, Eileen. What else would you call a woman with only one foot?" he answered and laughed.

She laughed along with him. "Oh, Nathan, you got me!"

The occasional jokes between them continued throughout the evening, along with conversations about his career and the different places he had traveled to with the FBI. He told her about the civil rights cases he had helped investigate over the years.

He expressed his feelings about the Medgar Evans case in Jackson, Mississippi, which was followed by the 16th Street Baptist Church Bombing in Birmingham in September of that same year. He told her of his return to Mississippi during the summer of 1964, where he helped investigate the death of three civil rights workers in Neshoba County. He even told her about the investigation in Miami.

"My word! Nathan, I don't think I know of anyone who has seen more inhumane acts than you. How in the world are you able to sleep at night? I think I'd have nightmares."

"I think of the good things people do when things like that happen."

"The good things?"

"Yeah, the good things, like the volunteers who were both black and white. That's bravery. I mean, to show up to help in some of the most volatile atmospheres filled with hate and random acts of violence… The volunteers go to those places to comfort the mothers, fathers, sisters, and brothers who have lost a loved one. With courage and determination, they rebuild from the ruins, sending a message to others that they will stand fast and continue their fight against hate."

"I think you're a very good man, Nathan Emerson."

They shared stories of the past and laughed many times. He didn't remember when it happened or how it happened, nor did he care, but somehow, they ended up holding hands on that pier as the moon found its way into the late-night sky.

How does one stop time? Nathan asked himself.

It was a long drive, but Emma and Ben reached Savannah in time to have a late dinner at Red's Steak and Seafood with Johnathan Davenport, one of Georgia's richest men, who also happened to be an old law school friend of Ben's.

Johnny, as he liked to be called, owned many cotton farms with clothing factories along the east coast of Georgia, South Carolina, and, most importantly, North Carolina. Most men would like to say they built an empire like that, but Johnny couldn't because he had been born into it. Ben knew that, and Emma suspected Ben of being jealous. She also suspected Ben had a plan, and he knew how to use Johnny and his family money to his advantage. Ben expected a great deal of financial support from Johnny, and Johnny anticipated much more from the future governor.

The two men had some things in common. Like Ben, Johnny was married, but unlike Ben, Johnny had five children at home in his Atlanta mansion. One of the other things they had in common was the company of women who were not their wives. Johnny was out tonight with his young girlfriend.

Libby was in her mid-twenties. She was blonde, and Emma thought she resembled Marilyn Monroe, whom she believed the young woman tried to mirror anyway. While Ben and Johnny discussed politics, the two mistresses boasted about their latest fashion purchases and their recently received gifts. With each new dress or handbag from France, the women made it a point to outdo the other.

Emma didn't care much for Libby and thought she was nothing more than a common whore. Like all common whores, she would be gone within a month or two, after Johnny grew tired of her. She had seen many whores like her come and go with Ben's wealthy friends, and she had grown accustomed to their presence and looked forward to their absence.

"If you would excuse me, I'd like to check my face before we leave," Emma said as she stood and started toward the bathroom.

"I'll join you, honey," Libby said as she stood and followed Emma.

Ben and Johnny stood slightly as the women left the table, and the men continued talking about what each one could expect from the other in the near future.

"I do like your purse," Libby said in a thick Southern drawl while looking in the mirror. Emma's purse was an expensive Chanel, given to her by Ben last Christmas.

"Well, thank you," Emma replied with a smile. The compliment had caught her off guard, and for a moment, she thought maybe she could like Libby.

"I had one just like it, and I gave it to my niece last week after Johnny bought me this new Chanel," Libby said quickly as she placed her new Chanel on the sink and looked through it. "I don't usually keep one longer than six months, as I find it out of fashion to do so," she said sarcastically as she traced her lips with bright red lipstick.

"Oh, I see," Emma replied as she turned and faced Libby.

"Well, that was very kind of you to give it to your niece. It seems you're livin' in high cotton these days. And I do mean high cotton. Who would've thought a simple cotton farmer could fare so well or even a simple whore for that matter?"

Libby placed her hands on the sink. "I've never—"

"And you never will. You're nothin' more than the current interest for that cotton farmer. In a couple of years, when you're still giving blowjobs in the back seat of a fancy car to some fat, rich, and married businessman in the parking lot of your trailer park, I'll be hosting a party at the governor's mansion."

"Johnny is gonna leave his wife for me, you two-bit—"

"Johnny ain't leavin' his wife. The whore he brought to dinner two months ago thought the same damn thing you do," Emma said as Libby's face turned a lighter shade. "Oh, you thought you were the only one. Bless your heart."

Libby just stood there, not knowing what to say or do.

"By the way, sweetheart, later tonight, when we all go back to the hotel, you should prepare yourself for what Ben and Johnny like to do at the same time. I won't ruin the surprise by telling you ahead of time, but if you need to go to the bathroom, I'd do it now."

Emma was pleased with herself as she walked out of the bathroom, where she left Libby standing in front of the mirror.

The passenger seat next to Stormie was comfortable, Nathan thought, as Stormie drove her new sports car slower than any car of its design should go. Nathan believed Stormie was in no hurry for the evening to end, just as he wished it would not. She had pulled her hair back into a ponytail, revealing her long thin neckline and a small light-brown birthmark. It was the shape of a circle below her right ear.

"Are you staring at me?"

"Actually, I was looking across, over toward the lighthouse." *Liar,* he thought to himself.

"That's too bad," she replied, not looking away from the road.

"Why?"

"I thought maybe you were looking at me, and a girl likes to be looked at."

He didn't really know what to say, so out of panic, he said the first thing that came to mind. "You ever been to the lighthouse over there?" *You idiot!* he thought.

"Yes, Sissy and I picnic there sometimes when we want to get away from the house on Saturdays or Sundays during the summer. The ocean pushes a nice cool breeze through the channel."

"Why would you want to get away from that beautiful home of yours on the water?"

"Because my husband doesn't go out of town every weekend," Stormie answered without hesitation.

Nathan didn't know how to respond but decided to change the subject. "Do you know where I can rent a boat?"

"Why in the world do you need a boat?" Stormie asked as she brought the car to a stop in the parking lot of the bed and breakfast.

"I need to go out on the water again tomorrow, but I don't want to bother the boys on a Saturday. I took up a lot of their time today."

"You don't need to rent a boat. Just come by tomorrow, and I'll take you where you need to go in my boat," Stormie said.

"I couldn't bother you again."

"No bother. I'll make another lunch, and we can even go by the lighthouse if you'd like."

"I'd like that, as long as you don't have anything else to do tomorrow," he said.

"How does nine work for you?"

"Fine," he answered quickly.

"Then nine it is."

Nathan sat there for a moment, trying to think of something to say. He looked toward the waterfront, and when he turned toward Stormie, he was met with her lips pressing against his. For a moment, the two were locked together. Stormie was the one who pulled away… but slowly.

"I'm sorry," she whispered while gazing into his eyes as she rubbed his arm with her hand.

Nathan slid his right hand along her cheek, under her ear, and cradled the back of her head as he pulled her closer.

Stormie knew what she should do but ignored those thoughts. He kissed her wantonly.

"Turn the car off," he whispered as he continued to kiss her lightly.

"I can't."

Nathan stopped and looked at her with eyes that held a burning fire of passion within them. She felt wanted, and she desperately longed for him. She reached up and placed her hands on the sides of his head.

"Not now, later," she said and kissed him once more. "I'll see you in the morning."

"Then morning it is," he said and opened the car door. He slowly got out while holding her hand.

He stood in front of the bed and breakfast until she was on the main road heading home before he turned and walked inside.

She sped through town, singing along with the radio. The words that blared from the speakers never had more meaning to her than at that very moment. *"You don't own me anymore."* She smiled and shook her head in disbelief.

What are you doing? she asked herself.

She thought back to the kiss. She thought of the two of

them sitting on the pier and how she enjoyed listening to his stories while holding his hand.

It felt so good!

How much she wanted him to lean into her and kiss her then. As she drove, she replayed the day over and over in her head.

She was so caught up in her thoughts, she failed to notice Sheriff Carter behind her. He turned on his siren and motioned for her to pull over. Stormie pulled into an empty parking lot and put the car in park. She waited for Sheriff Carter to walk up to her door.

"Evening, Mrs. Arrington."

"Evening, Sheriff. I don't believe I was speeding," she said as she looked up from the driver's seat.

"No, ma'am, you weren't. Ben asked that I look in on you while he was out of town. When I saw you go by back there, I said to myself, 'What could Mrs. Arrington be doing out this late?' I figured there must be something wrong. So here we are."

"Well, everything is just fine, Sheriff. You see, I bought this car the other day and just decided to take it out for an evening drive," Stormie answered as she noticed the sheriff looking at her black eye.

"It certainly is a fine car, Mrs. Arrington, but you should be careful and shouldn't be out running around like this when your husband is out of town. I mean, what would folks think or say?"

"I imagine they would say it's about time she enjoyed herself, or maybe, someone who really gave a damn would ask how she got that black eye—something you've yet to inquire about. Have a good night, Sheriff. And when you report back to my husband, make sure you don't leave anything out." Stormie pressed the gas hard, spinning the tires and throwing dirt and gravel onto the sheriff and his car.

He looked around the area to make sure he was alone before he opened the trunk. Once he was satisfied no one was watching, he placed the key into the lock and turned it to the right. Upon hearing the latch pop, he raised the trunk and reached inside. He placed both hands under the black wool blanket and lifted her body. He looked around once more and then walked backward away from the car, holding his victim in his arms.

She was heavy.

But hell, they are always heavy afterwards, he thought to himself.

The road was narrow with ditches on both sides, and it was the ditch to the left of him that he had to cross. He carefully stepped into the ditch, braced one foot along its edge, and lifted the other. The dirt beneath him shifted, and he slipped and fell backward onto the ground, with the lifeless body of Bessie Jones landing on top of him.

"Damn it!" He slid the body off and watched it roll into the ditch.

The blanket no longer covered her. Her eyes were open, her naked and tortured body glistened in the moonlight. She looked as though she were staring at a distant star. He sat in the dirt for a few more moments, hypnotized by it all. He then brushed himself off, picked her up again, and made his way to the water's edge.

Standing next to Galant Point with Bessie in his arms, he looked around the shoreline, making sure he was alone before carrying her into the calm water. He walked farther and farther into the serene bay until the water was up to his waist. He lowered her into the water but paused momentarily to take one last look. He thought she looked quite at peace. He kissed her one last time before pulling his arms away. He watched as she disappeared into the darkness below.

Deep down, Emma knew Ben had other plans for the evening that he hadn't shared with her during their drive into Savannah.

Emma sat on top of Johnny, naked, while an equally naked Libby sat across from her on his face. Libby caressed and lightly kissed Emma's breasts while she slowly moved back and forth on the wealthy businessman, his hands gripping her buttocks tightly.

Physically, Emma enjoyed the activities she was experiencing, but deep down, she was emotionally disconnected, and for the first time, she felt disconnected from the man she thought she loved. Now, as Ben placed the camera down and moved toward the bed, she found herself questioning her relationship and her connection to the man she thought she would one day marry.

The photos of the three of them would or could be used to blackmail Johnny into contributing money toward Ben's campaign, or ruin his life if Johnny refused. But would he use the photos for that?

I'm to be his wife, and it would harm him too. Wouldn't it? Emma asked herself.

She looked at Libby and thought, *She's the whore, not me, right?*

CHAPTER 13
EMMA

SATURDAY, JULY 10, 1965

Stormie had gotten up early and rushed to get herself ready for the day. She showered and spent more time than usual in front of the mirror, trying to conceal her bruised eye that had gotten darker. She had decided to wear her hair in a ponytail, in case they decided to go for a swim.

Wait. A swim! What type of bathing suit should I wear? she asked herself.

A one piece. No, wait, a two piece. No, that's too revealing, or is it? she thought as she held the two swimsuits in her hands. "Sissy!" she yelled, and after a moment with no response, she yelled louder. "Sissy! Are you here? Sissy!"

"Yes, Mrs. Stormie, I's comin'!" Sissy answered a few seconds before she entered the room, out of breath.

Stormie held the bathing suits out toward Sissy. "Should I wear this one or this one?"

"Is that all you wanted? Girl, I should tan your hide. I was getting them biscuits out the oven when you started screaming. I thought you done fell or something. You scared me half to death."

"I'm sorry! I'm just nervous about today."

"What you got to be nervous about?"

"I don't know," Stormie said shyly and turned away.

"Girl, you ain't falling for this man, is you?"

"No… I'm a married woman," Stormie said quickly and then hung the two-piece bathing suit back up.

"Yeah, a married woman who ain't had no man give her any attention in a long time," Sissy whispered deviously. She whipped the dishtowel toward Stormie and popped her in the butt before walking out of the room.

"I heard you!" Stormie yelled down the hall. "Besides, you don't know what I've had and not had!"

"I knows! I knows everything about my baby girl."

"You think you know!" Stormie yelled louder.

"Whatever, baby. But that man will probably like the two-piece you'll decide to wear anyway!" Sissy yelled from the end of the hall.

Stormie and Sissy worked quickly, getting the boat ready and packing food for the day trip. Stormie was nervous yet excited at the same time, and she ran around *"like a chicken with its head cut off,"* as Sissy put it.

Sissy was also excited and happy for Stormie, but she was worried as well. She knew Ben was an arrogant and vengeful man who would never allow anything that he believed was his to be taken away, and Stormie was his. Sissy believed he would kill Stormie before seeing her with another man. It wasn't that he cared about or loved Stormie—because he didn't. Ben was the type of man who was more concerned about his reputation and how he would look in the eyes of others if Stormie ever left him for another.

Stormie was standing in the boat with her hands on her hips, double-checking and then triple-checking everything, when Nathan pulled into the driveway. Sissy was standing on the dock, and she waved for him to come over. Nathan saw he had made the right decision to wear the swim trunks. He had spent an hour mulling it over in his room before finally putting them on and driving over.

Nathan was relieved to see that Stormie was wearing a thigh-length, white cotton pull-over cover that he could see through, which revealed a white two-piece bathing suit.

Stormie looked at Nathan as he walked in her direction, and her heart started beating faster. "Sissy, what am I doing?" she asked.

"Livin', baby. You finally livin' like you should've been doin' for all these years now."

"Hello," Nathan said when he walked onto the dock.

"Hello," Sissy and Stormie replied at the same time.

"Is there anything I can do to help get us on our way?" Nathan asked.

"No, we're all set. Come aboard," Stormie answered.

Nathan stepped into the boat with a small bag in tow, which contained clean clothes and his .45. He turned toward Sissy with his hand raised in her direction. "Can I help you down, Ms. Sissy?"

"I ain't gonna go anywhere. I don't like boats," Sissy answered.

"It's just the two of us," Stormie said as she started the motor.

Nathan sat in the empty seat next to her. "Okay then."

"Where we goin'?" Stormie asked over the roar of the motor.

"Phillips Island."

"Okay."

Nathan sat in the seat, trying not to stare at the boat's attractive captain as they bounced along the waves. Stormie adjusted the trim until the boat was skimming across the water as if it were on glass. She piloted the watercraft as well as any man could ever do. She looked over at her passenger, and the two shared a smile. They cruised under the Arendell Street Bridge, which brought them into Gallants Channel, where Nathan had been the day before with Willie and Sam.

After a few minutes, Stormie turned the wheel to the left and pointed the bow in the direction of an island. Nathan saw a brick chimney that sprouted out from among the few trees, on what he believed to be an uninhabited island.

She tapped Nathan on the shoulder and pointed at the anchor sitting on the deck of the boat near the front.

"Can you pull us onshore and set the anchor?" she yelled over the roaring motor.

Nathan nodded and moved toward the front. When they got closer to the bank, he jumped from the boat into the warm, shallow water. He pulled the boat forward onto the sandy beach and anchored it as Stormie turned the motor off.

"What is this place?" Nathan asked.

Stormie walked toward the front of the boat. "It was a fish plant a long time ago, but it burned down sometime in the fifties."

"The sheriff marked an 'X' on a map that he included in the file he gave me, which I think is right over there," Nathan explained as he pointed toward the south.

"Nathan, why are we here? What are you looking for?" she asked after jumping from the boat onto the beach.

Nathan hadn't shared that information with anyone except Preacher. Even the boys didn't know what he had been looking for the previous day. He looked out at the water and then back at her green eyes and decided to finally share what he kept from others.

"Have a seat," he said, pointing at a mound of sand on the beach.

Stormie grabbed a towel and laid it on the beach for the two of them to sit on. Nathan began from the beginning. He explained the missing girls had disappeared over three different weekends, and he didn't stop explaining everything until he got to the point where the two of them were sitting on the beach together. He even told her about being followed and how someone had shot at him at the cemetery.

"I'll be. I don't know what to say," Stormie said. She looked at her feet, which she was using to dig in the sand.

"There's not much to say. I just got to keep charging forward, hoping to find another piece of the puzzle, and that's why I'm here. Delia Snipes's body was found over there by Warren Prater," Nathan explained as he stood.

"What do you expect to find over there?"

"Nothin' at all, but I've gotta look," Nathan said and started in that direction.

Stormie got up and followed him down the beach. "I'm coming too."

When they arrived at the point on the map, Nathan searched in a circle about a hundred yards out from where he believed the "X" on the map was located. Stormie followed and helped him search, although she didn't know what exactly she was supposed to be searching for.

The two stayed on the beach for about an hour before getting back in the boat and heading in the direction of Harlowe Creek. Stormie controlled the boat once more over rougher water until they reached the area Nathan pointed at on the map. He didn't have high expectations of finding any evidence at the other two locations, and his expectations were even lower for finding anything in the middle of Harlowe Creek, where Ida Freeman's body had been discovered.

"Is there anywhere else you'd like to go?" Stormie asked as they drifted back toward Taylor Creek.

"No. Who owns those houses over there?" Nathan asked as he pointed toward the shoreline.

"A few people in town and some folks from out of town who vacation here."

"They're nice houses. Who owns that one?" Nathan asked, pointing toward a beautiful early-American plantation home. It had a long drive that seemed to disappear into a tunnel of Spanish Moss, which flourished on the sides and over the top of it.

"That's the Arrington House," she stated.

"Really? I thought you called your place the Arrington House."

"No, my place is the Arrington Home," she replied, emphasizing the word home. To Stormie, the two words were very different, in not only their spelling but their meaning.

"I don't understand."

"Well, you see, a house is something you live in that provides shelter. A home does that as well, but a home is where you're loved. That house is where Benjamin Arrington was born and raised," she explained.

"I get it."

"Good, so where to now?" she asked with a flirtatious smile.

"How about some place where we can see a lighthouse."

"I like the way you think," she said and winked at him.

Ben waited for the call to come in before he and Emma left for the day. Emma had become impatient, as she had grown tired of hearing Ben talk about the FBI agent over breakfast. She wanted to be on Tybee Island soaking up the sun. It was a glorious day, that the two of them were supposed to be enjoying together.

Emma paced back and forth in front of Ben, who was sitting on the bed.

"I don't know why we don't just go," she said.

"Emma, I told you we'll go after I speak to Dwight. Now stop your pacing. You're wearing out the carpet."

She stopped and stood in front of him. "Why am I here?"

"Because I need you, darlin'."

Need, always need, never love, she thought to herself. "Like you needed Libby and me last night?"

"Yes, and then some," he answered and looked up and reached for her hand. "You're probably the only person who really knows me. I need you."

Emma looked down and smiled. That'll work, for now, she thought to herself, right before the phone rang.

Ben picked up the phone and placed it to his ear. "Hello?"

"It's me," Sheriff Carter announced on the other end.

"I figured. What do you have for me?"

"You ain't goin' like it."

"What ain't I goin' like?"

"I followed him this morning, and he went over to your place."

"What's he doing there?"

"He ain't there, and neither is your wife. They went out on her boat."

"My wife and Agent Emerson went out on the boat together? Where'd they go?"

"I don't know. I ain't got a boat. I don't like how close he's getting to you… to us."

"Don't worry, Sheriff, this will help us."

"I hope you know what you're doing."

"I do. You just watch them when you can. And from now on, start letting other people around town know they've been seen together. A lot. Don't make a big deal of it, just kind of let it roll off your tongue in front of others."

"Okay. But what's that going to do?"

"Dwight, haven't you heard of a murder-suicide? It happens when two people who were once lovers are no more. Usually, one of them, the married one in our scenario, tries to end it, but the other one can't take the rejection, so he, Agent Emerson, kills Stormie and then himself."

"Problems solved," Sheriff Carter stated.

"Problems solved is right." Ben hung up the phone, smiling and shaking his head.

"It makes me nervous that you can come up with these plans so quickly, Ben."

Ben pulled her onto the bed with him. "It's only to take care of our problems and to help get us closer to the governor's mansion."

Nathan and Stormie finally reached Cape Lookout. He stood at the base of the lighthouse, looking up at the 163-foot tower while admiring the black-and-white diamond pattern that adorned the side of it.

"It's two hundred seven steps to the top," Stormie said as she walked up behind him.

"Really?"

"Yep. This old lighthouse was put into operation in eighteen fifty-nine. In eighteen sixty-four, Confederate soldiers tried to destroy it, but as you can see, they were unsuccessful."

"Sounds like there's a lot of history here."

"There's good and bad, like any other place, I guess."

"That's the way the world is," he said.

"So tell me about yourself, Mrs. Stormie Arrington," he said playfully.

"Well, before I got married, my name was Josephine; Josephine Mary Jane Abrahams," she said, looking at the blue sky above.

"Go on, tell me more."

Stormie smiled because it felt good that someone wanted to know her and took the time to talk to her. She liked the attention. She continued telling Nathan about herself. He learned that her father, Joseph Thomas Bannerman, had been killed in Key West, Florida, on September 2, 1935, the same day she was born, when a strong hurricane swept through the area where he worked with three hundred other people building Highway 1. Joseph was an engineer and had gone out with a surveyor to take some measurements when the storm pushed through.

"He never knew my mother had gone into labor with me. My mother said she thought the world was coming to an end. I mean, there she was giving birth to me as a record hurricane beat down on her. She found out about three days later that my father had been killed. They put up the Great Hurricane Monument near Highway 1 to honor the three hundred people who were killed that day. I don't remember it, but my mother and I attended the unveiling in nineteen thirty-seven."

"How did Josephine become Stormie?" he asked, encouraging her to continue past her father's death.

"Apparently, I was a bit of a smart aleck growing up and had a dislike for authority and discipline. I would, on some occasions, share my opinion when confronted by either, as Sissy explains it anyway. Folks eventually put two and two together, with the night I was born and my apparent dislike for authority, and would say things like, 'oh, you better watch it now, look at her. There's a storm a-brewing.' As you can imagine, I went from being Josephine to Stormie."

"I think I can see that," Nathan said as they walked back toward the boat to eat lunch.

"Oh, I don't know about that. You ain't seen nothin' yet. I'm a lady now. Can't you tell?"

"I can. So, where's your mother?"

"She passed away when I was ten years old," Stormie answered and looked away.

"I'm sorry. Who raised you from then on?"

"My daddy and Sissy. You see, my mother met Arthur

Charles Abrahams, a cotton farmer from Alabama, whom she eventually married. He adopted me and gave me his name on the same day he married my mother."

"Sissy, how long have you known her?"

"Since I was about three, I guess."

"You don't know?"

"Well, I remember Sissy just being there one day. The way my daddy explained it was that one late rainy evening in November, Sissy showed up naked and beaten on our doorstep."

Nathan's eyes widened. "What!"

"Yep, they didn't know where she came from, who she was, or what happened to her."

"That's awful. Didn't they ask her what happened?"

"I don't know really, and she's never said anything to me about it either. My parents asked around, and no one ever claimed to know her. They figured she was about fifteen years old and abandoned. Sissy was there in my life from then on. When I was growing up, she played with me, fed me, and after my mother passed, she kind of stepped in."

"How'd she get the name Sissy?"

Stormie laughed. "That's all me. She never told anyone her name, and a few days after she'd been with us, my mother caught her feeding me, and she started calling her Sister. I couldn't say Sister when I was three, so she became Sissy."

Over lunch, Stormie continued to tell Nathan about her life and how, after her daddy died, she'd met Ben, who had come into town on business. Over time, Ben would stop by, and eventually, he asked her to marry him. After they married, she and Sissy moved to Beaufort, where he was an established attorney.

Nathan learned that her father, Arthur, had amassed a considerable amount of wealth over the years, and when he died, he'd left it to Stormie. She had kept the house and farm in Alabama but sold much of the land around it at the advice of Ben.

Stormie and Nathan talked for hours, but eventually, they

loaded the boat and headed back toward her home on Taylor Creek. As they cruised, she would occasionally stop the boat and explain different points of interest along their route. She eventually stopped the boat, dropped anchor, and pointed out the wild horses that ran free on the outer banks of Shackleford Island.

She explained no one really knew where the horses came from, but it was widely believed that they swam to shore after the boats they were in sank during fierce storms. Nathan listened as his tour guide continued about the history of the area while they peacefully drifted. He was really enjoying the day and the company he was with. He didn't know how it could get any better.

"Wanna go for a swim?" Stormie asked as she removed her cover and stood there in her white two-piece bathing suit. The two smiled once more at each other, and she dove off the back of the boat.

When he arrived at the Arrington home, he saw the colored woman leaving. He didn't think anyone was home except for maybe her, and he'd thought she might be fun if he found her there alone. He could have stopped her, but he didn't have the urge to kill her like he'd thought he would.

He waited for nearly an hour before going to the back of the home and finding the kitchen door unlocked. A note sat on the counter where it would be easily found, and it read:

Stormie
Went to New Bern. Be back Monday.
Enjoy livin' baby!
Sissy

He looked around the house and didn't find anyone, but

he wasn't disappointed. He knew Ben and Emma were out of town, and he'd seen the FBI man and Stormie in her boat earlier when he was at Harlowe Creek.

He made his way into every room, closet, and drawer. He didn't know what he was looking for, but he would know it when he found it.

Nathan removed his shirt and stood on the back of the boat, looking at Stormie.

"Are you going to get in?" she asked as she treaded water behind the boat. She liked what she saw. She had imagined Nathan was well built, but she never imagined he would be as muscular as he was.

"Yeah. I just know it's gonna be cold, and I'm trying to brace myself for it," Nathan answered.

If he told the truth, he was amazed at everything that was happening, and he wanted to take it all in. He knew a simple leap from the boat was a leap into something big that could have consequences, both good and bad.

"Look out!" he yelled as he leaped into the air. He flipped backward and then splashed in the water, sending water up and onto Stormie.

Stormie wiped the water from her face, laughed out loud, and made her way to the ladder. She grabbed it and turned around and found Nathan behind her. He reached both arms around her and grasped the ladder with both hands behind her waist.

"I was beginning—"

He moved in closer and kissed her.

Stormie looked into his eyes, let go of the ladder, and wrapped her arms around his neck, her legs around his waist.

The two were intertwined, feeling their way around the other's bodies as they drifted along with the current. Neither knew where they were going, but they both wanted to go.

He spent the day roaming around the house. He lay on her bed, smelled her pillow, and put it in his arms and squeezed it tightly. She smelled much better than the others. He believed she even smelled better than Emma.

Eventually, he made his way into the laundry room, where he found Stormie's dirty clothes in a basket. He went through the pile, looking for the right pair, and as soon as he found them, he heard the sound of the boat returning to the dock.

He looked out the window and watched the two secure the boat, unload a few items, and walk toward the house.

They're not expecting anything. She's beautiful, he thought to himself as he placed her panties to his face.

CHAPTER 14
WARREN

Nathan and Stormie made it back to the house just before dark. He helped tie the boat off and carried their belongings to the house. The two entered the back door, where Stormie found the note Sissy had left.

You little… she thought to herself.

"Something wrong?" Nathan asked.

"No. Just a note from Sissy. She wanted to let me know she's going to New Bern until Monday."

"Okay. I guess I'll just—"

"Run up and take a shower. That's a good idea. I'll start working on a little something for dinner. You were planning on eating with me, right?"

"Yes. I brought clean clothes with me in my bag."

"Well, then you run on up and use the shower in my bedroom. It's the room at the end of the hall when you get to the top of the stairs. There should be clean towels hangin' up."

"All right then, I'll go on up."

"Just yell down if you need something."

Nathan left Stormie in the kitchen and made his way upstairs. He walked in the bedroom and saw a cherrywood

Victorian-style bed with a matching dresser, armoire, and nightstands. The bed was covered in a baby-blue-and-white quilt. Off to the right was the bathroom. Nathan walked in and began to undress.

Nathan was removing his shirt when he heard a noise like someone was walking in the hallway. He walked into the bedroom and looked around but didn't see anyone. He went to the door that led into the hall, but once again, no one was there. Nathan shrugged it off, walked back into the bathroom, turned on the water, and finished undressing.

This is great, he thought as the warm water relaxed his muscles.

Stormie was looking through the refrigerator when she found pork chops, spinach, and corn in the refrigerator. It made her smile. Sissy had prepared an evening meal for the two of them before she left.

"What am I going to do now?" she asked herself, right before she heard something or someone in the living room. "Nathan, is that you?" She walked out of the kitchen and into the living room.

Nathan was finishing his shower when he heard the wood floor creak in the bedroom. Once again, it sounded as if someone was walking around.

"Stormie, is that you?"

Nathan waited for an answer, but there was no response. He stood back under the water and finished washing off the soap. He was about to get out when the shower curtain slowly opened. Nathan was pleased to see Stormie standing there, naked. She smiled at him.

"I thought we could finish where we left off earlier," she said when he reached out for her and helped her into the shower. The two had gone pretty far with each other earlier out on the water. Now they were about to go much further.

Dinner stayed in the refrigerator as the two lovers spent the night in each other's arms until morning hours.

He had waited in the house for the pair to come inside. He hid in the closet, and when he saw the FBI man come into her room, he thought he was going to be discovered. He had prepared his knife and was ready to kill him if he had opened the door.

He waited to hear the shower being used before quietly making his out of the house. Once downstairs, he thought about taking her as she worked in the kitchen alone. But if she screamed, the FBI man could've possibly heard her. Getting caught was too risky. In the end, he decided to sneak out the front door when he had the opportunity, only taking the small souvenir with him for now.

Nathan and Stormie spent the next day by the water and in bed, talking and holding each other. Before they knew it, the day had once again turned into night.

"When do I get to find out about Nathan Emerson?" Stormie asked while lying on his stomach with his arms wrapped around her.

"What do you want to know?"

"Everything. Where are you from?"

"Well, I grew up near Winston-Salem."

"Really? Right here in North Carolina," Stormie said, surprised.

"Yeah."

"Tell me more." She wrapped the quilt around herself and laid her head against his chest.

"All right. My parents owned a small farm where they grew

peanuts. My father made most of his income by repairing cars and farm equipment. My mother did odd jobs and, of course, took care of the house and me. My father said taking care of me was a full-time job by itself. They were good parents, and they supported me in everything I did. I mean, every July twenty-fourth, they threw me an amazing birthday party. They were at every football game, and they were there when I signed my scholarship to play football at Oklahoma. Then, on December thirty-first, nineteen fifty-seven, they were driving down to Miami, Florida, to watch me play in the Orange Bowl when they were killed in a car accident as they got into town around eleven that night."

She sat up, looked at him, and caressed his cheek. "Oh, Nathan, I'm so sorry."

"I didn't find out about the crash until after we won the game against the Blue Devils. During the entire game, I kept looking for them in the area they were supposed to be sitting. Finally, after the game, I went into the locker room, and that was where the police were waiting for me. They pulled me aside, along with one of my coaches, and asked if I knew Robert and Sara Emerson."

"That's horrible! How did they know where to find you?"

"Apparently, they found one of my old jerseys in the back seat that my mom would wear to the games. They put two and two together and came to the stadium."

"That's horrible! How did you get through that?"

"Well, I had their funeral, and afterward, I went back to school to finish the year. I spent the summer at the farm, and in the fall, I started law school at Duke and stayed there until I graduated in sixty-one. One day, an FBI agent came by one of our classes and told us the FBI was looking for people with law degrees. I applied with the FBI in February, and in April, they offered me a job, and well, here I am."

The two of them took turns telling their life stories.

Stormie told him about going to school at the University of Alabama in Tuscaloosa and that she didn't like school very much. Her daddy wanted her to graduate, so she took extra classes over the summer and graduated in three years with a degree in history.

She also told him people had pressured her to get married after her father died. They told her a farming business of the size she now owned was no place for a woman. She had been invited to a party by an old college friend, and when she arrived, Ben was there. She shared how Ben had pulled out all the stops trying to impress her, and it had worked. She had been hypnotized by his charm. After about six months of dating, he asked for her hand, and she accepted.

Nathan told her about working on significant publicized cases involving civil rights violations and about the time he spent Thanksgiving weekend working in Dallas, the day before and after President Kennedy was assassinated.

"You were there?" Stormie asked and sat up once more.

"Yeah, I was there. When I told you I spoke to Mrs. Kennedy, well, that's when it was. I wasn't on the street when he was killed. I was driving around with some of the city cops. We were checking on some of the locals who had made threats to the president. The assassination came across the radio, and we were directed to go to the hospital and help with security there," Nathan explained.

"Is that when you spoke to the first lady?"

"Yes," he answered.

"I couldn't imagine."

"She was just sitting there, and no one was speaking to her. I still remember seeing her wearing her blood-stained clothes. I never felt more sadness for someone than I did at that moment. For some reason, I walked up to her and asked her if I could get her anything."

"I thought you were teasing me the other day," Stormie said

and then lay back down and pulled him close. She wondered what would come next for the two of them.

There's so much to learn about this man, she thought to herself before she fell asleep in his arms.

MONDAY, JULY 11, 1965

Nathan left Stormie's home just after noon and passed Sissy, who was coming up the driveway. He smiled and waved, and she smiled even more as she waved back at the agent. He shook his head, knowing she was very much aware that he had spent the weekend with Stormie. He and Stormie hadn't talked about their future. Neither acknowledged or even hinted that there was a future for them. They simply agreed to be professional in public and to contact each other when it was safe.

When Nathan entered his room, he found a note that had been slipped under the door. It was from Preacher.

I stopped by after church to tell you that someone has been spreading rumors about you and Stormie Arrington. Watch your back!
P.

Nathan shook his head in disbelief.

Did someone see us on the water together? Did someone see me at the house? The sheriff or one of the other tails may have, but I was careful not to be followed on Saturday… Wasn't I?

Nathan spent most of the day replaying the weekend in his mind. He then reviewed his case notes and looked over the files once more. He planned to travel to New Bern in the morning with the hope of locating Warren Prater. Before going to bed, he took heed of Preacher's advice and placed the chair under the doorknob before turning off the light.

TUESDAY, JULY 13, 1965

Nathan left Beaufort around ten and arrived in New Bern shortly after eleven. He drove to the US Marine base, and after stopping for gas, he was told that coloreds in the area ate at the New Bern Diner for lunch. He found the restaurant and took a seat at the bar. After a few stares from the other patrons and waiting for someone to take his order, the owner came over. He was a large black man with large hands, and he held a meat cleaver.

"You lost?" he asked.

"No. I'm Agent Emerson with the FBI, and I was hoping you could help me locate someone," Nathan answered as he displayed his credentials.

"I doubt I'll know who you're looking for."

Nathan saw where the conversation was going and didn't think he was going to get any information in the diner, so he decided to order something to eat instead.

"Can I have a menu, please?"

"Why?" the large man asked.

"Look, I'm just looking for a man named Hoot." Nathan barely got the name out of his mouth before a man at the end of the bar leaped from his chair and ran out the door. Nathan spun around and ran after him. He chased the man to the side of the diner, and that was where the race began.

The man had a head start. He leaped over fences and cut through people's yards, but Nathan stayed with him.

Nathan sprinted with everything he had. He was about to

lose the man when he ran into the side of a moving car. The man slid across the hood headfirst and came to rest on the other side. He tried to get up and run again, but Nathan grabbed him and held him to the ground.

"Stop! I just want to talk," Nathan pleaded.

"I ain't got nothin' to say, and I ain't did nothin'!"

"I know, so quit already!"

"Then what do you want?"

"I'm looking for a guy named Thurman. He goes by Hoot. Is that you?"

"No, man. Hoot's my uncle."

"What's your name?" Nathan asked, hoping for the answer he was looking for.

"I'm Warren Prater. I don't even live here. I'm just visitin'."

"Then you're the person I'm looking for," Nathan said proudly.

Warren gave the FBI man a curious expression. "Why you lookin' for me?"

"I'm looking into the deaths of the girls over in Beaufort. I was told you found Delia Snipes."

"I did, but I told Sheriff Carter everything," Warren said as he brushed himself off.

Nathan stood close to Warren, ready to chase him down if he tried to run again. "What about the camera and the pictures you took?"

"What are you talking about?" Warren asked as if he didn't know what the FBI agent was referring to.

Nathan dropped his shoulders and let out a deep breath. "The pictures you took with the stolen camera."

"Oh. I didn't do anything with them. I mean, I didn't get them developed or nothin'. I kept them in the camera."

"Where's the camera now?"

"In the trunk of my car, back at the diner."

"Let's go," Nathan said as he placed his hand on Warren's back and pushed him back in the direction of the diner.

Ben was getting agitated the longer he was on the phone with Sissy. He knew she was dodging his questions and providing half-truths when he questioned her about Stormie.

"I don't give a damn how busy you are!" Ben shouted into the phone.

"I knows you don't," Sissy said in return.

"You just tell Stormie I'll be back in town on Thursday and not Friday as planned."

"I'll tell her when I sees her."

"You do that!" Ben yelled as he slammed the phone back down. "Damn her!" Ben was frustrated, and he paced back and forth in the room.

"What's wrong? Why are we going back early?" Emma asked as she came out of the bathroom.

"We need to get ready for the parties this weekend."

"What's that got to do with anything?"

"I'm going to the costume party with Stormie on Friday," Ben said.

"Why are you bringing her? I thought we were spending this week and the weekend together after the party. You said she wouldn't go. What's changed now? Are you jealous because she's with the attractive FBI agent?" Emma asked as she walked back toward the bathroom.

Ben grabbed her and pushed her onto the bed. "I'm not jealous of anyone! Get that through your damn head! Now listen! I need to make it look like I'm a caring husband up until the time we put her in the ground. I need people to see us together. I need to dance with her, swoon over her, and make people think I love her."

"Okay, but why go back early?"

"If I know Stormie, she'll come up with an excuse not to go with me. We need her to go. I need Agent Emerson to go too."

"Why?"

"People in town need something to see and to talk about."

Nathan got the camera from Warren Prater and drove back to Beaufort as quickly as he could. Instead of going back to his room or to a camera store, he drove to the best person he knew who could develop film for him. Besides, he wanted to see Stormie again.

When he pulled up to the house, Sissy and Stormie were sitting on the front porch together. He parked the car and got out as Sissy walked inside and Stormie walked out to meet him.

"I was hoping to see you today," she said as she walked toward Nathan.

He smiled at her, and she put her arms around his neck and kissed him like she hadn't seen him in months. He loved the way she gave herself to him, and at that moment he knew she was what he needed and desired in his life.

"What brings you out here?" she asked as she ran her finger down his chest.

"I need a favor," he said as he reached in the car and took the camera out.

"Are you taking up photography now?"

"No. This camera has film in it. It's supposed to have some photos on it. Crucial photos. I don't know where else to go to get them developed."

"I can do it for you inside," Stormie said as she tried to take the camera away from Nathan. When he didn't release it, she asked, "What's wrong?"

"Stormie, the images that may be on here could be very gruesome. I need you to know that. If you're not comfortable with developing them, I'll understand."

"Are they pictures of the dead girls?" she asked.

"Maybe one of them."

Stormie thought for a moment. "Will it help you find who did it?"

"Yes, it could."

"Then I have to help you," Stormie said and took the camera from his hands.

Nathan followed her up the steps of the porch and into the house.

Nathan stood next to Stormie in the darkroom and watched as she worked on developing the film. He wanted to be in the room with her in case something horrible appeared in the photos.

Stormie had to squeeze past Nathan a few times as she worked to bring the images into focus in the trays. Her darkroom was the small bathroom off the first-floor hallway. Photography was nothing more than a hobby, so she didn't need any more space than what she had until now. She didn't complain about the crowding because she liked having Nathan close to her.

"Now what?" Nathan asked as he moved closer behind her and placed his hands on her waist.

She reached down and placed one of her hands over his. "We wait, and hopefully, the images will start to appear."

They watched as Stormie agitated the liquid. Soon, an image started to appear. Stormie prepared herself and took a deep breath. She thought she was ready for whatever was going to appear, but she was wrong. Suddenly, the naked and mutilated body of Delia Snipes became visible. Stormie gasped and turned and put her face into Nathan's chest.

"Don't look! Just tell me what to do," Nathan said as he turned her away from the images.

Stormie gave him instructions on how to move the photos to the distilled water to rinse them and how to hang them to dry. She waited with her eyes closed while Nathan completed the process for all ten photos.

The two finally emerged from the darkroom and went into the kitchen. Once more, there was a note left by Sissy:

Gone to a movie in town. Be back later.
Sissy

Stormie looked at Nathan and was not sure of what to say.

"I'll go and let you get back to your day," Nathan said.

"No, wait! Please stay awhile. I'd like to talk to you."

"All right." Nathan took a seat across from her at the kitchen table. He could see she was upset.

Stormie had been avoiding asking about the girls. She'd been curious ever since he told her about the case and Ben's and Ridge's relationship with the eugenics board. "All the girls who have died were killed. That's what you think. Right?"

"Yes, based on what I saw in the darkroom and everything else I've found, it leads me to believe they were all killed. I can certainly say Delia Snipes wasn't struck by a boat propeller. Someone used a knife to do what was done to her."

Stormie took a second to think. "You went to Charlotte that day we had lunch together, and found those girls' names on the list from the eugenics board."

"Yes."

"All three girls were sent for sterilization, all three were killed, and all three had ties to two men who worked with the eugenics board in the past."

"Yes."

"Judge Ridge and the apparent monster I'm married to," she stated.

Nathan was surprised as to how fast Stormie had put things together. "Well…"

"Do you think there's some conspiracy to kill the girls? Who else is involved? Is there anyone else involved?" she asked quickly.

"I know Sheriff Carter has been following me a great deal. Jack Walters has done the same at least once. Now, there is a third person following me as well."

"The third one is the one who you think shot at you in the cemetery, correct?"

"Yes," Nathan answered, looking at Stormie.

She sat there quietly, looking at the floor.

"Why don't you take Sissy and leave?" he said more than asked.

"No, I can't! Ben would come for me, and he wouldn't stop until he found me. After the other night, I'm sure he'd kill us both," Stormie replied and then moved to the sink to fill a glass with water.

"What are you going to do?"

"Help you. If Ben's a part of these girls being killed, I want him stopped," she said and turned around to face Nathan.

"I can't have you do that."

"No arguments. I've made my mind up, and I've already decided." Stormie walked to the refrigerator and removed some leftovers.

Nathan sat there, not saying anything. He didn't know what to say.

"Do you like dumplings? You're joining me, right?"

"Yeah," he answered.

I'm with you till the end, he thought to himself as he watched her move around the kitchen. He had already decided he would protect her against anything and anyone.

The two of them ate dinner together in the kitchen. Nathan told her of the rumors swirling around town. Stormie simply shrugged it off and decided people would make their own minds up. Eventually, she led Nathan into the living room, where they sat on the couch with Stormie curled up next to him. Before long, they saw the headlights of Sissy's car coming through the front window.

Stormie sat up and looked at Nathan. "What should or could I even tell Sissy?"

"Everything. If I'm not around, then the two of you need to watch out for each other, especially if you think Ben's behavior is getting worse, which it sounds and looks like it is."

"I agree."

When Sissy came inside, Stormie brought her into the living room and sat her down, where she and Nathan shared everything with her. Sissy didn't say anything or do anything to interrupt them as they gave her all the details.

"Now that you know everything, do you want to leave?" Stormie asked while holding her hands on her lap.

"Are you leaving, baby?"

"No," Stormie answered quickly.

"Then you know I ain't leavin' neither," she replied.

"That's what I thought," Stormie said and kissed her cheek.

Nathan made it back to his room around eleven. He sat on the bed to look over the photos. He hadn't had an opportunity to view them at Stormie's home. The photos were amateurish at best, and many were out of focus. Delia's injuries could be seen, but they couldn't really be made out. It was the last photo he looked at that provided him with what he thought he needed. Delia's breasts had been cut off with a knife or some other cutting tool, but it certainly was not a propeller with its rapid chopping motion.

Nathan stood and walked to the bed. He looked out the window at Sheriff Carter, who was standing under the streetlight. The sheriff had followed him from Stormie's home. It made him nervous that the sheriff knew he was at Stormie's. He believed it was Sheriff Carter who spread the word about him spending time with Stormie.

He's not even trying to hide anymore. I guess I won't either, Nathan thought to himself.

CHAPTER 15
PIRATES

Nathan pulled into the parking lot of the coroner's office at ten o'clock. He didn't know what to expect from Doctor Glenn. He was going to confront the doctor with the photos and ask him why he had ignored the apparent mutilation to Delia's body, which Nathan believed had been done with a hand cutting tool and not a boat propeller.

The waiting area of the office was messy, and no one sat at the receptionist's desk. Nathan rang the bell numerous times before a small man wearing a lab coat came through a side door. The man was in disarray, with his hair uncombed, face unshaven, and clothes wrinkled.

"Are you the county coroner?" Nathan asked as he displayed his credentials.

"Yeah. How can I help you, Agent?" he asked with a slightly slurred speech.

"Are you the one who examined the remains of Delia Snipes, then decided she died accidentally and was later struck by a boat propeller?"

The man rolled his eyes. "Maybe, I don't remember."

"Well, I need you to remember. Look at this photo and tell me why, in your expert opinion, you thought she was hit by a boat propeller when these injuries were clearly inflicted with a straight-edged cutting tool."

The coroner didn't bother to look at the photo. "Son, in this county, you do as you're told. If the sheriff said that's what happened, then that's what happened. I'm too damn old and too damn sick to really care anymore."

"Don't you care about the oath you took?"

"All my patients these days are dead before they get here. I like it that way. No one cares. Besides, the oath doesn't matter to me when it comes to people who are already dead."

Nathan dropped his hands to the counter. "So you're standing by what you wrote?"

"Why wouldn't I?"

"Because of this!" Nathan said as he aggressively held the photo out for the doctor to look at.

"All you have is one grainy, black-and-white photo that shows someone's body has been torn to shreds by something, something I think was a propeller. Now, I'm still drunk from last night, but I can still see that the photo isn't all that great."

"You're a disgrace."

"I know, but I don't really give a damn," the doctor said and walked out of the waiting area.

Nathan walked out of the office and into the parking lot, where he found Sheriff Carter leaning on his car, drinking from a coffee cup.

"Morning, Agent Emerson."

"Good morning, Sheriff Carter."

"How was your meeting with Doctor Glenn?"

"Fine."

"It's usually better to catch him later in the day, after he's had a nap and before he starts drinking again," Sheriff Carter explained and took another sip from his cup.

"Apparently."

"You know you can ask me for help anytime. I could have told you about the doc if I knew you were coming by here to see him. It would've saved you the trip. What do you have there?" the sheriff asked, looking at the photo in the agent's hand.

"It's a photo of Delia Snipes's body," Nathan answered.

"Where did you get that?" Sheriff Carter asked, dumping his coffee into the grass.

"It just came to me in the middle of the night."

"What do you mean it just came to you in the middle of the night? If you got something new, then you need to share it with me," he stated.

"I only need to share it if it's evidence, and I haven't decided if it's evidence yet."

"Look here, young man—"

"No, you look here. I've put up with your bullshit ever since I arrived. I'm an agent of the federal government. I'm going to do what I need to do to solve these cases. Now get your fat ass off my car. I got things to do!" Nathan yelled and moved past the sheriff.

Nathan was furious, and the time for tact was over. The past week and a half had finally pushed him over the edge. If the sheriff was going to play games, then he was going to let him know where he stood and how he was going to play it. If he played it right, the sheriff would get pissed off and make a mistake.

It's time to put a little pressure on the Four Horsemen, Nathan thought.

"If you're lookin' for trouble, you goin' to get it!" Sheriff Carter told Nathan as he climbed into his car and backed out of the parking space.

THURSDAY, JULY 15, 1965

Nathan had spent most of the previous day with Preacher at his church and then ate dinner with him and his family that evening. He gave Preacher an update on what he had uncovered over the previous days and thanked him for the note he had left in his room concerning the rumors. He told Preacher that Sheriff Carter was most likely the source. Preacher asked if there was any truth to the rumors, and Nathan felt he could not lie to his old friend, but he also thought it best not to tell him the entire truth.

Nathan informed Preacher that he and Stormie had been spending a lot of time together on her boat, looking over the locations where the girls' bodies were found, and she had developed the photos from the camera Warren Prater had given him. Preacher accepted the explanation and did not pry any further.

Preacher told Nathan he needed to attend the annual Pirate's Ball that would be held Friday night at the town hall. He explained the attendees would eventually find their way to Judge's Revenge. Preacher told him anyone who's anyone in North Carolina would be in town over the weekend attending the event. He also told him people were saying that there was another party going on this weekend as well.

Nathan took Preacher's advice and decided he should attend the ball. When Nathan went into town, he found a store that rented costumes specifically for the Pirate's Ball. The shop was large, and it was spread out between two adjacent stores. Inside, various costumes were hanging everywhere, and shoppers crowded together, browsing the racks.

As he moved from rack to rack, looking over the collection of pirate clothes, Nathan spotted Rhett Jenkins skimming the racks himself. Rhett looked at him and nodded. Rhett looked around, and when he felt no one was watching, he walked over to Nathan.

"Sorry about the other day, but the sheriff was watching us both. He came by late the previous day and ran George and Otis off before you got there. One of my guys told me so when I came back from my fishing trip later that evening. Then he called the morning before you came by and told me I better not talk to you and to run you off if you came by," Rhett explained.

"No need to apologize. I understand, and I appreciate the information. What happened to your hand?" Nathan asked and pointed toward Rhett's right hand, which was bandaged.

"When you own a fish market, you'll eventually cut yourself cleaning fish," Rhett explained, holding up his hand.

"You going to the ball?" Nathan asked.

"Yeah. It's kind of expected if you own a business in town to be seen at these types of things."

"I get it. I guess I'll see you there," Nathan said.

"Maybe, for about thirty minutes," Rhett said and then walked away.

Nathan walked to the back of the first shop and spotted Stormie. She was entering a makeshift dressing room with a shower curtain for privacy. Nathan made his way toward the dressing room and looked around to see if anyone was watching. Once he felt it was safe, he stepped inside the curtain and quickly closed it behind him.

"What?" Stormie said as she jumped slightly, obviously surprised by her visitor.

Nathan grabbed her half-naked body and kissed her deeply. "I've missed you," he said softly.

"I've missed you too. Ben's home, and he's forcing me to go to the Pirate's Ball tomorrow evening," she whispered.

"I'm going too. That's why I'm here."

"Great! I'll go out and find your costume. Just watch me, and I'll point it out," Stormie said with a mischievous grin.

"All right," Nathan said. He kissed her once more and stepped out of the dressing room.

As Nathan browsed the store, he occasionally picked up a costume and placed it up to himself, pretending to make it look as though he was measuring it for fit. He watched Stormie exit the dressing room area, and without pause, she walked to a rack that had costumes of a better quality hanging on them. She took one out and placed it on the end of the rack.

She looked at Nathan and pointed at it while mouthing the words: "this one."

She then walked to the counter, paid for her own costume, and left the store. Nathan made his way to the rack and picked up the costume she'd laid out for him.

Really, Stormie! This is the one? he thought to himself as he walked to the counter to pay for the rental.

FRIDAY, JULY 16, 1965

Sheriff Carter arrived early to the Pirate's Ball to meet with the others. He wore a costume that resembled a night watchman of Colonial America. He carried a lantern and a nightstick to complete the ensemble. He found Arrington, Walters, and the judge in the back room, sitting around a table.

"Nice costume, Sheriff Carter," Judge Ridge announced as Carter walked in.

The judge was wearing the same outfit he wore every year. It was a long black robe that he topped off with a white curly wig, which was already twisted. The judge had apparently started the party before he even arrived.

"Come on over and sit down. I want to explain something to everyone," Ben stated.

Ben was dressed as none other than Blackbeard himself. Jack Walters sat next to him, dressed as a colonial businessman. Sheriff Carter walked over and sat without saying anything.

"I guess the rumors are moving around town quickly. People have been coming up and asking questions about Stormie and me."

"Well, I did what you told me to do. I mentioned to some people that the two of them had been seen together a lot since you were out of town," Sheriff Carter explained.

"Good. Jack, tonight you stay with Emma. She already knows the two of you need to make it appear as if you're together. I'll be with Stormie, and I'll eventually cause a scene with her that everyone sees. After tonight, I need to be the innocent husband whose wife is having an affair with a stranger in town."

"Be careful. I heard Agent Emerson was in the costume shop picking up his costume for this evening. So he'll be here," Jack said in warning.

"That's fine. It's all part of the plan," Ben replied.

"I don't know if him being here is a good idea," Sheriff Carter said.

"Why?" Ben asked.

"He confronted me on Wednesday at the coroner's office. It didn't go well. He's doing whatever the hell he wants, and he doesn't care who knows it, and he damn sure made me know it."

"He will if I decide to have him escorted out of town. He doesn't have any evidence. Who does he think he is?" the judge stammered.

"He does have something. He showed Doc Glenn a photo of Delia Snipes's body," Sheriff Carter said.

"Where'd he get that?" Jack asked as Ben sat there, thinking.

"I don't know, but he has it."

"No matter. We still move forward with what we're doing. We have the Gentlemen's Social tomorrow night. We need that to happen," Ben explained. "Let's just get through tonight, and we'll go from there."

The Pirate's Ball was in full swing when Nathan arrived. The first thing he noticed was a makeshift pirate ship table display with the familiar skull and crossbones on it. The town attendees were all dressed as either pirates, gentlemen, loose women, or ladies. There appeared to be more loose women than ladies. Only one person was wearing a blue, English officer's uniform. Nathan thought it was tight around the collar, but he liked how he looked in it. He still didn't know why Stormie had selected that particular costume for him to wear.

Nathan walked around, mingling with other people, and even stopped for a snack at the refreshment stand. As he was drinking tea from a plastic cup and pretending to listen to a couple explain the history of Blackbeard, Nathan browsed the crowd and finally found her. Stormie was standing next to her husband, wearing an elegant cream-colored gown adorned in colorful beads.

Stormie was following her husband around as he'd ordered her to do before leaving their home earlier. She, too, was looking around the room for someone, and finally, she saw him across the way. He looked charming and handsome in his costume. She watched as he made his way toward her, which made her smile even more.

"Good evening," Nathan said as he walked up to the group

Stormie and Ben were standing with. "It seems I've found Blackbeard himself," he said to Ben.

"Good evening, Agent Emerson. It appears you have. Now, I do like your military uniform, but for the life of me, I don't understand who you're supposed to be," Ben said and laughed out loud.

Nathan wasn't quite sure either. "Well, I don't—"

"My dear husband, do you not recognize Lieutenant Robert Maynard right before your very eyes? You, Blackbeard, of all people should recognize Lieutenant Maynard. After all, he is the one who tracked you down and killed you in hand-to-hand combat. He then celebrated his victory by cutting off your head and tying it to the bow of his ship."

The sheriff, Judge Ridge, Jack, and Emma just stood there, along with the other people at the party who were all at a loss for words. Emma was the first to say something.

"I do believe that is the most descriptive and gruesome story I've ever heard. I mean, I've never—"

"Oh, I'm sure you've heard worse, Emma. You do work for an attorney."

"That was quite the story, my dear, and if my memory serves me right, that's how I, Blackbeard, met my untimely demise. May we drink in my memory," Ben said as he raised his hand in the air for a toast with the group.

"Hear, hear," the group cheered and drank from their glasses.

Nathan made his way around the ballroom, occasionally stopping to visit with the residents. He watched the Four Horsemen as they worked the room, contacting one powerful man after another. Nathan was sure he recognized two sitting congressmen, two former governors, and one former senator.

There were many men he didn't recognize, but Nathan was sure they were wealthy people who would be donating to a future Benjamin Arrington campaign.

Nathan made his way toward the back of the building, toward the bathrooms, and found a hallway where he could find some privacy. He walked down it a short distance and found a chair to rest. He didn't like mingling, and he hated crowds more. He was sitting there when he heard the high heels of a woman walking down the hallway toward him.

"I thought you would never find me," he said to Stormie, who was now standing in front of him.

"I had to wait until I could get out of there," she said as she moved closer to him.

Nathan stood, took her into his arms, and kissed her passionately. She held him tightly, not wanting to let go. He was tired and wanted to leave.

"I wish we could run away together and leave this place," he said softly.

"So do I," she whispered back.

The two embraced each other for a long time and then they turned to walk back down the hallway. When they reached the end, Nathan kissed Stormie once more and motioned for her to step out first. As Stormie walked out from around the corner, Ben was standing there with three women and two men, talking about a painting on the wall. Before she could stop him, Nathan walked out behind her.

"What do we have here?" Ben walked toward his wife. "You do know this is a married woman, do you not?" he asked Nathan loudly.

"I do. What do you think happened?" Nathan asked as the others watched on.

"Well, I don't know."

"Nothing happened," Stormie said as she started to walk past Ben.

Ben grabbed her by the arm and turned her around, which angered Nathan. He clutched his fist and looked Ben in the eye as a larger crowd gathered. Ben decided to seize the moment. He released Stormie and walked up to Nathan, then looked around the room and moved his head to within inches of the FBI agent.

"How did you find the comfort of my bed?" Ben whispered, leaning in closer to Nathan.

Nathan ignored the question and just looked at him. Ben didn't get the response he was looking for. He looked at Stormie, smiled, and turned back toward his adversary.

"Well then, how did you enjoy fucking my whore wife?" Ben asked in a whisper only Nathan could hear.

Nathan reacted just the way Ben was hoping he would. He pushed Ben to the ground and charged after him as other men grabbed Nathan, stopping him. Sheriff Carter came over and looked at both men.

"What's going on here?" he asked.

"Nothing, Sheriff Carter. Agent Emerson and I were just reenacting the fight between Blackbeard and Lieutenant Maynard. Weren't we, Agent Emerson?" Ben said as he stood.

"Whatever you say," Nathan answered and walked out of the building.

Nathan drove back to his room and took off his costume. He lay on the bed for about two hours. He was angry. He knew he should not have pushed Ben Arrington. He knew Ben had been baiting him.

Why did I take the bait? You idiot! he thought to himself.

He was running the scene in his head again when there was a knock at the door. Nathan jumped to his feet and grabbed his .45. He walked to the door quietly and listened.

"Nathan, are you in there?" Stormie whispered.

Nathan opened the door. She'd been crying, and there were marks on her neck. He reached for her, pulled her inside, and shut and locked the door behind her. Neither one said anything. They just held each other as she wept.

"What happened?" he asked as he examined her neck.

"After you left, people started talking in circles about the two of us. I told Ben I was leaving. He tried to stop me, but I got in my car and drove home. Ben came home a short time later to yell at me. He said I had embarrassed him and that I was a whore. I gave it back to him and told him I knew he had been having an affair with Emma and that I had pictures of them in some hotel room. He went crazy. He grabbed me by the neck and demanded I give him the photos."

"Where was Sissy?"

"I sent her to New Bern because Ben told me before the ball that he was not staying with me this weekend. He has the Gentlemen's Social tomorrow night at the Arrington House, and he is staying there all weekend."

"Did you give him the photos?"

"Yes, but I have another set he doesn't know about. I thought he was going to kill me tonight," she said. She closed her eyes, leaned into him, and cried some more.

"That will never happen," Nathan said as he held her tightly.

"There's something else."

"What is it?" he asked.

"When Ben mentioned the Gentlemen's Social tomorrow night, I thought about all the previous Gentleman's Socials. I looked at the calendar in Ben's office at home and wrote down the dates when he had socials earlier this year," she said as she handed him the folded paper.

"What are you thinking?"

"I want to know if they match the dates the girls went missing," she answered.

Nathan's eyes widened. He went to the dresser and opened the drawer with the case file. He browsed the reports and discovered that both Delia and Rose were last seen on the same days that a Gentlemen's Social had been held.

"Was I right?" Stormie asked.

"Yes."

"I don't want to go home, Nathan!" Stormie declared as she sat on the bed.

"You're not; you're staying with me tonight." He walked past her and checked the lock on the door once more. He then wedged the chair into place under the doorknob.

He drove around town, looking for something to do. He wanted to take advantage of one of the many intoxicated women leaving the Pirate's Ball, but he decided against it. He knew the Gentlemen's Social was being held tomorrow night, and it would be safer to find someone there to play with.

The time grew closer and closer to take down the men he hated the most, especially Ben Arrington. He, most of all, deserved what he was planning.

They all deserve to die, but Ben Arrington deserves it the most! he thought to himself. He moved the knife back and forth under the light of the streetlight and thought about Ida.

Ida's Story

SATURDAY, MAY 29, 1965

Ida Freeman was making her rounds at the party when she caught the eye of Johnathan Davenport. Johnny, as he liked to be called, enjoyed the Gentlemen's Social more than most men who were there. He liked the light-skinned girls Ben Arrington provided during the evening.

Usually, by the end of the night, he found his way upstairs with one or maybe two of the girls, if he was willing to pay more for it of course. Johnny knew he would only get one evening with any one girl because they would never agree to be with him again. He had a reputation for not being very gentle with the girls, but he didn't care. After all, he didn't care what some *"half-breed"* said or thought about him.

Ida saw Johnny watching her. She was aware of his behavior in the bedroom, as she had heard rumors about how he was, but she also knew he paid more for what he enjoyed doing. If she were lucky, he would pay her enough money, and with it, he would be her only customer for the evening. She thought she may even get to go home early if he paid her enough. Ida made her way toward him, making sure she kept his attention by running her hands along her hips and breast. Johnny waited on the sofa, hypnotized by her seduction.

"May I sit next to you?" she asked and sat down before he answered. She placed her arm around his shoulders and rubbed her breast against his arm.

"Yes. Please have a seat," Johnny finally answered.

"Are you having a good time?" she asked.

"Not yet, but the night is still young," he said flirtatiously.

The two sat on the sofa very close to each other for nearly fifteen minutes before heading to one of the many bedrooms upstairs. Johnny opened the door for her and followed her inside. Ida walked toward the bed and placed her purse on the nightstand under the lamp. She then turned around to face Johnny, who was no more than a foot away. He smiled and looked deep into her eyes. He had already taken his penis out and was stroking himself. He leaned forward to kiss her. Ida placed her right hand on his chest to stop him but used her left hand to caress his manhood.

"I know you want and need it, baby, but we need to get the business part taken care of first," Ida stated.

"I'll pay afterward. Let's just keep going," Johnny said.

"No, you'll tell me what you want, and I'll tell you what it will cost before we do anything. I need to make sure we have an understanding."

"I want to fuck you!" Johnny said excitedly. He pulled the top of her dress down, baring her breasts.

"All right, but how?" she asked.

"From behind." Johnny spun her around and pulled her dress up over her hips.

"Okay, but take it easy, and no rough stuff. And I want two hundred dollars."

"Okay, but I get to do what I want," Johnny replied quickly and threw money on the bed.

The men and women at the party were dancing, laughing, and having a good time when they heard a woman screaming upstairs. Everyone stopped and looked up toward the balcony and saw Ida come running out of the bedroom. Her nose was bleeding, and she appeared to be frightened. Johnny went out behind her, zipping up his pants and laughing madly.

"You're a sick bastard!" Ida shouted as Sheriff Carter grabbed her and escorted her outside to the back of the house.

Ida was still screaming and causing a scene outside. Sheriff Carter tried to calm her but was not being successful. Finally, out of frustration, he slapped her across the face with his right hand.

"Shut the fuck up!" he yelled.

Ida held her face as she looked at the sheriff. "Is that what you white men like to do? Beat women?"

"You need to leave now."

"Why, Sheriff Carter? Do I embarrass you? Are you afraid I'll call attention to what you sorry bastards are doing out here? What would you do, Sheriff, if I called the FBI and told them how you send poor half-breeds like me off to be made sterile so that you, Ben Arrington, and his friends can fuck us without worrying about getting us pregnant and taking a chance on us having your bastard child?"

"Leave, and you better keep your mouth shut if you know what's good for you," Sheriff Carter warned.

Ida stepped toward the sheriff and spit in his face. She then walked off the porch toward the driveway. Sheriff Carter used his handkerchief to wipe his face off and watched Ida until she disappeared in the darkness.

Ida was out on the highway next to the water's edge when a car pulled up beside her. She stopped, placed her hands on her hips, and looked into the sky. The driver leaned over and opened the door. Ida looked at him, shook her head in disbelief, and climbed inside.

"You know, you ain't no better than me," she said and looked out the passenger side window toward Taylor Creek.

"Why do they think they can treat us this way?" Ida asked as she began to cry.

The driver didn't say anything. He did not place the car in drive. He put his hand on her shoulder and then reached down between the door and seat and retrieved his knife.

"Sometimes, I wish I could just climb into a boat and drift out to the sea. Maybe I'd wash up on some distant shore somewhere. The people who live there would treat others fairly, no matter their skin color. I think that…" Ida trailed off when she felt a knife slowly slide in between her ribs and then deeper into her heart.

Ida slumped sideways against the door. Her face pressed against the window, where she could see the light of the moon shining over the water. Her killer started back down the highway, while Ida watched as fond memories appeared but then faded into the shadows of Taylor Creek. She smiled when she saw a small boat drifting with the current toward the ocean.

Chapter 16
Gentlemen's Social

Nathan kept Stormie in his room for the better part of the day, out of sight. He only left the room to get them something to eat. When he returned, he laid out his plan for the evening with Stormie.

"I think you should go to New Bern and stay with Sissy. I'm going to your place and taking your boat to the Arrington House, where I'm going to try to get close enough to see what's going on inside tonight."

"It's a good plan, but there's only one thing wrong with it."

"What's that?" Nathan asked curiously.

"I'm going with you."

"No, I don't—"

"No matter what you say. I'm going," Stormie stated.

Before Nathan could say anything more, there was a knock at the door. The two looked at each other, and Nathan placed his finger to his mouth and nose.

"Don't say anything," he whispered. He then grabbed his pistol and quietly walked to the door.

"Who's there?"

"It's Preacher."

Nathan opened the door and allowed Preacher to enter. Preacher looked at Stormie sitting in the chair across from the bed. He looked at Nathan and handed him a sheet of paper with a name on it.

"Who's this?" he asked.

Preacher looked at Stormie once more.

"It's okay. You can speak in front of her. She knows everything," Nathan said.

"There's another girl who's missing. Bessie Jones," Preacher explained.

"When did she come up missing?" Nathan asked.

"No one knows for sure, but she does the same work as the other girls. Her father is a drunk, and he's been telling people she's missing."

Nathan went back to his file. He took out the list from the eugenics board and looked over it. He sat on the edge of the bed and looked over at Stormie. "She's on the list."

Sunday, July 19, 1965

Nathan and Stormie left her house in the boat right after midnight. The two wore darker clothes, and they had covered the boat's navigation lights before leaving the dock. The night was dark, as the increasing thunderstorm clouds veiled the full moon above. Stormie kept the boat at a slower speed as it glided along the calm waters of Taylor Creek. The lights from the docks offered visibility as the two cruised by each property until she saw the familiar house in the distance. She idled the engine and then shut it off entirely when they got closer to the dock that led to the Arrington House.

Nathan climbed onto the dock and held the boat still while he peered through the darkness toward the lawn and beyond it to the house.

"Don't tie on. Just hold the boat close to the pier," Nathan whispered to Stormie.

"Why?"

"In case we have to leave in a hurry."

"Nathan," Stormie said softly as he turned to leave.

He turned back toward her. "Yes?"

"Be careful. I don't want anything happening to you. I think—"

Nathan pulled her to him and kissed her. "I know, me too," he said and ran into the darkness beyond the edge of the dock, leaving Stormie in the boat, alone and speechless.

Nathan ran toward the house, carefully remaining concealed in the shadows. He stopped just short of the back of the house. The music was loud, but he could hear people laughing and dancing to the music of Gary Lewis and the Playboys.

He wanted to see inside, so he started to move closer, but from the corner of his eye, he saw Sheriff Carter pulling up and parking toward the back. Nathan dropped closer to the ground. Carter was not in his uniform, but he still carried his gun and badge on his belt. He got out, opened the back door, and let three colored girls out. They were all dressed in evening dresses in various colors.

"Now you ladies go inside and be nice to the guests," Sheriff Carter ordered as he pointed at the back door and followed them inside.

Nathan started to get up and move toward the side of the house again when the back door flew open. He quickly dropped down once more. Nathan watched as Dolly, the woman he saw at Judge's Revenge the first night he was in town, came outside while being followed by a man in a suit.

"C'mon, darlin', have some fun with Old Jeb, dammit!" The intoxicated man begged as he ran his hands over her body. The two made their way to a car parked along the edge of the woods.

"I don't think you can even do it. You too drunk," she said.

Nathan ignored them. He carefully made his way to the side window and hid in the bushes. He then lifted his head slowly and peered inside. He saw mostly white men with young colored women everywhere. Some people were drinking, laughing, and dancing. Others were getting more acquainted with each other before going upstairs.

Nathan continued looking through the window until he thought he'd seen enough. He ducked and turned to go back the same way he had come. Cautiously, Nathan eased out of the bushes. He looked toward the car for Dolly and the man in the suit. Nathan scanned the darkness and saw the two of them in the back seat of the car. The couple was oblivious to him or anyone else, including the person lurking in the bushes next to them.

Nathan watched as the man made his way closer to the car. He squinted his eyes for a better look, but all he could make out in the darkness was his silhouette.

Suddenly he saw it! The shadowy figure carried a knife in one hand, and he was getting closer to the car.

"Stop!" Nathan yelled. He ran across the yard toward the dark figure, who quickly turned and ran into the thick brush after being discovered.

Dolly and the man stopped what they were doing. They exited the car but didn't see anything except the rustling of the brush.

"Who was that?" Dolly asked.

"No one. Let's get back to it."

Nathan ran after the dark figure with his pistol in hand for about two hundred yards before he lost him in thicker brush. Nathan dropped to a knee in a small opening and listened for any movement in the blackness surrounding him.

You got to get him! he thought to himself.

Nathan heard a sound to his right and spun with his gun pointed outward, but he wasn't quick enough. His assailant kicked the gun from his hand and landed a solid punch to his jaw. It sent him backward, slightly putting him off balance. As Nathan tried to steady himself, he saw the blade of the knife being swung toward him. He attempted to move backward, out of the way, but he wasn't able to avoid the knife's edge as it sliced through his left arm just above his elbow.

Nathan fell to the ground, close to where his gun had landed. He saw the attacker coming at him once more with the knife over his head. Nathan reached out for his .45 and rolled to his right. He fired two shots behind his back and heard the attacker scream. Nathan kept moving and fired four more shots until he landed on his knees. He looked back at his intended target, who had apparently run away once more.

"Who the hell's out there?" Sheriff Carter yelled out from the back of the house.

Nathan got to his feet and ran farther into the brush. He made his way along the beach and back to the dock, behind the cover of the trees that bordered the property. When he made his way down the pier, he found Stormie still waiting for him just as some of the guests from the party started walking toward the water.

"Get us out of here!" Nathan yelled to Stormie. He jumped in and fell to the bottom of the boat, bleeding badly from his wound.

"What happened? Are you okay?!" Stormie called over the motor as she piloted the speeding boat toward open water.

She waited until she had the boat well away from Arrington

House before she shut the motor off and dropped down beside Nathan. He was bleeding. The wound was so long and deep, she could see exposed muscle. "I gotta get you to a hospital!" she cried, using a towel to wrap his arm.

"We can't,' Nathan said as he sat up.

"Why not?"

"Hospitals ask questions, and they'll call the sheriff," he explained.

"I know where we can go," Stormie said. She placed a folded blanket under his head, turned the boat back on, and sped off into the night.

Preacher was in bed when he heard the knock on the door at two in the morning. He was hesitant to open it until he heard the familiar voice of Nathan on the other side. Stormie had driven the boat back to her home, gotten Nathan into his car, and driven him to Preacher's house. Stormie had remembered that Preacher's wife was one of the few colored nurses in the county, and she knew she would help.

Preacher's wife, Regina, prepared her surgical tools and gave Nathan some old pain medication she had left over from Preacher's hernia surgery. Regina was diligent, and she worked as quickly as possible to clean and close the wound. Stormie was by Nathan's side when he passed out, and she remained there, holding his hand.

Preacher sat in a chair facing the front door, with his double-barrel shotgun in his lap. He didn't know if anyone would come looking for his friend, but he was going to be ready if they did. Willie and Sam were told to sleep on the floor in their room. They did as they were told, but they kept the door open and watched the adults until they fell asleep.

Charlie White made it a few hundred yards from where Agent Emerson had shot him. He stopped in a small opening in the woods next to the side of Taylor Creek to tend to his stomach wound. He was angry with Sheriff Carter, who had made him sit in the woods all night while everyone else attended the party. He was also angry with Agent Emerson for interrupting him doing what the sheriff had him in the woods to do. Finally, he was upset with himself for getting shot, once again, by the agent.

"Dammit!" he called.

I had him, and my knife was ready! It was going to be quiet, just like the sheriff wanted. Until that damn FBI man yelled out, Charlie thought to himself and then angrily stabbed his knife into the ground next to him.

Charlie blamed the FBI man for ruining everything. The only satisfaction Charlie had was that he had gotten the FBI man good, even though the agent wasn't the person he was there to kill. He knew knife wounds could be worse than any bullet if the cuts were long and deep enough, and Charlie believed the one he had delivered to the FBI man was just that. For a moment, Charlie lay his head back and enjoyed the thought of the FBI man in pain.

"Who dat?" Charlie asked when he heard someone coming out of the woods next to him. He gripped his knife tightly and got ready for round two, but then he saw the face of the person as he emerged from the brush into the dim light of the partially covered moon.

"Oh, it's you. Well, just don't stand there. Help me up and get me to a hospital," Charlie said as he started to stand.

"What are you—" Charlie was grabbed by the hair.

The person pulled Charlie's head back, dug a knife into his

neck, and made a cross-directional cut across his throat. Charlie gargled and tried to use his hands to stop the attacker, but it was useless. Within seconds, Charlie felt himself slipping into blackness.

He waited there, looking at Charlie at his feet. He knew he'd been careless tonight. Charlie had almost got him. He heard the cars in the distance starting up and driving away from the house. Finally, after he was sure Charlie was dead, he walked back toward the house to see if there was anyone left to play with. He left Charlie's lifeless body in the woods, in a pool of his own blood, with his knife still in the ground next to him.

Ben stood on the dock, looking out over Taylor Creek for the boat he had heard speeding off into the darkness. He believed it carried his wife and her new FBI friend, who had apparently made an uninvited appearance at Ben's Gentlemen's Social. He bent down, and with his finger, he wiped through a dark red liquid on the dock. Ben was confident he knew who the trespassers were, and he decided it was about time to finally deal with them once and for all.

"I don't know what happened, and I can't find Charlie anywhere," Sheriff Carter announced as he walked up to Ben on the dock.

"He's probably hiding because he screwed up again."

"Probably, but who fired those shots? I made sure he didn't have a gun tonight."

"I believe it was the FBI," Ben said smartly.

"What do you want to do about Charlie?"

"Nothing for now, but we need to be rid of all of our problems quicker than I once thought," Ben said as he turned toward Sheriff Carter.

"What do you want me to do tonight?" Sheriff Carter asked.

"Nothing. But tomorrow, why don't you pay Agent Emerson a visit and see how he's fairing," Ben said as he wiped the blood from his finger onto Sheriff Carter's shirt.

Nathan awoke and found Stormie sitting on the floor. Her head was on the edge of the couch next to his. She was asleep, so for a few minutes, he just watched her. He questioned whether he could protect her or not. He stroked Stormie's hair while thinking back to the boat and how, right before he had left her there, she was about to say something meaningful and important—something he felt and that he wanted to say as well but hadn't brought himself to deal with yet.

I've only known her for a short time. Can I really be falling for this woman? Have I've already fallen for her?

Across the room, Nathan saw Preacher sleeping in a chair. He faced the front door with a shotgun between his legs. Nathan knew he was at the end of his rope last night, and so did Preacher. But his old friend wasn't going to let anything happen to him while he recovered.

"I see my patient's awake," Regina whispered as she walked out of the kitchen carrying a glass of water for Nathan. She was wearing her nurse's uniform and was about to leave for work.

"Yeah. How long have I been here?" Nathan gently sat up, took a long drink from the glass, and looked at Stormie, who remained asleep.

"Since about two o'clock in the morning."

"I don't remember much after getting here."

"That's because I gave you plenty of pain medication. I didn't want you feeling anything as I was stitching up that arm.

There are over thirty stitches in your arm. I had to stitch you up inside and out."

Nathan shook his head. He looked down at the bandage and then at Stormie.

"She ain't moved from your side since you passed out last night. I offered her our bed to sleep in, but she wanted to be right next to you."

"I passed out?" Nathan asked.

"Yes. You lost a lot of blood. The cut was bad. I didn't know if I could stop the bleeding or not. To tell you the truth, I was really worried. We all were."

Nathan looked down at this arm. "Looks like you did a great job. I'm still here," he said and smiled at her.

"Well, of course you are! I couldn't let the man who saved my husband's life die on my couch, could I?" Regina said as Stormie began to wake up.

Stormie took a minute to gather her senses, but then she remembered where she was and the events of the previous evening. "Nathan, you're okay!" Stormie said and sat up.

"I'm fine," Nathan assured her as he caressed her cheek.

"You alive?" Preacher asked as he stood. He placed the shotgun against the wall and stretched his arms out wide.

"I'm alive," Nathan replied.

Preacher moved his chair closer to the couch and sat. They were all glad to see their friend conscious once again. Nathan explained to the three of them about what had happened when he left Stormie at the boat. He told them he didn't get a good look at the man who had cut him, but he was sure he had hit him with the blind shot he fired from his .45.

"I'll call some of the local hospitals when I go in for my shift," Regina said as she got ready to leave.

"Good, and thank you again for saving my life," Nathan said.

"Don't mention it. I'll call my husband later when I find

out if anybody came in with a gunshot wound," Regina replied. She kissed her husband and walked out the door.

"What're you going to do now?" Preacher asked.

"I think we need to get out on the water and start looking for Bessie," Nathan answered.

"Where are we going to look?" Preacher asked.

"If we can get some people to drag the waters and search the area from Taylor Creek into Harlowe Creek and then around Galant Point, we may find her if our guy put her in the water like the others—and if he's the one who took her," Nathan explained.

"I'll let everyone know this morning when my congregation meets. We'll get everything organized and meet you out there tomorrow, bright and early."

"Sounds good. If you have Bessie's address, I'd like to go by there and speak to her family after I get cleaned up," Nathan said.

"I'll get it for you and call you with it later."

Nathan and Stormie started for the door. "By the way, thank you and your family for saving my life."

"No thanks needed. I owed you anyway."

Nathan and Stormie left Preacher's and drove to Nathan's room, where he cleaned himself up and put on clean clothes. He waited until Preacher called with the address for Bessie's home before leaving.

Nathan and Stormie drove to Stormie's house. Once inside, Stormie discovered Ben had removed most of his clothes from the bedroom closet, and some of his personal items as well. Nathan went from room to room with his .45 in hand, making sure they were alone. He then locked all the doors and windows. Stormie took a quick shower, and when she came out of the bathroom, she found Nathan sleeping on the bed. She set her alarm clock for two o'clock and lay beside him. They both needed the rest.

Chapter 17
Wesley Jones

Nathan and Stormie arrived at 610 Maple Lane in Morehead City at four. The house believed to be where Bessie Jones had lived sat alone at the end of the street. It was more of a rundown shed than a home, and the surrounding yard was unkempt with car parts, toys, and trash spread about. Nathan knocked on the door while Stormie stood behind him. He waited a few minutes, and when no one answered, he knocked again but much louder than the first time.

"Who there?" a man asked from inside.

"Agent Emerson with the FBI," Nathan answered.

The door slowly opened, and the man looked them both over before inviting them inside. He directed them to sit in two of the four dining chairs in the living room, which were the only items of furniture in the room. The man was white, and he had bloodshot, watery eyes. He was unshaven and unwashed. His clothes were filthy, and he spoke with slurred speech.

"You find my Bessie?" he asked. He picked up a half-empty bottle of whiskey from the floor and drank from it.

"Not yet," Nathan answered.

"Why you here then?"

"I wanted to ask you a few questions about Bessie," Nathan answered.

He drank from the bottle again. "Like what?"

"Are you Bessie's father?"

"Yeah. I'm Wesley Jones."

"When was the last time you saw Bessie?"

"She didn't come home on Thursday. I think it was the eighth," Wesley answered and drank from the bottle once more.

"I have Bessie's name here on a list. The list has the names of people who were sent to the eugenics board for a medical procedure that made them unable to have children," Nathan explained.

Wesley quickly glanced at the paper Nathan held. "I know what it is."

Nathan looked over at Stormie and then back at Wesley. "Can you tell me why Bessie's name is on the list? Why was she sent in for the procedure?"

"She got arrested for getting paid to have sex with men. Her lawyer man worked it out with the court," Wesley answered suspiciously.

"Who arrested her, and who was her lawyer?" Nathan asked.

Wesley didn't say anything right away, he thought about the question before answering. "Sheriff Carter arrested her, and her lawyer was that little man at the courthouse."

"Was his name Jack Walters?"

"Yeah, he's the one who paid me," Wesley stated.

"Paid. Why did Jack Walters pay you?"

"She came home and told me they wanted her to do it, get fixed and all, and I told her to tell them no, so she did. The next thing I know is Walters is coming over and telling me it was the right thing to do and that he would give me a hundred dollars if I made sure Bessie went along with it."

"And you thought that was the right price for your

daughter… not to ever have children?" Stormie asked sarcastically.

"Yeah. We ain't got money like you, lady. A hundred dollars is a lot to me and mine. Who are you to judge me?" Wesley asked, raising the tone of his voice while he stood.

"We're no one. We'll be on our way," Nathan said as he ushered Stormie out the door.

"You see Bessie, you tell her to come home! I need her here! You tell her!" Wesley yelled as he followed them out to the car and watched them drive away.

Sheriff Carter was a visitor Emma was surprised to see on her doorstep. She had spent the better part of the day at the beach and had been pleasantly surprised to find Ben in her house when she returned late in the afternoon. The two had eaten dinner together and were getting ready to settle in for the night when the sheriff knocked on the door.

"I need to speak to Ben," Sheriff Carter said to Emma as he walked in, not waiting for an invitation.

Ben walked into the living room from the bedroom. "What is it, Dwight?"

"I found Agent Emerson and your wife at his place earlier today. I followed them to Bessie Jones's place and then to Stormie's house. After a few hours, I drove back to Arrington House and walked around the property. I found a blood trail by the dock, and I followed it back into the woods to an opening where I discovered a few .45 shell castings," Sheriff Carter stated.

"Okay. We heard the gunshots last night. Did you find anything else?" Ben asked.

"Yeah. I found another trail of blood and followed it."

"And what did you find?" Ben asked impatiently. He was growing tired of the sheriff's slow-paced explanation.

"I found Charlie White's body."

"Oh my!" Emma said and placed her hand over her mouth.

"What happened? Did Agent Emerson kill him?" Ben asked.

"I don't think so. Charlie was shot, but his throat was cut too. I think the gunshot wound was by Agent Emerson, but I don't think the agent took the time to cut his throat. And there's something else," Sheriff Carter said.

"What?" Ben asked.

"I think Charlie knew who cut his throat."

"What makes you think that?" Ben questioned.

"His knife was in the ground next to his body. Charlie White was meaner than a rattlesnake, and I've seen him in a fight. I know how well he used that knife of his. It makes no sense that it would still be in the ground. Charlie White would have fought back with it."

"Maybe the gunshot wound was too bad, and he couldn't fight back," Emma said.

The sheriff shook his head. "No, I've seen plenty of gunshot wounds like his in Korea. He was hurt, but the bullet went straight through. I could've had Doc Glenn patch him up, and he would've been fine in a few weeks."

"So we still have a problem running around out there," Ben said as he sat on the sofa and thought for a few minutes. "What about my wife and Agent Emerson?"

"As far as I know, they are thicker than thieves. They're never apart, and they're still at your place right now," Sheriff Carter replied.

Ben stood and walked back toward the bedroom. "We end this Friday."

"How?" Sheriff Carter asked.

"I'll let you know tomorrow. Leave Charlie where you

found him for now. Take photos and collect evidence. You make certain the evidence points to Agent Emerson as the one who killed him."

"Okay, but I hope you got a really good plan." Sheriff Carter said before he left.

Nathan thought it best to spend the night at Stormie's home, where he reviewed everything he knew thus far. Stormie sat beside him in the kitchen and listened as he ran through his thoughts out loud about what he knew. Stormie asked questions, hoping it would help Nathan's deductive reasoning, along with coming up with answers to his questions.

The two of them knew that Rose, Delia, Ida, and Bessie were all on the list from the eugenics board. There was even a Dolly on the list, and Nathan believed it was probably the same Dolly from the party. They also determined the parties were most likely political fundraisers, of sorts, in an effort by Ben to win favor from influential men in and around the Southern states for his campaign when he ran for governor.

But he still had questions.

Who was the shooter in the cemetery?

Who vandalized the church?

Who attacked me with a knife? Was it the same person who was killing the girls?

Why were the girls being killed in the first place?

All the girls except Bessie were reported missing after the weekend following a Gentlemen's Social…

Were the Four Horsemen killing the girls, or were they protecting someone else?

Stormie had called Sissy in New Bern and told her to stay there until she heard from her again. Sissy was hesitant, and at first, she refused until Stormie told her Nathan was staying with her. Stormie was concerned that Ben could or may be responsible for the girls' deaths in some way, and it made her sick to think about what could possibly happen to Sissy.

"Do you think Ben is the one killing the girls?" Stormie asked as they lay in bed next to each other.

"I don't know, but my gut says no," Nathan answered.

"Why?"

"I think whoever is killing the girls enjoys what he does. There's something sinister and grotesque in what happens to them. I don't doubt that Ben would kill if he got something out of it financially or politically, but he wouldn't kill for the enjoyment of it, and I think the one who is killing the girls does."

"I hate that I married such a man. What do we do now?" Stormie asked.

"We need to find Bessie before Sheriff Carter does."

MONDAY, JULY 20, 1965

Nathan received a call from Preacher at a little after seven in the morning, and he told him he had everybody coming out to help look for Bessie. He had people to walk the shoreline, people to drive boats, people to drag the bottom where they could, and others bringing out food to feed everyone.

Nathan thought about calling the bureau in Washington, bypassing Agent Smith, and informing them about what he had found. After some time, he decided to wait until he found Bessie. Bessie's body would prove his theory on the girls being murdered, which would lead to Sheriff Carter's cover-up, Ben Arrington's involvement, and anyone else who was a part of it. Bessie Jones's body would be enough to launch an official investigation.

Nathan was sitting on the edge of the bed when Stormie came back into the bedroom, carrying a tray with breakfast on it. She placed it on the dresser and turned and smiled at Nathan. He smiled back, then rushed over, swept her into his arms, and kissed her.

Nathan and Stormie were scheduled to meet Preacher and the other volunteers at Gallants Point. They took Stormie's boat and docked it along with the other volunteer boats on the pier. Preacher was true to his word. People were running around, doing just about everything.

The volunteers were both white and black folks from the community. Rhett Jenkins was there helping to organize the search, and he had two of his boats already on the water, dragging the bottom. Nathan was pleased to see the turnout of volunteers. It seemed many people knew 'something' was wrong in Beaufort but didn't know what to do about it. Nathan figured out that the 'something' that was wrong in Beaufort was the Four Horsemen.

Nathan and Stormie walked from her boat toward the shore. Rhett was giving orders to his crew on the third boat, which he was about to go out in. The crew moved around quickly, placing gear in its correct spot and preparing the boat to leave the dock. Nathan looked on the boat as the men hurried about it, and one of the people he recognized was the large man from the courthouse when Stormie called up to the man.

"Amos!" she called as she moved closer to the boat.

"Hi, Mrs. Stormie," he said, smiling as he walked to the

edge of the boat. He was wearing coveralls, a sleeveless shirt, work gloves, and rubber boots.

"How in the world did you get Judge Ridge to let you come out here?"

"I told him I's sick. Besides, Mr. Rhett pays me more, and I just want to help," Amos replied.

"We're glad you're here," Stormie said and turned back toward Nathan.

"I thought I saw him at the courthouse the other day," Nathan said as he and Stormie walked away.

"Yes, he works there during the week and some weekends. The judge has him clean and do other maintenance around the courthouse. He always greets everyone and speaks to them kindly. People say he's touched. I think the judge takes advantage of him. He doesn't pay him very much and treats him poorly. I don't know why he continues to work for him."

"I wouldn't," Nathan stated frankly.

Over the next two days Nathan followed up on possible leads while Stormie and Sissy delivered meals and other supplies. The number of volunteers dwindled with no luck in locating Bessie Jones. Her father, Wesley, had showed up for the first day but wasn't seen again. Rhett had used his boats and crew for two days more, but by Thursday, he had only one boat left in the search that he captained himself with one other crew member.

Sheriff Carter made it a point to come by and watch in the mornings and then returned in the late afternoons. He never spoke to Agent Emerson or Stormie. Ben Arrington came by too, but only Stormie had seen him parked on the bridge over Taylor Creek. He had come by the house at least once, and he left a note saying they needed to talk about how they would end things and divide their property. He indicated he would meet her at their home at six this evening if she were willing to talk.

In his note, Ben had also prepared what he thought was an equitable split of assets. She was surprised at what Ben was willing to do. He had indicated he would not go after her family money if Stormie and Sissy left North Carolina. She was to leave him the sole owner of Arrington House and Arrington Home. The money currently in their joint account was to be his along with three hundred thousand dollars from her accounts in Alabama. Stormie estimated it would cost her about four hundred thousand to escape Ben Arrington. She would still have the four million in her bank account in Alabama, along with her property. Ben also expressed she should seek the advice of an attorney in Charlotte once they came to an agreement.

Why does he want to make a deal? she asked herself.

THURSDAY, JULY 22, 1965

Ben arranged to meet his men at the courthouse, where he discussed his strategy concerning the next two days. He was eager to get things done and move on with his plans to be the next governor of North Carolina. Ben had what he felt was enough support, and if things went as planned, he would be taking office in January of 1969.

Judge Ridge was the last to show up, and the four men sat in his chambers where Ben laid out the details and gave each man his job.

"Does everyone know what they're doing?" Ben asked the group.

Jack sat in the chair nervously, shaking his leg. "There seems to be a lot that needs to happen, Ben, for this to work," he said.

"Yeah. If one thing goes wrong, we're all done," Sheriff Carter added.

"Just follow the plan. Ben knows what he's doing," Judge Ridge stated and drank from the flask he carried in his pocket.

The four of them left the courthouse, each with a job to do. Ben knew his part in it would be the most difficult, but he'd figured she deserved what she had coming to her.

It was after five thirty when Nathan and Stormie heard over the radio that Rhett Jenkins had found something he was bringing to shore. He indicated it was a body. Nathan asked if it was Bessie, and Rhett informed him he didn't know because it was in bad shape. Sheriff Carter heard the transmission, so he rushed from the courthouse and drove to the dock that Rhett was going to tie off to when he arrived.

"I want you to go," Nathan said to Stormie.

"Why?" she asked.

"You don't need to see this. I've seen this before, and you don't want that memory," Nathan explained.

"Okay. I'll go meet Ben at the house and listen to what he has to say."

"I'd rather you reschedule the meeting with him. I'm worried about you. I would like to be there," Nathan said as he held her hands on the dock.

"It'll be okay. Sissy will be there. I spoke to her last night."

"If this is Bessie, then I think I'll be done here. The bureau will send more agents out here, and they'll take over the case and I'll call Washington."

"What will you do when that happens?" Stormie asked as she pulled him closer.

"I'm leaving the FBI. I've already decided," Nathan answered.

"Where will you go?" Stormie asked worriedly.

"I don't know. Wherever you'll be, I suppose," Nathan said and kissed her quickly.

"We can decide later, but I hear California is nice," Stormie said and happily ran off the dock toward her car.

"California?" Nathan asked aloud.

Rhett eased his boat to the dock, and his crewman jumped off and tied it on. Rhett looked at Nathan and was about to tell him something when Sheriff Carter walked up to the men.

"Whatever you got in that boat falls under the jurisdiction of my county, and I'll be conducting the investigation," Sheriff Carter ordered as he stepped up onto the boat.

Nathan grabbed Sheriff Carter by his pistol belt and pulled him back off the boat, causing him to fall backward onto the dock. Nathan felt a sharp pain in his injured arm, but he didn't allow it to show on his face.

"You son of a bitch!" Sheriff Carter said as he went to pull his gun out of the holster.

Nathan quickly took it out of his hand and backhanded him across the face. He threw the gun toward shore into the shallow water, picked the sheriff up by his shirt, and pushed him toward shore.

"Get your ass out of here! This is now an investigation that falls under the Federal Bureau of Investigation. If you so much as come around it again, I'll see that you are placed in a federal prison for interference."

"You can't do this," Sheriff Carter declared as he walked into the water to retrieve his gun.

Nathan held his own gun at his waist. He wasn't sure what the sheriff would do, but he wasn't taking any chances. After the sheriff left, Nathan finally attended to his arm that was aching and bleeding through his shirt.

CHAPTER 18
HIM

Stormie got back to the house and found Ben's car in the driveway. She sat in her car for a few minutes before getting out. Stormie was nervous and didn't know what to expect. She didn't see Sissy's car, which made her even more nervous. Stormie looked at the front of the house and thought about driving away, but then she saw Ben walk out onto the porch.

"You comin' in?" he yelled. He motioned with his hand for her to come inside and then he turned and walked back in the house.

Stormie took a deep breath, got out of the car, and walked up to the front door. She paused, took another breath, and stepped inside.

It'll be okay, she told herself.

Ben was smiling at her when she walked in. She smiled back and then noticed he was wearing black leather gloves. Without warning, Ben took one step toward her and punched her in the face, knocking her backward onto the floor.

Stormie was disoriented and confused. She soon felt another blow to the side of her head that laid her flat. She tried to collect her thoughts and sit up, but once again, she was attacked by Ben, who was kicking her in her lower ribs.

She screamed as she felt bones break. "Don't, Ben!" She cried out in pain as she held her stomach.

Ben was unstoppable. He reached back with his right hand and punched her again, this time putting her entirely on her back. Stormie was still conscious but not completely aware of what was happening. Ben straddled her and delivered one clenched fist after another to her broken and bleeding face. He was in a fit of rage. He shouted unrecognizable obscenities as he beat her. Stormie finally went unconscious, but Ben couldn't and wouldn't stop. He punched and kicked her until he had nothing left. Out of sheer exhaustion, Ben finally spilled onto the floor next to her body. He lay there for some time, resting and listening to her labored breathing, hoping each one would be her last.

Nathan looked over Bessie's body, which rested on the boat's deck. Her body was bloated, and it had decomposed moderately during her time in the water. Nathan could still determine her breasts had been cut off, that she had been stabbed multiple times in the vaginal area, and that she had been eviscerated. He used Stormie's camera and took photos. This time, there would be no question as to what had caused the injuries to her body.

Nathan thanked Rhett Jenkins for his help, and the two men waited until the coroner from another county arrived to take Bessie's body away. Nathan wasn't letting anything happen to the evidence he had and needed, to bring down the Four Horsemen and whoever had killed the girls.

He knew the men were involved in some way, and he was going to prove it.

Ben went to the kitchen and got a glass of water. He removed his blood-soaked gloves and washed his hands, then walked back to Stormie, who was still lying on the floor. He drank the entire glass and shook his head from side to side, listening to her quietly whisper, *"Nathan, Nathan."*

Ben walked back into the kitchen, placed the empty glass on the counter, and thought for a moment. He then walked back into the living room, picked Stormie up off the floor, and threw her limp body over his shoulder. Ben uncaringly carried her out the front door, across the lawn, onto the dock, and then dropped her into Taylor Creek. He waited a moment as Stormie disappeared into the depths below.

That wasn't so hard, he thought as he walked away.

After leaving the house Ben drove to Judge's Revenge. The others were already there, waiting for him to arrive. Ben walked in and told Jack to pour him a double shot of bourbon. Ridge had closed the bar early and sent his employees home. He was getting drunker by the minute.

"Now what?" Jack asked after handing Ben his drink.

"We wait," he said and threw his whiskey back. He grabbed a napkin, dipped it in a pitcher of water, and cleaned his wife's dried blood from his expensive shoes.

"Wait for what?" Jack asked.

"Hell, I imagine."

Rhett Jenkins took Nathan back to Stormie's house in his boat and dropped him off on the dock. Nathan was making his way toward the house when he saw an ambulance race out of the driveway. Sissy ran down toward him, screaming. Nathan heard the desperation in her voice, so he ran toward her. Sissy exhaustedly fell into his arms on the lawn.

"My baby, my poor baby, I think he's done killed her!" Sissy said over and over again.

"Sissy, what are you talking about? Where's Stormie?" Nathan said frantically.

"They're taking her to the hospital!"

"What happened?"

"I come home, and I find a lot of blood in the house. I started running around, looking for Stormie. I couldn't find her nowhere, so I ran out here and found her lying on the bank, half in the water and half out. She was bad, Mr. Nathan. She was having trouble breathing, and her face was swollen up somethin' awful. I didn't recognize my baby!"

"Let's go!" Nathan said. He picked her up and hurried to his car.

Nathan and Sissy made it to the hospital shortly after the ambulance arrived. They rushed in but were stopped by hospital staff. They were told to wait in the waiting room. After waiting for almost two hours, Regina and a doctor came out. She found Nathan, Sissy, and Regina's family sitting together. Nathan jumped up and walked to them, followed by the others.

"Is she okay?" Nathan asked.

"She will be, but she's had some traumatic injuries. She has multiple facial fractures that will require surgery when she's well enough, and she has multiple broken ribs and a punctured lung. To be honest, I don't know how she survived," the doctor stated.

"Can I see her?" Nathan asked as Sissy cried. Preacher put his arm around her and moved her toward a chair.

"Yes, but she's in a lot of pain. Try not to excite her."

Nathan made his way down the hall and opened the door to Stormie's room. He stood there for a minute, looking at her lying helplessly on the bed. She was unrecognizable.

He caught himself on the wall, as his legs felt weak under him. He moved closer to Stormie and saw that her left eye was swollen shut. Her right eye had a cut over it, which ran along her eyebrow. Her forehead was swollen and bruised, and her lips were cut in two places. He sat on the edge of the bed and took her right hand in his. She squeezed it slightly and let out a slight moan. He leaned down toward her face and kissed her lips while a tear dropped from his face onto hers.

"I said I wouldn't let anything happen to you. I'm so sorry," Nathan whispered in her ear.

"I love you," she whispered faintly.

"I love you too. Just lie here and think about sitting with me on a nice warm beach in California. I'll be back," he said.

"Can we come in?" Preacher asked from the door.

"Yes," Nathan answered as he wiped his face.

Nathan got up, and Sissy sat and took his place, holding Stormie's hand. Sissy rubbed Stormie's arm, kissed her hand, and brushed her hair away from her face.

"You'll be okay, baby. I'm right here," Sissy said reassuringly.

Nathan walked out of the room, and Preacher followed him into the hallway.

"Nathan, where are you going?" Preacher called.

"To get Ben Arrington!" Nathan yelled angrily as he passed the nurses' station, startling the three nurses sitting there.

Emma was at home, packing her belongings like Ben had instructed her to do. He told her she would be leaving in the morning for Destin, Florida, and that he would be joining her shortly. She was happy things were in motion for them to be together, and she was ready to go. She danced to the sound of the Beatles singing *"Ticket to Ride."*

She moved from room to room as she filled one suitcase after another with clothes from her drawers. She was finally happy. Ben and she would be together, and she would be the next first lady of North Carolina.

"Mrs. Benjamin Arrington," she said to herself.

She opened her closet and was surprised to find someone standing there. Emma started to scream, but he placed his hand over her mouth and then pushed her to hold her against the wall.

"I wish we could've had some time to play, but I got to be somewhere else!" He slid the knife between her ribs as she desperately tried to push him away. He looked her in the eyes, kissed her lips, and let her body fall to the floor. He then cut her dress away and took his trophies before leaving.

Nathan found Ben's car in the parking lot of Judge's Revenge. He parked his car and slowly made his way to the front. He peeked in from the side window and saw Ben sitting at the bar with Jack Walters. The judge was standing on the other side, pouring drinks, while Sheriff Carter sat at a table by himself near the front door.

Nathan placed his gun in the small of his back and entered the bar quickly. Sheriff Carter stood and reached for his gun but wasn't quick enough. Nathan delivered a right cross to his jaw, and as he stumbled backward, Nathan grabbed his head and drove it into the bar, knocking him out.

He then grabbed the bourbon bottle with his left hand and swung it into Jack Walter's head, knocking him to the floor. Nathan winced in pain. The swinging of the bottle partially reopened the cut in his arm. Judge Ridge yelled in protest as he grabbed his pistol from under the bar and aimed it at Nathan. Nathan pulled his gun from his back and shot Judge Ridge in the chest just as Ridge fired his own gun.

The bullet caught Nathan in his right shoulder. His gun flew from his hand onto the floor to his right. Nathan moved toward it and leaned over to pick it up just as Ben kicked him in the ribs.

Nathan rolled to his right in pain and saw Ben going for the gun. Nathan scrambled to his feet, grabbed a chair from the floor, spun it in a circle, and brought it down on top of Ben, who had the gun in his hand. The chair broke as it slammed onto Ben's back and sent him to the ground. The gun once again was on the floor, away from both men. Nathan ran over and delivered a hard kick under Ben's chin, sending him backward as he tried to stand.

Nathan was hurting, but he was emotionally charged. Ben had a beating coming to him, and Nathan was the man to deliver it. Ben got to his feet and looked Nathan in the eye. Both men were determined, and neither were backing down.

Ben charged forward and delivered three quick jabs to Nathan's injured shoulder and then one to his jaw. Nathan moved back against the bar with Ben in pursuit. Ben tried for a punch to the jaw, but Nathan blocked it and returned a quick jab, catching Ben in the eye and knocking him to the floor. Nathan jumped on top of him and delivered repeated punches to his face.

Nathan was still punching the downed Ben when the butt of Sheriff Carter's gun came down hard onto the back of his head. The room went black, and Nathan fell forward on top of Ben.

Sheriff Carter stumbled to the bar with his gun in his hand where he examined the butt of his pistol that was now broken. He then looked at the unconscious FBI man on the floor.

After resting for a moment, Sheriff Carter collected himself and then placed Nathan in handcuffs while Jack closed the blinds. Ben finally got up and made his way to look over the bar. Judge Ridge lay dead in a puddle of beer, whiskey, and blood.

"This is not what I expected!" Jack yelled as he frantically walked back and forth.

"Shut up!" Sheriff Carter yelled.

Ben walked to Nathan's gun and picked it up. He then stood over Nathan.

"You can't kill him here! That's not part of the plan! The judge getting killed wasn't part of the plan! The plan is gone! Oh, shit! We're screwed. The FBI will be here, and we're all done," Jack shouted, continuing his hysterics.

"Shut up!" Sheriff Carter yelled again.

"Fuck you, Sheriff Carter, and fuck this whole thing! What are you going to do now, Ben? What?!" Jack yelled.

Ben turned, pointed the gun at Jack's face, and pulled the trigger. Jack Walters fell to the floor next to Nathan.

"What? Why did you do that?" Sheriff Carter asked, surprised.

"You knew it had to be done," Ben said. "Jack and the judge were our weak links. They would have eventually talked. Now, either we can continue with our plans, or you can shoot me and come up with something on your own."

"Well, tell me what you're thinking, since things have now changed a bit. By the way, at the end of this new plan, there better be a million reasons why I am going to go through with it," Sheriff Carter said, holding his gun by his side.

"Dwight, I need you, and you need me. I'll give you one and half million reasons to stay with it," Ben said as he placed the gun on a table.

"I'm listening."

"You see, Agent Emerson fell in love with my wife, and

when she tried to break it off, he started following her. He followed her to Arrington House the other night and killed poor Charlie White, whom I had hired to be my wife's private security. We even got the shell casings from his gun to prove it. He then followed my poor wife to our home, where he attempted to profess his love for her. When she denied him once more, he beat her severely and threw her in Taylor Creek to die. He then showed up and tried to kill me tonight. Judge Ridge and Jack tried to stop him, but he ended up killing them both, and he was about to kill me when you showed up and stopped him," Ben explained.

"You beat Stormie to death?" Sheriff Carter asked, surprised again.

"No," Ben replied uncaringly. "I beat her and threw her into Taylor Creek. She drowned."

"Agent Emerson will tell a different story. The FBI will listen to him."

"Dead men tell no tales," Ben said in return.

"We're going to kill him too?"

"Hell yes. Take him to the station. Put him in a cell. Tomorrow, spend the day writing the report the way I explained it. Then send a copy by courier to the FBI. Later in the afternoon, call the FBI and tell them you and I are on our way to Charlotte to bring him in. Let them know you're concerned about his safety and want him out of your town. By the time the FBI gets here, Agent Emerson will have already attempted to escape. And well, you had to shoot him during his escape attempt."

"You think that'll work?"

"Yes. People do crazy things when they're in love."

FRIDAY, JULY 23, 1965

Sheriff Carter left Judge's Revenge just after midnight, with Nathan still unconscious in the back seat. He got to the station and took him in through the back door, out of view of any witnesses. He placed him in a cell and left him there. A short time later, he returned to the bar. He took photos of the crime scene and collected evidence and then he and Ben met with Doc Glenn, who arrived to collect the remains of the deceased.

Doc Glenn and his assistant left some time around noon with the bodies of Judge Ridge and Jack Walters. They were on their way to retrieve Charlie White's body from the woods where Agent Emerson had killed him and left his body. Doc Glenn and his assistant left the bar believing Agent Emerson had murdered the two men during his attempt at killing Ben Arrington. Ben and Sheriff Carter knew the two of them, especially the assistant—Jennifer, the town gossip—would spread the news of what had happened. The news of the scandal would be all over town by tomorrow.

Ben and Sheriff Carter decided to meet later in the afternoon at Arrington House to finish off Agent Emerson, if he lived that long. Sheriff Carter had examined the agent's wounds at the jail and knew they were serious.

Sheriff Carter eventually left Ben at the bar, went back to the station to finish the report, and sent it off to the FBI as planned.

Ben had remained at the bar and drank heavily. After his tenth shot, he staggered to the bathroom to clean up. He looked in the mirror, and for the first time, he didn't recognize the man staring back.

You'll be okay. Get it together, Ben thought to himself as he bent down to clean off his shoes.

When Ben was finished, he walked back out to the main bar area, where he was surprised to find a familiar face standing in the center of the room.

"What the hell are you doing here?" Ben asked angrily as he walked up to the man.

He just stood there, staring at him and not saying a word.

"I asked you a question!" Ben yelled.

The man reached back and swung the leg of the broken chair at Ben's head. Ben went to the ground. He tried to stand back up, but a second blow was delivered to the back of his head, rendering him unconscious.

Sheriff Carter had had a long day. He took a nap after sending the report to the FBI, and when he woke, right before five o'clock in the afternoon, he called the FBI's office in Charlotte. He spoke to the special agent in charge, who, in Sheriff Carter's opinion, sounded eager to get his men out to Beaufort to help with the investigation. Sheriff Carter explained to Agent Smith that he and Prosecutor Ben Arrington were driving Agent Emerson back to Charlotte later tonight. He then went back and got Nathan from his cell.

"Where are you taking me?" Nathan asked as he was being dragged by Sheriff Carter to his car outside.

"Don't worry, son. It'll all be over soon," Sheriff Carter answered as he sat the groggy and weak FBI agent in the back seat of the police car.

Preacher and his sons had driven around town, and after about an hour, Willie saw Nathan's car at Judge's Revenge. The three of them stayed out of sight. They watched as Doc Glenn and his assistant removed two bodies from inside. They then followed Sheriff Carter to his office and waited. Eventually, they watched from across the street as Sheriff Carter loaded their injured friend into his police car. They followed the sheriff to the Arrington House driveway and made sure to drive past without stopping so they wouldn't be noticed. They parked farther down the road, where the car couldn't be seen from the house.

"What are we going to do, Pops?" Willie asked.

"I'm going up to the house. The two of you are going to stay here for forty-five minutes, and if I'm not back by then, take the car and go get your momma. Have her bring help," Preacher said and got out of the car.

"Pops, I'll go with you," Willie pleaded.

"No! If I don't come back, I need you to get help. Do you understand, son?" Preacher asked, raising his voice.

"Yes, but I don't like it," Willie confessed.

"I'll be okay," Preacher said. He grabbed the back of his son's head and hugged him and then reached over the seat and pulled Sam into the embrace.

Sheriff Carter pulled up next to the house and was surprised to see the man who walked out. The man made his way to the car just as Sheriff Carter got out. Nathan was lying in the back seat, drifting in and out of consciousness. When he felt the car stop, he heard the engine shut off and Sheriff Carter talking to someone.

"What are you doing here?" Sheriff Carter asked right before the knife sliced across his throat. His eyes widened, and he reached up with both hands and tried to close the gaping wound as blood spat out from his carotid artery. He dropped to his knees and reached for his killer's legs.

Nathan maneuvered himself up next to the door and peered out the window. On the ground was Sheriff Carter, rolling from his stomach to his back as blood sprayed into the air. Nathan looked at the killer as he slowly opened the back door.

"Amos," Nathan said before passing out.

CHAPTER 19
'GIVE THE DEVIL HIS DUE'

Nathan woke and found himself still handcuffed, sitting in a chair across from Ben Arrington, who was tied to another chair. He was in a bedroom that was nicely decorated. The room smelled of gasoline and liquor. On the wall across from him, just above Ben, was a painting of Arrington House. Nathan believed he was in one of its bedrooms, but he didn't know how he had gotten there or what was going to happen to him.

"About time you woke up," Ben said drunkenly from his chair.

Nathan looked around the room. "What's going on?"

"I think that damn nigger is going to kill us," Ben answered confidently.

To Nathan, it appeared Ben Arrington had been in the chair for a while, and he had accepted his fate. Nathan tried to sit up more, but he couldn't find the strength.

"You ain't going nowhere, boy. You're white as a ghost. I'm betting there ain't much blood left in you. You don't know it, but you're knockin' on heaven's door as we speak," Ben said and lightly laughed.

"Yeah, well, what are you doing then?" Nathan asked.

Ben laughed out loud. "I think we both know it ain't heaven's door I'm knockin' on, now is it?" he finally answered just as the two men heard footsteps coming up the stairs.

A few seconds later, Amos darkened the door, carrying a can of fuel. He didn't look at Nathan. His attention was solely on Ben Arrington. Ben looked up at Amos and laughed out loud once more. Amos poured fuel onto the prosecutor's body.

"Yeah! Baptism by fire! Burn the sins away!" Ben yelled and tilted his head back when Amos poured the fuel on his head.

"Amos, why are you doing this?" Nathan asked.

"Because he made me who I am," Amos stated as he set the can on the floor.

"How'd I make you, boy?" Ben asked.

"When I was sixteen, I was accused of raping a white girl. You was my lawyer. You came to see me in jail in your fancy suit and them shoes with silver buckles on the top. You said don't worry, that you'd make sure I was all right. But they still came and got me later that night. They all came dressed in their white gowns and hoods, coverin' their faces and all. They took me to the woods and tied me to a tree. I was screamin' for 'em to stop."

"I remember that, but I couldn't stop them. I didn't even know what they were going to do," Ben said.

Amos bent over and placed his hand on the man's shoulder. "You sure about that, Mr. Ben?"

"Yeah. I'm sure," Ben answered, while Nathan sat there and listened.

"I don't thinks you're telling the truth. Because when they pulled down my pants and backed the truck up to me with that torch on it, I saw you climb out of the other side. I knows it was you because you were still wearing those same fancy shoes with the silver buckles," Amos said as he dug into his pocket and pulled out a lighter.

"Amos, I can help you. I have evidence that can put him away for a long time," Nathan said.

"No, no. You see, Mr. FBI man, I did rape that white girl all those years ago. I liked playing with girls like her, but Mr. Ben and his friends saw to it that I'd never be able to use my man parts anymore to play with girls when they took that torch to me!" Amos said and lifted the lid to the lighter.

Amos looked at Ben and back at Nathan.

"Just because you remove part of the man, it doesn't stop the urges. I still liked girls, but now I enjoy killing them more, but it's not the same," Amos admitted as he placed his thumb on the wheel of the lighter.

Nathan knew it was now or never. He looked at Ben, who was looking up at Amos.

"Let's go, boy! Let's give the devil his due!" Ben yelled and started laughing madly.

Nathan jumped from his chair with all the strength he could muster and managed to be out the door just as Amos lit the lighter. The room exploded, sending Nathan over the rail to the floor below. He landed hard, knocking himself out as flames quickly swept through the old house. Preacher ran to the front door and saw Nathan on his back, covered in flames. Without thinking, he ran in and placed his arms under Nathan's shoulders and dragged him out of the house.

Once outside, Preacher rolled Nathan over and over, desperately trying to extinguish the flames. He saw Willie and Sam speeding down the driveway, and he waved them over. The burns were horrible along Nathan's torso, face, and legs. His arms and hands were practically unburned, as they were behind his back, still cuffed together.

Willie drove across the lawn as the fire raged out of control, engulfing the once beautiful home. Preacher yelled for Willie to help him load Nathan into the car. From inside the inferno came the sounds of Benjamin Arrington still laughing madly, and then they listened as the laughter turned into horrific, blood-curdling screams.

"Amos killed the girls, and he just killed Ben Arrington," Nathan whispered before passing out again.

"What do we do, Pops?" Willie shouted while Sam looked on.

"Get in and drive," Preacher said as he climbed into the back seat with his dying friend.

Regina was getting ready for work when she heard a knock on the door. She peeked out the window and saw three men dressed in suits standing in front of the house. She opened the door slightly, and one of the men introduced himself as Agent Smith with the FBI as he showed her his credentials. Agent Smith and his men had sped to Beaufort after his phone call with Sheriff Carter.

"I'm looking for a Mr. William Turner. Do you know where I can find him?" Agent Smith asked.

Smith and his men didn't find Agent Emerson at the sheriff's office, or the sheriff as expected when they arrived. Since Turner had invited Emerson out to Beaufort in the first place, Smith figured his home would be a good place to start in locating the lost agent.

"That's my husband, and he's at the hospital," she answered.

"I hope everything's okay," Smith said and looked back at the other two agents.

"Yes, a friend of ours was injured, but she's recovering," Regina explained.

"Well, that's good to know. We're here looking for Nathan Emerson as well. Do you know where we can find him?"

"No, I don't."

"Well, he's a dangerous man. We got here as quickly as we could. We went by the sheriff's office, but no one was there. I know your husband has been in contact with Agent Emerson, so we decided to come by here," Agent Smith explained.

"Yes, he has, but we haven't seen him in a few days now."

"Well, thank you for your time."

Agent Smith and the two men left the Turners' home. They were in a hurry to get to the hospital. Agent Smith wanted to know who the injured friend was, but he didn't want to ask Turner's wife.

"Why are we going to the hospital, Agent Smith?" the agent who was driving asked.

"I want to know who Pastor Turner is seeing at the hospital. We didn't see or pass a police car on our way down here. We should've seen them if they were on their way to Charlotte with Emerson."

"Maybe they went a different way," the driver suggested.

"No. The sheriff sounded really excited on the phone. He was determined to get Emerson out of here. He would've taken the quickest route, and that's the route we came in on," Smith explained.

"We better find him. It's not looking good for us in this investigation. If we go down, then you go down, Smith," the man in the back seat said as he looked out the window.

"I know. We'll get Emerson and kill him before we get him back to Charlotte."

"It sounds like he got himself into some trouble while he was here," the driver said.

Smith scoffed. "Damn sure does. Good for us though!"

Regina took a shortcut to the hospital and went straight to Stormie's room. She found Stormie still unconscious, and her husband was gone.

Sissy had gone outside for a break. She was standing at the corner of the building when the three FBI agents arrived. Sissy saw one walk inside while the other two came over and smoked a cigarette near the corner where she was, but they did not see her.

"This better be quick. I want this all over, and I want that rat Emerson in the ground tonight," one of the men said.

"Don't worry, I think Agent Smith will get the information we need. We'll find Emerson, and we'll be out of here pretty soon. Then we'll be back in Miami doing what we do best: making money. Agent Emerson will be dead along with any other loose ends in this town," the other replied.

Regina was coming downstairs when she saw Sissy hurrying along the hallway. Regina told Sissy about the FBI men coming to her house, and Sissy told her what she had heard the FBI men say outside.

"What do we do?" Sissy asked frantically.

"I don't know, but—" Regina saw Sam coming in through the emergency room. She ran over and hugged him. "Where's your father?"

"He's in the car with Willie and Mr. Nathan. He's hurt bad," Sam said.

"Who's hurt bad?" Regina asked quickly.

"Mr. Nathan. He's been burned bad, and I think he's been shot," Sam said through sobs.

"Sissy, stay with him," Regina said. She ran out the doors, while Sissy comforted the distraught Sam.

When Regina got outside the hospital, she found Preacher and Willie getting ready to take Nathan out of the car. She ran over and stopped them. She looked at the severely injured Nathan in the back seat and didn't recognize him.

"Amos killed Ben Arrington and tried to kill Nathan." Preacher quickly explained as he began to lift his friend out of the backseat.

"You can't bring him in. There are three FBI men here, and they're here to kill him," she explained.

"Why?" Preacher asked in bewilderment.

"I don't know, but they are."

"He needs help now!"

"I know." She said and then thought about it for a moment. "I got it! I'm going back inside to get some supplies. Stay here until I get back."

Preacher did as his wife said, while keeping an eye out for the FBI men while he and Willie waited in the car with Nathan.

Regina ran inside, and a few minutes later, she returned with a gurney and bandages. She wrapped Nathan's face and torso. Then she and Preacher loaded him on a stretcher.

"I'll take Mr. Arrington inside," Regina announced and looked directly into her husband's eyes for his approval.

Preacher didn't know what she meant at first. Then suddenly, he understood what needed to be done. "I got it. You take good care of… Mr. Arrington," he replied and kissed her.

"This is all on you now. Come up with a good story," Regina said as she took the injured *"Benjamin Arrington"* inside.

Chapter 20
Some Secrets Must Be Told

Jaxson had stopped reading and listened intently as Stormie Arrington, and William Turner Jr told the story of FBI Agent Nathan Emerson. When they finished, Jaxson looked off toward Taylor Creek, deep in thought.

Stormie picked up the photo once more and looked at the clearly visible University of Oklahoma class ring that Jaxson had found on the finger of the man whose face was bandaged. It was the same man Stormie had fallen in love with so many years ago. The man wrapped in bandages, with the University of Oklahoma ring was the man she knew as Nathan Emerson, but he had lived the remainder of his life, from that night on, as Benjamin Arrington.

"So your father, William Turner, Preacher, came up with the cover-up story?" Jaxson asked.

"We all did," Stormie answered. She exhaled a long breath, knowing the secret had to be told. "Preacher told Agent Smith that he and his sons had gone to Arrington House that night to look for Ben. They saw Sheriff Carter fighting with Amos in the front of the house. Amos got loose and ran inside, and Sheriff Carter followed. A few minutes later, without warning, flames were coming from the upstairs area of the house and then there was an explosion shortly after. Preacher, without thinking about his own safety, ran into the house and found Ben Arrington lying on the floor, covered in flames. Preacher dragged him out of the fire, and that's when Ben told Preacher Amos had kidnapped him and was going to kill him when the sheriff arrived and stopped him. During the commotion, Agent Emerson somehow got out of his handcuffs and shot Ben, who tried to stop him from escaping. He then ran away, never to be seen again." Stormie explained and then took another long breath before starting again.

"Agent Smith stayed in town long enough to take photos and to collect what evidence he needed to point blame onto Agent Nathan Emerson for multiple murders. He left Beaufort with the other two men. He eventually returned and questioned me a few weeks later when I was conscious. I confirmed I had a brief affair, regrettably, with Agent Emerson and that I tried to end it. Agent Emerson became violent and tried to kill me. They also tried to speak to Ben. Unfortunately, Ben's throat was damaged by the fire, so he had to write his statement. He remained in bandages for the better part of six months, healing from the burns to his face. Agent Smith took those photos of me and Nathan that night." Stormie paused and looked over at Will.

Will reached over and took Stormie's hand and nodded his head with an approving smile. "The bodies of Amos, Sheriff Carter, and the real Benjamin Arrington were never recovered from the fire. My father and I returned that night and made sure that everything that needed to disappear in the fire did so. Later, Rhett Jenkins helped remove the fire debris from the property, and he, along with my father, dumped it all somewhere deep in the Atlantic Ocean. Rhett admitted to my father, sometime later, that he was the one who had discovered Ida Freeman's body and that he had called the sheriff anonymously."

"What about Agent Emerson's car?" Jaxson asked.

"My father took Nathan's car and hid it in the woods," Will replied. "He kept its whereabouts a secret. The car remained hidden until a few days ago when the road crew found it and alerted you."

Jaxson then listened as Stormie described how she and Nathan had moved with Sissy to California, where the couple lived as Mr. and Mrs. Benjamin Arrington. Nathan went into real estate law, where he was very successful. She told Jaxson it had been easy for them to start over in California because no one knew them there. Sissy eventually married her man friend from New Bern, and the two of them lived in California as well, until Sissy passed away ten years ago.

Nathan still had many scars from that night, but Stormie never saw anything except the man she had fallen in love with on Taylor Creek. Will told how his father had secretly married Nathan and Stormie on the dock of their home overlooking Taylor Creek a year later. Stormie never sold the home, and she and Nathan had occasionally returned in secret to Taylor Creek and cruised the waters in her boat. The two remained together until his death last year.

Jaxson thanked Stormie and Will for sharing the truth with him, and the three of them decided it was time for it to be told. It was time for Agent Nathan Emerson to be found.

Agent Locke returned to Charlotte, and he began a follow-up investigation. He found that Agent Smith, along with a few other agents, had been executed by drug smugglers in Miami in 1971. At the time of his death, he was under investigation by the bureau.

After a lengthy review by his supervisors, Agent Locke, along with Stormie and Will, were able to resurrect Agent Nathan Emerson posthumously. Mrs. Nathan Emerson was presented with a plaque from the president of the United States in recognition of her husband's selfless sacrifice in the pursuit to correct an injustice done to others.

The marriage certificate Preacher had completed was also recognized and accepted by local officials, finally recognizing Stormie as Mrs. Nathan Emerson

ONE MONTH LATER

Jaxson sat in his recliner, relaxing while he watched the national evening news. He was finally finished with Agent Nathan Emerson's case and was looking forward to starting something new in the morning. He expected he would be back in his office tomorrow. There, he would review unsolved cold cases or find answers or new leads on new cases that different law enforcement agencies needed help with.

"In national news, law enforcement officials are still searching for the former police officer Jacob Mean, who is wanted for questioning in the murder of at least three people."

"Wow! I bet Axel is going out of his mind right now," Jaxson whispered to himself. Axel Frost was the detective that Jaxson had worked with during the Pikes Peak Killer investigation previously. Jaxson knew that Jacob Mean was a friend of Axel's.

"In other news, the body of a young woman was found earlier this morning under a beach house in Pensacola, Florida. The beach house belongs to a missing woman, but authorities are not saying if the body is that of the missing woman," the female news correspondent announced live. She stood in front of the yellow-and-black police tape protecting the crime scene in the background.

Television viewers had a great view of the large beach house, which was illuminated with the use of large floodlights.

Jaxson was intently listening to the news when his cell phone alerted him to a text.

I was pleased with how quickly you solved the Nathan Emerson case in Beaufort, North Carolina, after nearly fifty-five years. I look forward to seeing how fast you solve your new case in Pensacola, Florida.
SKO

Jaxson was confused by the text. He thought about everyone he knew with those initials but couldn't come up with anyone. He was looking through his contacts in his cell phone when it rang.

"Hello?" he answered.

"Jaxson, Steve Overton here," the man on the other end announced. Jaxson recognized his boss's voice.

"Steve, what can I do for you?"

"Sorry to call you so late, but we need you down in Pensacola, Florida."

"Yeah, I just saw on the news that a woman's body was found under a beach house. Why am I going out to investigate a homicide?" Jaxson asked. Usually, his involvement in a homicide required there to be something serial in nature, which needed at least two victims. Before Steve could answer, Jaxson knew the answer to the question.

"They've already found three bodies, and there may be more," Steve explained.

"Yeah, all right, I'll leave in the morning."

"Good. Someone from the Escambia County Sheriff's Office will meet you at the airport."

"All right, but before you hang up, did you send me a text right before calling me?" Jaxson asked as Overton ended the call.

He looked at the text message once more and saw it

originated from a private number. Once again, he thought of everyone he knew with the initials SKO, but still, there was no one except his boss who had initials that were even close to SKO. Jaxson shook his head and decided it wasn't something he needed to focus on right now.

Jaxson got online and made his flight arrangements. He packed his suitcase and went to bed so he could get some sleep before catching his early morning flight. As he lay there trying to fall asleep, he once again found himself thinking about the text message.

"Who is SKO?" he asked himself.

ROSES
IN THE
SAND

AGENT JAXSON LOCKE FBI MYSTERY THRILLER SERIES BOOK 3

Prologue
Roses in the Sand

Agent James Carter sat naked in the wooden chair, trying to collect himself. His thoughts were confused, he was disoriented, and he was tied to the chair. But his biggest concern was the man who sat across from him. Carter briefly looked around the dimly lit room but couldn't find anything that would hint to his location. From what he could tell, there was no window, no door, and no sounds coming from outside the room. Cool air crossed over his body as the vent, which sat directly over his head, pulled the air from the room. As the air moved from the floor to the ceiling, he felt cold at first, but then he became warm as his body began to burn in different places along his arms and legs.

"Well, you got me here; now what?" Carter asked.

The man sitting across from him did not answer. He just sat there, observing his prey.

"Aren't you going to say something, or are you one of those serial killers who gets off on trying to scare your victims before you kill them? Because if that's the case, plan on being disappointed. I've accepted the choices I've made in my career, and I knew this situation was a possibility when I decided to join the task force to hunt you down. I came to terms with what could happen a long time ago. So I'm not screaming or begging just to entertain the likes of you," Carter explained as he tried to adjust his legs and hands. They had been tied tightly in place.

"I don't plan on trying to scare you, Agent Carter," the man answered, breaking his silence.

"So you're not going to kill me?" Carter asked suspiciously.

"Oh, I plan on killing you, Agent Carter. As a matter of fact, you're dying right there in that chair within the next few minutes," the killer remarked in a deep, clear, and confident voice. Agent Carter knew it was him. *"Him"* being SKO, the serial killer who had already killed two other agents before Agent Carter had been assigned to track him down. Agent Carter had spoken to SKO numerous times over the phone, and he thought he had gotten to know him. He also thought he had been closing in on the killer right before the killer captured him.

Agent James Carter had been tracking the infamous serial killer for six months. As he sat there, recalling the night's events, he shook his head, angry at himself. He knew he had let his guard down last night, and that was when SKO had made his move and got the drop on him. The liquor, the woman, and the atmosphere of the evening had been too much. They were going to be his downfall. SKO was the moniker the serial killer had given to himself some months back. The number of people SKO had killed was unknown, but it was over two, and two victims were all the FBI needed to label him as a serial killer.

"How are you going to do it? Are you going to cut my throat like you did to Agent Wilks, or are you going to bludgeon me to death like you did to Agent Bellows?" Agent Carter asked in a now dry, raspy voice. His throat was becoming hoarse, and his eyes started to burn, just like the other parts of his body.

"No on both assumptions. I have something special in

mind for you," SKO answered as he stood from the chair and moved closer to Agent Carter. When he was only a few feet away, Agent Carter noticed SKO was wearing a spit shield and rubber gloves. He was also covered from head to toe in what appeared to be a rubber suit.

"What are you wearing? Are you planning on stepping outside the box and killing me in one of the ways the drug cartels kill their enemies? Maybe you have a chainsaw somewhere behind you with my name on it. C'mon, when we getting started? I'm not begging. I won't give you the satisfaction! You crazy sick fuck!" Carter yelled from the confines of his chair.

"I've already started, Agent Carter," SKO answered calmly.

"What do you mean? What did you do to me?" Carter asked as the burning in his body worsened. Dark bruises were surfacing along his arms.

"I've given you something, Agent Carter, and it's starting to work." SKO moved closer to his victim for a better look.

"I was close to capturing you," Carter managed to say through the intense pain.

"You were never close! You followed the road I laid out before you. Now it's time for me to move on to another opponent," SKO advised the dying agent.

"What... What's happening to me?" Carter struggled to ask.

"The tissue in your body is eroding. In other words, you're bleeding from the inside out. When the chemical has run its course throughout your body, you'll be nothing more than a liquid mess on the floor while your bones will still be intact in that chair. Well, that's what I was told would happen by the man who sold it to me anyway. I'm actually excited to see if it really happens," SKO explained as he walked around the chair, observing the visibly melting man.

"Wait..." Carter said out loud.

"Wait? Are you begging? I thought you said you weren't

going to. Now I'm disappointed in you, Agent Carter," SKO admitted despairingly.

"I'm… I'm not begging. Where did this stuff come from?" Carter asked.

"Does it matter?" SKO asked back.

"To me, it does," Carter admitted right before his left eyeball slipped out of its socket and fell to the floor.

"Let's just say I got it from the man from Medan," SKO answered softly as he pushed a pencil into Agent Carter's leg.

"You'll never find anyone better than me," Carter managed to say as the skin on his face slowly slid downward.

"Very little pain, from what I gather. Very interesting," SKO said as he continued to observe the dying FBI agent. "By the way, I've already found someone else. I'm sending him to Pensacola, Florida. I'm interested in seeing how he performs on the case down there." SKO walked away just as Agent Carter's face completely slipped off the bone and slid down his chest and onto his lap.

Chapter 1
'Jerry'

Pensacola Beach, one of the three small communities that make up Santa Rosa Island, had been evacuated two days prior to the arrival of Hurricane Jerry, a category three hurricane. Yesterday morning, three hours before Hurricane Jerry was predicted to make landfall, the National Weather Service downgraded Jerry to a category one. Deputy Brian Kennedy was assigned to patrol the residential and public areas along Pensacola Beach east and west on Via De Luna Drive from Fort Pickens Road to public parking Lot H. Deputy Kennedy had been awake for twenty-four hours, running from one call for service to another, assisting twenty to thirty citizens who had refused to evacuate the island after getting advanced notice to do so. During his shift, he broke up one hurricane party at the high-rise condominiums on the west side of the island and ordered three small business owners to leave or get arrested, and to top it all, he rescued one terrified Shih Tzu puppy from the rising waters. The dog's collar identified the brown-and-white puppy as "Pumpkin," who had become Deputy Kennedy's partner for the remainder of his shift.

Deputy Kennedy was tired, overworked, and irritated.

By the time he backed his green-and-white cruiser under Todd's beach house on Ariola Drive, he was all too ready to fall into a deep sleep. He placed the cruiser in Park, locked the doors, and grabbed Pumpkin from the passenger seat. He made his way into the dark beach house, sat on the couch, lay back, and closed his eyes, with Pumpkin resting comfortably on his lap. The beach house belonged to Todd Warren, who was an old high school friend of Brian's, and Todd had given the deputy permission to use his beach house if he needed to during the storm. The wind blew the rain against the side of the beach house as Deputy Kennedy quickly sank deeper into unconsciousness. It was about twenty minutes past midnight when Tina, one of the county dispatchers, called for Deputy Kennedy over the radio.

"Four Adam Thirty-Eight," Tina announced and then waited a moment for Deputy Kennedy to answer.

"Four Adam Thirty-Eight," Tina announced a little louder once more over the radio.

"Four Adam Thirty-Eight, go ahead," Kennedy answered, half asleep. He sat up, startling the puppy.

"Four Adam Thirty-Eight, I know it's been a long shift, but we need you to respond to sixteen sixteen Ariola Drive in reference to a possible DB," Tina advised.

"Roger. Did I copy that correctly? It's a possible DB?" Deputy Kennedy asked. He knew DB was the acronym for a dead body. Kennedy wanted to make sure he had heard his dispatcher correctly.

"That's correct," she answered.

"Is there a reporting party?"

"Negative, the call came in anonymously."

"Anonymously. Really?" Kennedy responded surprisingly.

"Roger, Four Adam Thirty-Eight. I don't have another unit clear right now, but as soon as I do, I'll roll one your way for cover."

"Don't send a cover unit. I'll advise when I get there. I've been on Ariola all night, and there's no one out here but me. It's probably just some prank caller. I can't see anyone finding a DB this late at night, especially since there isn't anyone out here but me and my partner."

"Partner? Four Adam Thirty-Eight, I was told you were a lone unit tonight," Tina replied.

"I am. I'll explain later. Go ahead and show me en route."

"Roger, Four Adam Thirty-Eight. By the way, the DB is supposed to be under the house near the back."

"Roger."

"Roger, Four Adam Thirty-Eight. Twenty-four, twenty-five hours."

Deputy Kennedy stood up, stretched, held Pumpkin under his arm, and walked back out to his cruiser. The night air was cool. The strong, seventy-five mile-per-hour winds from Jerry were blowing the rain in from the Gulf of Mexico as a brilliant flash of white light streaked across the dark sky, followed by loud claps of thunder. Deputy Kennedy took a deep breath and held Pumpkin tightly as another flash lit the night, followed by another clap of thunder just above them. He quickly unlocked the passenger door and placed Pumpkin in the seat. He then walked out to the end of the driveway where it met the road and looked down the street through the darkness toward 1616 Ariola Drive. All the residents had been evacuated, and the power was out along the island. There should not have been any visible lights for miles in any direction, but there on the south side of the road, Kennedy noticed a small light moving about from the road toward the beach house. He squinted his eyes and tried to see through the darkness when another flash of light suddenly streaked through the night sky, revealing the silhouette of someone holding the light. "Hmmm, who is that?" Deputy Kennedy said quietly.

Kennedy went back to his cruiser and climbed inside, then

petted the frightened pup and used the radio to call dispatch once more.

"Four Adam Thirty-Eight."

"Four Adam Thirty-Eight, go ahead."

"Four Adam Thirty-Eight. Dispatch, why don't you go ahead and start another unit this way. It looks like there could be someone out here."

"Four Adam Thirty-Eight, are you on scene?"

"Negative. I'm just down the road from the beach house, and I can see someone moving around, carrying a light."

"Roger, Four Adam Thirty-Eight, I'll get a unit headed that way, but it may be a little while."

"Roger. I'll continue to the house. It's probably just a homeowner who refused to evacuate. I'll keep you advised."

"Roger, Four Adam Thirty-Eight. Twenty-four thirty hours."

Deputy Kennedy placed the car in drive and pulled out of Todd's driveway and onto Ariola Drive. He kept the cruiser lights off and allowed the car to move slowly toward 1616 in the Drive position without the use of the accelerator. As he got closer, he could see the light again, but now it was moving around under the beach house. When he was about three properties away from 1616, he placed the car in Park and called the dispatcher once more.

"Four Adam Thirty-Eight."

"Four Adam Thirty-Eight, go ahead," Tina replied.

"Four Adam Thirty-Eight. Show me on scene."

"Roger, Four Adam Thirty-Eight. Your cover unit is a few minutes out."

"Roger," Kennedy said.

"All units be advised, this channel is Code One for Four Adam Thirty-Eight at twenty-four thirty-five hours," Tina announced to all other deputies on the same channel. The Code One gave Deputy Kennedy priority use of the channel until he felt he was safe, by announcing he was Code Four and that dispatch could clear the Code One.

Deputy Kennedy reached down to plug his earpiece line into the radio on his belt and then looped the earpiece around his ear. He wanted to maintain noise and light discipline when he approached the unknown person or persons. Deputy Kennedy opened his cruiser door and once again stepped out into the hurricane environment. Before he could close the door, Pumpkin jumped out and ran toward 1616 Ariola Drive.

"No! Kennedy whispered, but it was too late. Pumpkin quickly disappeared into the darkness as she ran toward the light in the distance.

Deputy Kennedy ducked and quietly moved closer to the houses on his right. He decided to go around toward the back of the homes that lined the Gulf of Mexico. As he approached 1616 Ariola Drive, he used the sound of the waves breaking against the shore to cover his approach while keeping his flashlight off. When he got closer, he could see that some of the bottom blow-out panels of the beach house were missing. It appeared a surge of water had passed under the beach house, removing the bottom panels during the peak of Hurricane Jerry.

The light Kennedy had observed earlier continued to move back and forth, shining over the ground below it. It appeared as if a person was holding a flashlight, and he or she was moving it clumsily across the ground. Kennedy cautiously moved closer with his pistol drawn and aimed in the direction of the unknown figure holding the light. When he felt he had the element of surprise, Deputy Kennedy flipped his flashlight on and pointed it toward the figure.

"Sheriff's Office! Slowly turn around and face me," Deputy Kennedy ordered from behind one of the beach house support piers. He waited for a moment, but the person did not comply with his command.

"Turn and face me with your hands in the air! Kennedy yelled just as a bright white light streaked across the sky, revealing the unknown figure. Thunder clapped, and the deputy's eyes widened.

"What the…"

Lightning flashed overhead, exposing a female mannequin hanging from the trusses of the beach house with the flashlight tied to one of its hands. The deputy moved closer and saw Pumpkin standing under the mannequin, where she was tied securely to one of the support piers.

Deputy Kennedy quickly dropped to his knee, pulled the flashlight down, and used his light to survey the area around him.

"Who's out there?" he yelled as he passed the beam of light from one side of the house to the other, looking for a suspect.

"Four Adam Thirty-Eight, are you Code Four?" Tina asked after not hearing from the deputy for a few minutes.

Kennedy was about to answer when off in the distance, toward the water, he heard the unmistakable sound of a boat engine starting. He reached to his side for his more powerful flashlight, turned it on, and pointed it in the direction of the Gulf of Mexico. A few hundred yards offshore, he saw a large, fifty- to sixty-foot fishing vessel motoring its way out to deeper waters.

"Four Adam Thirty-Eight, Deputy Kennedy, are you Code Four?" Tina asked once more.

"Four Adam Thirty-Eight. I'm Code Four, and you can drop the Code One. Do we have any watercraft on the water near my location?"

"Negative, Four Adam Thirty-Eight."

Deputy Kennedy watched as the vessel's operator turned off its outside lights and went dark after reaching cruising speed. In its wake, Kennedy could see what appeared to be a small inflatable raft drifting in the surf back toward shore. He turned, put his light on the excited, barking Pumpkin, and walked toward her.

"I know, somebody's playing a very dangerous game with us," Kennedy said as he placed his pistol back into his holster. When Kennedy was almost to the excited pup, he tripped over something and fell to the wet sandy beach.

"Damn it!" Kennedy said out loud as he rubbed his knee in the dark.

"What did I trip over?" he asked himself and used his flashlight to survey the ground behind him.

"Holy…" Deputy Kennedy yelled as the light from his flashlight revealed the head and hand of a woman protruding upward out of the sand.

"Four Adam Thirty-Eight!" Kennedy shouted into the radio. "Four Adam Thirty-Eight, DISPATCH!" "Four Adam Thirty-Eight, go ahead," Tina answered quickly after hearing the excitement in the deputy's voice.

"I need additional units to my location, as well as major crimes. I need a perimeter set up as far as Panama City to the east and Fort Pickens to the west. I need units looking for a fifty- to sixty-foot fishing vessel, making its way to shore from the Gulf side of the island."

"Four Adam Thirty-Eight, roger. What do you have out there?"

"I got a DB at 1616 Ariola Drive!"

About the Author

Michael grew up in Pensacola, Florida, where he spent the summer months as a youth at the beach, tubing down the river or splashing around in a pool near his grandmother's home. After graduating from high school, he joined the US Army and served in the Military Police Corps. After nearly seven and a half years, Michael left the military. He took a position at the Colorado Springs Police Department, where he served the community for ten years. An injury on duty forced him into early retirement from policing. Currently, Michael is the Department Chair of the Criminal Justice Department at a local community college. Michael earned a Bachelor of Science in Sociology with an emphasis in Criminology from Colorado State University and a Master of Criminal Justice from the University of Colorado.

Michael started his writing career as a ghostwriter for a publisher of textbooks. Eventually, he co-authored a textbook. Michael has always had the desire to write fiction. Through the encouragement of his family and friends, Michael started writing mystery fiction and hasn't stopped. Michael's wife, Stefanie, still catches him daydreaming as he drives down the highway thinking about different stories. The facial expressions that he makes reveal to her that somewhere in his mind, he's reviewing a chapter, scene, or dialogue between characters for a new book.